BAD KARMA

RICHARD CHARTRAND

 FriesenPress

One Printers Way
Altona, MB R0G 0B0
Canada

www.friesenpress.com

Copyright © 2023 by Richard Chartrand
First Edition — 2023

This is a work of fiction. Any names, characters, businesses, events or incidents, are fictitious. Any resemblance to actual persons, living or dead, or actual events is purely coincidental.

All rights reserved.

No part of this publication may be reproduced in any form, or by any means, electronic or mechanical, including photocopying, recording, or any information browsing, storage, or retrieval system, without permission in writing from FriesenPress.

ISBN
978-1-03-918870-9 (Hardcover)
978-1-03-918869-3 (Paperback)
978-1-03-918871-6 (eBook)

1. FICTION, THRILLERS, CRIME

Distributed to the trade by The Ingram Book Company

CHAPTER 1

NO REMORSE, NO MERCY

Marine veteran Malcolm Jennings pointed his pistol at CEO Jamie Stonely, who sat behind his mahogany desk in his Manhattan apartment. Stonely stared at the silencer aimed at his chest.

Founder of the privately held conglomerate Stonely Holdings Inc., Stonely arranged business mergers and acquisitions. His talent had made him a success story. But his brilliant financial schemes had caused the layoff of thousands of workers. One of those workers had been Malcolm's father.

Malcolm's team had entered Stonely's apartment dressed in electricians' uniforms, claiming to be troubleshooting the building's fire alarm system. Wasting no time, Malcolm, with a steady hand, had pressed a gun in Stonely's chest, and ordered him to his den. Malcolm's recent recruit, Duke, a giant of a man, stood beside Stonely. Duke held his arms crossed over his chest.

"Bring up your bank accounts on your laptop," Malcolm said.

"Stop pointing this gun at me. I'm doing what you asked."

Stonely, sweat beading on his forehead, called up his local bank accounts. The laptop's screen displayed two Citibank accounts totalling $250,000.

Malcolm's wife, Gerta, a cyber expert, had taken a seat beside Stonely. "Start a transfer of funds and then turn the keyboard over to me," she said.

Stonely did as he was told. Gerta, with fingers tapping expertly on the keys, transferred the funds into a hidden account in cyberspace. She returned the keyboard to Stonely, and nodded to Malcolm.

Malcolm leaned forward. "Bring up your offshore accounts."

Stonely stared at Malcolm with raised eyebrows. He leaned back in his chair. "I don't know where you got your information, but there are no offshore accounts." He pursed his lips. "You've got all the liquid money I have. My accountants invested the rest in real estate and in company shares. It will take weeks to liquidate those."

Malcolm let out a deep breath. "Don't bullshit us. We have read your communications with the Cayman National Bank and Fidelity Bank. We know about the accounts. Bring them up on your screen."

Stonely stared back wide-eyed. "What the hell are you talking about?"

"We've read your communications and internet transactions."

Stonely looked stunned. He regained his composure. "So big deal! As chief executive of a holdings company, I contact bank managers to discuss investment opportunities every day. My staff opens these accounts out of courtesy. They contain token amounts. Besides, I've no access to them." Sweat mixed with cologne ran down his neck. Wet patches appeared under his armpits.

"Token amounts? You've transferred over fifty million dollars to those accounts in the past two years."

Stonely sat still and showed no sign he would comply.

"Tell you what," Malcolm said. "Bring up one account and if the amount is reasonable, say twenty-five million dollars, we'll call it a day."

"I suggest you leave right now with the money you've stolen from me already and save us time and trouble."

Malcolm pressed the tip of the silencer against Stonely's left knee.

"I suggest you bring up those accounts now and save yourself a lot of suffering."

"Now hang on. Fuck. Let me open one of these accounts." Stonely called up the website of the Cayman National Bank. He opened an account. The balance read twenty-five million dollars. He looked up at Malcolm. "You're in luck." Stonely started the transfer of funds, and Gerta took over the keyboard, entered the destination, and completed the transfer.

Stonely looked at Malcolm and spoke through clenched teeth. "You got what you came for. Now get the hell out of my apartment before security figures out what you're up to and calls the cops."

Malcolm turned to Gerta. "You've sent this man an email warning?"

Gerta nodded.

Stonely, looking perplexed, asked, "What are you talking about?"

Gerta answered, "The email we sent you four weeks ago about your having masterminded the bankruptcy of Windy City Machining, leaving the workers with no pensions or health benefits. We asked you to make reparations, but you ignored our request."

"That weird, untraceable email? That was you guys? How the hell did you get my personal email address?"

Malcolm shook his head. "You're not a good listener, are you? I meant to talk to you about my father, but I see I would waste my breath. Time for you to hang."

"What the hell is this? Are you guys some kind of cult? Your threats don't scare me." Stonely shouted for help at the top of his lungs and stood from his chair. Duke pressed Stonely back into his seat.

Malcolm signalled to his long time teammate, Larry, who had been standing guard by the door. Larry ran over with a roll of duct tape. He expertly covered Stonely's mouth, and bound his hands and legs.

Malcolm nodded at Larry. "The rope."

Upon hearing these words, Stonely bolted upright in his chair, and kangaroo hopped toward the door. Duke grabbed him in a body lock, lifted and carried him into the living room. Stonely swung his shoes backward and struck Duke on the shins, to no effect. Duke stood his captive upright on a chair below the edge of the apartment's mezzanine.

Larry dug through a duffel bag. "Fuck." He looked up at Malcolm. "The rope's back in the van."

"There's no time to return to the van. Improvise."

Larry searched and returned with a twelve-foot extension cord. He grabbed butter from the fridge, greased one end of the cord and improvised a slipknot. He ran up to the mezzanine and tossed the noose to Duke below. Duke placed the noose around Stonely's neck and pulled it snug.

"Do we have to do this?" Gerta said. "Just shoot him with a silencer. That's more humane."

Malcolm considered for a moment. "The suffering this man caused my father and his coworkers, was that humane?" Malcolm paused, then added, "The team voted on this. No remorse, no mercy."

Gerta lowered her gaze. Everyone's eyes were on Malcolm.

Someone knocked on the apartment door. Gerta looked up at Malcolm, wide-eyed. He jerked his head toward the entrance. Gerta tiptoed to the door and peered through the peephole. A doorman stood in the hallway.

"In a minute," Gerta shouted as she ran to the bathroom. She stripped down to her panties, mussed her hair, wrapped a bath towel around her shoulders, and ran back to the door. She opened it a crack and leaned in. "Yes?"

"Hello, ma'am. A neighbour reported loud noises coming from this unit. Is everything alright?"

"Loud noises?" Gerta appeared to be searching her mind. "Well, Mr. Stonely has been quite frisky today. I'm sorry we alarmed the neighbours. I'll tell Mr. Stonely to cool his passion." Gerta winked.

"I'm glad all's well. Have a pleasant afternoon." The doorman left.

Gerta hurried back to the bathroom and dressed.

Malcolm signalled Duke, who kicked the chair from under Stonely. The man grunted as his weight pulled the noose tighter. He jerked his bound legs repeatedly, and arched his back, like a diver reaching for the surface. He pulled on his arms, twisted his shoulders, attempting to free his hands.

"I can't watch this," Gerta said. "I'll be having nightmares." Her face was white. She left the room.

Larry, his face pale, looked down from the mezzanine. "I've seen worse, but I think I may chuck my cookies."

Duke looked up at Stonely. "I feel sorry for the bastard, but did he not expect someone to come calling someday with a score to settle?"

Malcolm watched Stonely's engorged face and blue skin, and felt a mix of sadness and revulsion. He could summon pity, but not mercy. Malcolm knew his father would not approve of such a severe punishment, but he burned with anger and a desire for revenge.

After four minutes had passed, Stonely's body relaxed and hung limp. His tongue protruded from his lips, and his glassy eyes stared into the distance. Fluids stained his trousers, and the smell of urine and feces filled the room.

"That part I don't like," Duke said as he pinched the bridge of his nose.

"Okay, guys, cleanup time." Malcolm turned toward the kitchen and called out, "Gerta, it's all over."

Gerta appeared carrying a duffel bag. She pulled out a stack of white cloths and five spray bottles of cleaning solution. Everyone grabbed a cloth and a bottle and, retracing their steps, swiped every surface they had touched.

In less than five minutes, the team had returned the cloths and the spray bottles to the duffel bag. Gerta switched on a signal jammer she carried from a shoulder strap. It would block nearby digital cameras, but not the closed-circuit cameras. Everyone lowered the brims of their caps, and Malcolm led. The crew darted down the service stairwell to the underground parking garage.

When they reached the garage, the team loaded their toolboxes and equipment cases inside two cargo vans. Teammate Steve had stayed behind in one van as a lookout. When Larry and Duke climbed aboard, Steve said, "You lucky devils. You got to see the action while I was twiddling my thumbs down here."

"You should be glad you missed the finale," Larry said.

Malcolm climbed behind the wheel of the lead van and Gerta took the passenger seat. As they emerged from the underground garage, they faced an NYPD cruiser with roof lights flashing. The cruiser blocked the exit ramp.

"Shit!" Malcolm cursed.

A patrol officer walked over to his van. He examined the logos, which read Fiber Optics Solutions, then leaned through Malcolm's lowered window. "Driver's licence and vehicle registration, please."

Malcolm passed the documents over. "Anything the matter, officer?"

"We've received a 911 call from a resident who heard someone calling for help from the unit below." He looked up at Malcolm. "What was your business in the building?"

"We were installing an energy management system in penthouse unit 1501," Malcolm said. "We didn't hear any calls for help."

The officer walked behind the van and opened the rear doors. Electrical tools, tool bags, and cases lie on shelves and on the floor of the cargo area. He closed the doors, walked over to Steve's van, and repeated the procedure. He returned to his cruiser, documents in hand, and tinkered with his onboard computer.

Malcolm turned to Gerta. "This is the acid test for the identities you've created."

"I'm thankful he wasn't wearing a body cam," Gerta replied.

Malcolm brought his hand up and palmed the holster beneath his jacket. He remembered having chambered a cartridge in his Glock. It was ready to fire.

The officer returned, handed the documents back to Malcolm, then to Steve, and waved them on. Malcolm drove past the police cruiser, and Steve followed. Another cruiser stood at the building's entrance. Malcolm drove past at a slow speed.

The vans left Manhattan by the Lincoln Tunnel. The latest variant of the pandemic had reduced the city's traffic to a trickle. They quickly emerged on the New Jersey side of the Hudson river. Gerta guided Malcolm to a warehouse in the borough of Hawthorne.

Once arrived at the warehouse, Malcolm and Gerta walked through the front entrance and met with proprietor Gunter Klein. Gunter was a long-time friend of Gerta's uncle Karl. Karl Wagner owned a machine shop in Chicago.

Gunter hugged Gerta. "It's good to see you, Gerta. Thank God you're safe. I was worried." Gunter turned to Malcolm and shook hands with him. "Good to see you, Malcolm." He then extended an arm toward the warehouse. "I've cleared a bay for you. Drive your vehicles inside and do what you have to do. Let me know if you need anything."

Gerta placed a hand on Gunter's arm and said, "Thank you so much, Mr. Klein. Uncle Karl said we could count on your help and your discretion."

"Always glad to help, Gerta. You're like family to me."

Malcolm and Steve drove the vans indoors.

"Let's get to work," Malcolm said.

Like a well-trained backstage crew, the team pasted new logos on the vans and replaced the licence plates. Gerta replaced the vehicle registration papers and applied new peel-and-stick VIN labels over the dash-mounted ones.

The substitution work completed, Malcolm waved Steve over. "Give me a five-minute head start. Stick to secondary roads as planned."

Malcolm and Gerta shook hands with Gunter and thanked him for his help. They climbed into their van and led the way out of the warehouse and back onto the road.

When the city was behind them, Gerta said, "We collected over twenty-five million dollars, but we took a lot of risks."

"We avenged my father. The money is secondary."

Gerta maintained a worried look. "There's enough here to split with the team, and help the families Stonely has harmed. We could stop now."

Malcolm paused, then said, "I'm not resting until I've avenged the death of my kid brother, Eddie. I want to see the man I hold responsible, Carl Tillman, hang." He felt his blood boil and his nerves tingle.

Carl Tillman was the former CEO of the military contractor Grenadiers Military Resources, in Canada. Malcolm's brother, Eddie, was tortured and murdered by insurgents during an ambush in Fallujah, Iraq.

Gerta rested a hand on Malcolm's arm. "I understand."

Malcolm asked, "How much has the bastard stashed overseas?"

Gerta considered this for a moment, then said, "Over thirty million dollars."

"That's good." Malcolm considered, then said, "Working in Canada will allow things to cool down on this side of the border. What's the guy's setup again?"

"He's retired in a country mansion near the city of Kitchener, Ontario."

Malcolm ran a scenario in his mind. "He'll have a private security team guarding the property. We'll need a larger team for that job."

"When would you like to do this?"

"How long do you figure for us to design a plan, buy what we'll need, and for you to prepare the documents?"

"Three months, at least."

"That makes it September. A beautiful time of year in Canada."

Malcolm drove quietly for some time, then said, "Hey, how about a few days' vacation for the entire team before we tackle that next job?" Malcolm thought some more. "I'm thinking countryside, an inn with a barbecue pit, even a campfire. What do you say?"

Gerta smiled. "That's a great idea! After this last job, the crew could do with some fun and relaxation. I'll look on TripAdvisor. Maybe an Airbnb on a farm? How does that sound?"

"That would be perfect."

Malcolm leaned over and planted a kiss on Gerta's cheek. "Let's get back to Chicago, to our electrical jobs. We need to maintain our cover."

Malcolm's and Steve's vans rolled along highway 46, one mile apart, headed for Chicago. Malcolm was already planning the next job in his head.

CHAPTER 2

MALCOLM (FIVE YEARS EARLIER)

Malcolm received a medical discharge from the Marine Corps following a battlefield injury in Afghanistan. He enrolled in an electrician's course courtesy of Veterans' Affairs.

Malcolm sat at his desk in his Chicago apartment. He leafed through his course notes, put the binder down, and walked over to the kitchen. He opened a cupboard door looking for the Earl Grey tea bags. The package was empty. He threw the empty package in the kitchen garbage container and closed the cupboard door with a bang. He walked back to the living room, picked up a book from a bookcase, sat and read for five minutes, then put it down and returned to the kitchen.

Gerta had been watching this. "Malcolm. You're bored. Why don't you go out for a walk? Or better still, it's Saturday. Take your father fishing?"

"Yeah. Good idea."

"Take him to Humboldt Park, then bring him over for dinner. If you catch some largemouth bass, I'll cook them."

Malcolm walked over to his daughter's bedroom. The door was open and Danielle was working on her laptop.

"Honey? Want to come fishing with me and grandpa?"

Fifteen-year-old Danielle answered without taking her eyes off her laptop. "No, thanks, Dad. I must study for my exams next week. Say hi to grandpa for me."

Humboldt Park, in the suburbs of Chicago, provided an oasis to fishers and birdwatchers.

Malcolm's father, Ronald Jennings, sat at the bow of the rented fifteen-foot aluminum rowboat. He was attaching a lure to his line.

Malcolm sat at the stern. He stretched his long legs between the tackle boxes and winced from the pain in his left hip. Malcolm had joined the Marines at eighteen, served first in Iraq and then Afghanistan, and had made captain before a Taliban bullet shattered his left hip and left him with a limp. His medical discharge ended his military career at forty-five years of age.

Ronald stared at Malcolm. "That hip injury is still bothering you?"

Malcolm shrugged his shoulders. "Sometimes."

"Do you miss the army?"

"I miss the camaraderie, but not the never knowing when you'll be shot at or when your vehicle will drive over a roadside IED." Malcolm paused before adding, "I'm still angry about Eddie's death."

Malcolm's younger brother, Edmund, had followed in his footsteps, and had enlisted with the Marines at eighteen. After the sudden death of their mother, Malcolm and Edmund grew close to their father. The three worked side by side on projects in the garage, fished and hunted on yearly trips.

Edmund had later left the Corps and joined a private military contracting company, Grenadiers Military Resources, and had been deployed to Iraq. Insurgents killed Eddie and three fellow soldiers during a medical convoy escort duty in Fallujah.

Ronald looked at his son with sadness. "You and Eddie have always been close. I, too, haven't made peace with Eddie's death."

Malcolm paused before answering, "It's not so much that Eddie died in combat; it's the greedy decisions made behind the scenes that anger me. I vowed to avenge his death. Those responsible with sending him and his teammates on that assignment without support will pay for that."

"Whoa! Don't you go and play God, Malcolm. "Vengeance is mine," said the Lord. Leave retribution to Him."

"God, if he exists, will render judgment in the afterlife, but, on this earth, it's our job to do it. If our legal system can't get the job done, then I will, when it comes to my loved ones."

Ronald was silent for a moment, then said, "I can't imagine what it must have been like when they sent your platoon to recover Eddie's and his comrades' bodies. They shouldn't have sent you on that assignment."

"The major didn't know Eddie was my brother. I didn't tell him, and I told my comrades not to tell, either. I wanted to go and get Eddie back." Malcolm rubbed his eyes. "The insurgents had dragged him and his teammates behind trucks through the village streets. They doused the soldiers with fuel, set them ablaze, and hung them from the underside of a bridge. We brought the four bodies back to the base to be returned home."

"That must have been hard."

Malcolm spoke through gritted teeth. "I blame the military contractor for not providing backup."

Ronald rubbed his hands together. "I've joined the other three families in a class action suit against the military contractor. I hope it will serve as a warning to the other contractors to better protect their soldiers."

Malcolm took slow, deep breaths to regain his calm. Dr. Reid at Veterans' Affairs had diagnosed Malcolm with PTSD and warned him of the symptoms: depression, nightmares, and episodes of pent-up rage.

Ronald stared at his son. "I worry about you. You're the quiet type. Your scars run deep. You must have lived through some nasty stuff."

"No worse than my comrades, but I'll admit that recovering Eddie's body was a low point."

Silence settled over both men. Malcolm cast his fishing line in the water. Ronald did likewise. The men fished quietly. They caught two largemouth bass.

Ronald broke the silence. "I have some bad news to share with you."

Malcolm's eyebrows rose.

"The shop closed last week. The company declared bankruptcy. They've given me my termination package already."

"Bankruptcy? How is that possible? Windy City Machining has been making auto parts since you joined them, fresh out of trade school. The automotive industry is still going strong."

Ronald lowered his head. "I can't say it came as a complete surprise. They've been neglecting the building and the equipment for some years now."

"I don't want to belittle the hardship it must be for you, Dad, but weren't you close to retirement, anyway? Another two years, right?"

"True, but the bankruptcy trustees plundered the company's self-administered pension and health benefit plan to pay debtors. This couldn't have happened at a worse time."

Malcolm stared at his father, waiting for the rest of the bad news.

"They've diagnosed me with lung cancer, stage 4."

"Lung cancer? Stage 4? That sounds serious Are they absolutely sure?"

"Dr. Feingold put me through every test imaginable, MRI, the whole shebang. He says I have six months to get my papers in order."

"Six months? We'll get a second opinion."

"Dr. Feingold wasn't alone in this. He had other specialists looking at the results of the tests. A whole group of specialists. They sat around a table with me to discuss the few options available to me. There's no cure possible, but they can keep me out of pain until the end."

"I can't believe this, dad. You don't even smoke."

"Smoking isn't the only cause of lung cancer." Ronald reflected for a moment. "Dr. Feingold said we can never be sure what caused it, but the metallic dust floating around the machine shop wouldn't have helped. The union has been pushing the company to upgrade the ventilation system for years, but management has been dragging its feet. Now it's plain why."

Malcolm looked intently at his father. "Don't worry about money, Dad. You sign up for the best treatment available. Gerta and I will support you."

Ronald's face turned sombre. "Dr. Feingold has lined up chemo and radiation treatment, and he's referred me to an at-home nursing care agency for an oxygen machine and a morphine pump." Ronald looked down and wrung his hands. "My savings will only cover part of the cost, but I'll mortgage the house to cover the rest. I'll die penniless but debt free." Ronald paused, then said, "There'll be nothing left for you, Gerta, and Danielle. I feel bad about that."

"Don't worry about that, Dad. Get the best care. We want you to be as comfortable as possible. That's the important thing."

Malcolm mulled something over. "This bankruptcy is suspect. Draining the employees' pension plan can't be legal. We'll get legal advice."

"Our union has a law firm looking into it. I'll give you our shop steward's name and number. He can give you the details."

Malcolm's face turned red as he spoke through clenched teeth. "If this bankruptcy was part of a financial scheme, I promise you, Dad, I'll serve rough justice to those responsible."

"Whoa! Leave this in the hands of the union's lawyers, Malcolm. Don't go off seeking revenge on your own."

Ronald reeled in his line, signalling the fishing was over. Malcolm sat silently, looked over the lagoon surface, and surveyed the green shoreline. Wood ducks and Canada Geese swam nearby. Eastern kingbirds and red-winged blackbirds hopped on the branches and weeds along the shoreline.

Mr. Jennings died six months later. The trade union's lawyers reported that liquidating self-administered employee pension and health plans to cover company debts was legal.

Malcolm learned that the bankruptcy of Windy City Machining had resulted in a rise in share value for the parent company, Stonely Holdings Inc., and that the board of directors awarded themselves and their CEO, Jamie Stonely, $1 million bonuses. Besides this windfall, CEO Stonely had exercised his executive share options, which netted him over $20 million.

Malcolm vowed revenge.

CHAPTER 3

GERTA (THREE YEARS EARLIER)

Gerta and Danielle cleaned up after a light lunch. Mother and daughter stood side by side at the counter, doing the dishes. Gerta gave Danielle the last wet plate, dried her hands on the dish towel, and said, "Time to go pick up Dad."

"Is it okay if I stay home? I must work on my application for Marine Corps Training."

"Sure, honey. Grandpa will understand. He is so proud of your school marks."

Gerta's father, Albert Mueller, was undergoing chemotherapy for stage 4 stomach cancer at the outpatient clinic at Northwestern Memorial Hospital in downtown Chicago. Malcolm and Gerta had rented a three-bedroom apartment on North Fremont Street in the Lakeview neighbourhood. Gerta's father had moved in with them. The apartment was a twenty-minute drive from the hospital. The location was convenient to Malcolm's new job as apprentice electrician on North Elston Avenue, and within walking distance of Danielle's high school. But it was a fifty-minute drive to Gerta's contract assignment at the FBI field office on West Roosevelt Road.

Gerta climbed behind the wheel of their black Jeep Wrangler, steered the vehicle toward Lake Shore Drive, then climbed on the southbound ramp leading downtown. The highway hugged Lake Michigan and offered pleasant vistas: Belmont Harbor, North Avenue Beach, Oak Street Beach.

After exiting at North Michigan Avenue, Gerta proceeded south along the Magnificent Mile for some six blocks. She turned left on a side street, and parked illegally in front of the Arkes Pavilion. She ran to the pavilion entrance.

Albert Mueller sat on a bench in the lobby. Father and daughter hugged, then ambled toward the car. Albert steadied himself on Gerta's arm. She helped her father climb into the jeep.

"So, Dad, how are you feeling?"

"Glad to be on the right side of the grass. Thanks for picking me up, honey."

As the jeep zoomed north along Lake Shore Drive, Albert stared at the whitecaps covering the blue grey lake. He broke the silence. "Dr. Goldfarb mentioned the chemo was effective in slowing down the cancer. He figures I have another six months before my grand departure."

"Dad, don't talk like that. Nobody knows what the future will bring."

Albert followed on his train of thought. "Soon he'll be prescribing stronger painkillers. They'll make my mind foggy."

"It's one day at a time, Dad. We'll deal with it when it comes."

He turned to Gerta. "I'm not saying this to be morbid. I'm worried time is running out for me to teach you about running the printing equipment. Once I'm doped up with painkillers, I won't be able to teach you anything about printing security documents. The cops are already watching my comings and goings like Russian spies. It's hard enough evading their surveillance as it is."

Albert's employer, an international security document printer, had fired Albert with cause six months earlier for refusing to get vaccinated. Albert had become an anti-vaxxer after his sister died of a vaccine injury. The company lawyers had exploited a loophole in the government's workplace vaccination law to refuse him a severance package and extended health benefits. He had retaliated by masterminding the robbery of security printing equipment and software. The police had charged him with conspiracy to commit a robbery, but their case rested on circumstantial evidence alone. The cameras and all door alarms had been turned off during the robbery. Albert was out on bail.

Gerta turned to her father. "Don't worry, Dad. The software part is a natural for me, and as for operating the printers and laminators, uncle Karl will help me with those."

Karl Wagner wasn't Gerta's uncle but a close friend of the family. He had emigrated from West Germany at the same time as Albert Mueller. Both men had settled in the Lakeview neighbourhood and become close friends. Karl owned a machine shop and a moving company. He had transported the stolen printing equipment to a secret rental office in the Chicago suburbs. Albert had handpicked some equipment for himself and had Karl sell the rest on the black market. The two friends had split the proceeds.

Albert looked at Gerta. "Nothing would please me more than if you used this equipment to teach a lesson to those corrupt executives and their lawyers who use legal loopholes to avoid paying severances to their employees. I have enough money to pay for the medical bills and the lawyer's fees, but there'll be nothing left."

Gerta turned to her father and rested a hand on his arm.

Albert covered her hand with his own. "It was generous of you and Malcolm to invite me to move in with you after I sold my house. I'm glad I won't be around for the trial."

"Dad, please don't talk like that."

"It's just that I would like to help you and Malcolm with your projects. And there'll be Danielle's university tuition soon."

"Oh, Dad, stop worrying so much about money. We'll manage."

"I'm very proud of you, Gerta. A graduate of Caltech, and a computer programmer for the NSA and the FBI. Unbelievable. You have your mother's brains. If only she was here to see you. Breast cancer took her so young."

Gerta nodded.

Albert turned his gaze toward the lake. After a while, he said, "Malcolm looks happier these days. He's stopped brooding over the injustices of the world. It's good to see."

"Yes, he's finally shaken off that depression. He was never one to worry about money, but those disability checks are small. But thanks to VA's education program for veterans, he's got his master electrician's ticket, and he enjoys his work."

"That's great news."

"Malcolm's employer is retiring, and Malcolm wants to buy the business. We have money for a down payment from the sale of the house, and the owner will assume a mortgage for the rest." Gerta turned to her father and smiled. "We'll be proud owners of an electrical contracting business."

"That's great news. And you with your programming contracts, things are looking up for you guys."

Gerta hesitated before adding, "The FBI is not renewing my contract."

Albert stared ahead and bit his lips. "The bastards. I'll bet the conspiracy charges against me played a part."

Gerta turned toward her father. "That's okay, Dad. I'll be handling the books for our new business."

After brooding for a few minutes, Albert said, "Danielle's still doing well at school?" Without waiting for an answer, he added, "I'm so proud of my granddaughter. Strong-willed and smart, like her mother. No drama queen, that one. You think she'll carry through with her plan to get a university degree?"

"I think so."

"She might get a sports scholarship at those fancy schools. She's a good basketball player. I love to watch her play at school tournaments. And she came in first at that high school marathon."

"No. She doesn't play or run at scholarship level, but her school grades are good, and she has good work habits. She wants to join the Marines and, if she's accepted, they'll subsidize her studies at the state university. There's nothing to stop her."

"She's following in the footsteps of her father and her uncle Eddie," Albert said.

They rode north along the shoreline of Lake Michigan, a sea of blue-grey water.

Albert Mueller died six months later, before his case went to trial. Gerta resolved to put her father's security printing equipment to good use.

CHAPTER 4

MALCOLM RECRUITS HIS TEAM

For the past four years, Malcolm had nursed the desire to dispense rough justice to the executives he blamed for his father's needless suffering and his younger brother's death. Malcolm had bought a small electrical contracting business, offered generous early retirement packages to the existing employees, and now could hire men of his choosing. He felt he finally had the resources to put his plan into action.

His first hire was his former combat companion and trusted friend, Larry Schmidt. Larry had requested an early discharge from the army in order to follow Malcolm into civilian life. The two had enrolled in electrician courses and stayed close friends.

When Larry reported for his first day at work, the men hugged, sat in the shop's office, and reminisced about their army days.

"I appreciate this opportunity to work alongside you again, Malcolm. Thanks for hiring me."

"I did you no favour. You're a qualified electrician, and I too look forward to working with you."

Malcolm placed a hand on Larry's shoulder. "I'll never forget the support you showed me after we recovered Eddie's body in Fallujah. You stood by me as I found my way out of a very dark place."

"It's what friends do."

Malcolm nodded, then said, "Are you keeping up with your yoga and meditation?"

"I have to, for my sanity. The army taught me well on how to kill, but on how to deal with my emotions, not so well. Especially after they sicced us on Iraq based on false intelligence. I've built up a lot of resentment and anger towards our leaders."

After a quiet moment, Malcolm broke the silence. "Gerta told me you instructed her to deposit half your paycheck in your mother's bank account. I've always admired how you've supported your single mother. How is she doing?"

"She is doing all right. Thanks for asking. She still lives in her apartment in Queens. She's retired now."

Larry sat, pensive, then said, "My dream is to buy Mom a small bungalow, in her neighbourhood, close to her friends and her support system. She could do a little gardening in her own backyard. She tends a small plot in a community garden, but it's not the same."

"I remember you telling me she was mistreated by her long-time employer. That she lost her house in the ordeal."

"Yes, she did," Larry's tone hardened. "She had worked her way up to executive secretary when the CEO fired her, without a severance, after she rebuffed his sexual advances. She sued for wrongful dismissal, of course, but the company's lawyers walked all over Mom's legal aid greenhorn." Larry gritted his teeth in anger, then added, "I sure would like to pay back that bastard for the hurt he caused my mother."

"I know how that feels," Malcolm said. "If you ever decide to do something about it, you can count on my help."

Malcolm's next hire was Steve Adams, a former combat companion in Afghanistan.

"Thanks for hiring me, Malcolm. And thanks for offering a decent wage. Since my dishonorable discharge, with no pension or benefits, I've been working for minimum wage."

"I'm doing you no favour. You have electrical experience. You learned the trade from your stepfather."

"True. Even after I left home at sixteen, I worked as an electrician's helper before I joined the Marines at eighteen."

"That had to be tough on you, leaving home at sixteen."

"When I asked my stepfather to pay me for helping him, he said I should be thankful for the room and board and the pocket money he provided. I left."

"How are your stepparents?"

"They're fine. I stay in touch with my stepmother, and I visit her when I pass through Chicago."

Malcolm let a moment pass then said, "I will never forget that you saved my life, in that Afghan village, when our jeep rolled over an IED. We survived the explosion, but a group of insurgents opened fire on us. A bullet struck me on the hip, and I fell unconscious. I learned afterwards that you had stood by my side and kept the insurgent at bay until reinforcement arrived."

"We have my grenades to thank for saving both our lives," Steve said. "There's nothing like hand grenades for keeping the enemy at a distance. It's lucky they didn't have grenades themselves."

"I'm grateful to you and your grenades, then."

Both men chuckled

Steve shook his head, then said, "I paid dearly for my affection for my little friends. You remember? The warrant officer would not issue more than two hand grenades per soldier, even after I argued for more. So, one night, I removed two cases of grenades from stores and stashed them away for future use. I got discovered and here I am."

"And I'm glad you're here," Malcolm said.

CHAPTER 5

MALCOLM LAYS OUT HIS PLAN

Malcolm decided to put his revenge project into action. He assembled his core team, Gerta, Larry, and Steve, at the neighbourhood Denny's restaurant. He already had Gerta onboard, but he needed the help of the others.

"I want to pay back the bastards responsible for the suffering my Dad and my brother Eddie went through," Malcolm said. "I want them to hang. But I can't do this alone. I need your help."

"Whoa!" Steve said. "There are a few scumbags I'd like to beat to within an inch of their lives, but murder them? I don't know."

"I'm with you with killing the bastards," Larry said. "But how do you propose to do this without getting caught?"

Malcolm had the answer ready. "With expert planning, flawless execution, and some reserve money in case things go sideways and we have to live on the run."

"I like the idea of reserve money, but how much money are you talking about and where would you get it?" Steve asked.

Malcolm turned to Gerta.

Gerta leaned forward, then said, "Malcolm's two targets have fortunes hidden in Cayman banks. Jamie Stonely, CEO of Stonely Holdings Inc., has fifty million, and Carl Tillman at Grenadiers Electronics of Canada has thirty million."

"How do you know this?" Steve asked.

"While programming at NSA, I hacked into their surveillance software. Once in, I can read the targets' internet communications and listen to their phone conversations. They're all stored in NSA data banks."

Larry and Steve looked on, slack jawed.

"But you guys will have to force the bank account passwords out of them. Then I'll transfer the funds into an untraceable account."

"I know how to squeeze the passwords out of the fuckers," Steve said. "I'll put a grenade in their mouths, wrap my finger around the pin and look them in the eye."

Larry poked him in the ribs.

Malcolm let the chuckling pass, then said, "After we've covered our expenses, there'll be plenty of money left over for us to start fresh with new identities if we need to."

"But how can we avoid getting caught?" Larry said. "We gave DNA and fingerprint samples when we joined the Marines. The FBI has those on file."

Malcolm turned to Gerta. "This plan won't stand a chance without you."

Gerta addressed Larry and Steve. "While on contract for the FBI, I did programming on their databases. I programmed in a backdoor. I can get into their databases without a password. I'll go in and replace our DNA and fingerprint files with fake ones."

The men exchanged a look with raised eyebrows.

Larry turned to Gerta and asked, "But how long before they find out?"

"I don't know, but I monitor my backdoor regularly, and when they find it, I'll know."

"And then what?"

"They'll close my backdoor and they'll eventually discover what I did to the files." Gerta turned to Malcolm.

"That will mean the end of the operation. We'll have to disperse and disappear," Malcolm said.

The men stared at him blankly.

"Disappear? Let's talk about how we'll do that," Larry said.

"With the security printing equipment and software my father left me, I can print passports, social security cards, driver's licences, and credit cards." Greta said. "I've stored the printing equipment in a rented office under a fake name."

Larry and Steve nodded their heads and looked impressed.

"What about being caught on camera during the operation?" Larry asked. "They have cameras everywhere these days."

"We can block digital cameras and cell phones with a signal jammer," Gerta said. "But not the closed-circuit cameras. Against those, we'll have to wear long brim baseball caps and hide our faces."

"What about witnesses? Larry said. "Will we wear masks?"

Malcolm hesitated before answering. "We won't wear masks. If we plan this properly, there won't be any eyewitnesses. If there are, despite our precautions, we'll have to silence them permanently. It's the only way to ensure a clean getaway."

Larry and Steve locked eyes and were silent. The men straightened and stared back.

"I don't like the hanging part," Larry said. "It takes time to hang a man. And he'll put up a struggle and create a racket."

"I'll hire a muscleman. Someone strong enough to hold the target while we tape his mouth, arms, and legs," Malcolm said.

"Still, the struggle could attract attention. Using a silencer would be faster and quieter."

"I agree with Larry," Gerta said.

Malcolm bit his lips, then said, "I want them to hang. In honour of Eddie."

Gerta put a hand on Malcolm's arm. "Let me send an email to the targets before we strike. I'll make it untraceable. If they show remorse and offer reparations, then the hanging is off."

Malcolm considered, then said, "Okay. You give them four weeks' notice. No more."

Larry gave Malcolm an anxious look, and said, "If we get caught, we'll face life imprisonment or worse, the death sentence."

Malcolm paused, then answered, "I've consulted a criminal lawyer. He said juries and judges rarely award a death sentence when there are no eyewitnesses to a murder."

"Life in prison is no fun either," Steve said.

Malcolm locked eyes with the men. "We must stand honour bound to spring from jail any of us who gets arrested. After our first job, we'll have enough money to put together a solid escape plan for whoever's arrested."

Larry and Steve looked at one other and nodded.

"So, after we take care of these two targets, I get my share of the money, and it's over?" Steve asked.

Malcolm crossed his arms and leaned back in his chair. "I've only got these two targets in mind."

Larry raised his hand. "I'm in if we include the bastard that hurt my mother, the one I told you about."

"Okay, we'll add him to the revenge project," Malcolm said.

Steve raised his hand, and asked, "Can I leave whenever I want to, and take my share with me?"

"That's fine by me," Malcolm said. "But keep in mind we'll need more men for some of these operations, and that will mean smaller shares."

Steve mulled something over in his mind, then said, "I'm in, but on one more condition. I don't execute anybody. But you can count on me to shoot our way out of any jam."

"I can live with that," Malcolm said.

Gerta looked at the three men, got their attention, then said "I have a condition, as well."

The men stared at her.

"That we dedicate twenty percent of the funds to helping the families that were hurt by those executives' financial schemes."

Malcolm searched the men's faces for approval.

Steve was first to speak. "I like the idea. Makes me feel like Robin Hood."

Larry nodded his agreement.

Gerta released a deep breath. "Good."

Malcolm looked into the eyes of his teammates and exchanged a nod with each one.

"Good. Gerta and I will plan the first job; Jamie Stonely."

Malcolm and Gerta stayed behind after the men had left.

"We need to inform Danielle of this revenge project," Gerta said. "If we get discovered, we'll be on the run and her life will be affected. That would limit her career prospects. She'll be known as the child of assassins."

Malcolm bit his lips, then said, "The project won't be a complete shock to Danielle. I've shared my desire to avenge dad and Eddie with her already, and she said she understood. But now it's for real." Malcolm considered, then said, "You could create a new identity for her as a backup plan. We'll collect money on those jobs, and we'll be able to help her build a new life."

"You *have* given this a lot of thought. Even so, we need to review the risks with her and to hear her out." Gerta considered for a moment, then added, "She'll be home from the base this weekend. Let's go over this with her on Saturday."

Gerta looked up at Malcolm, placed a hand on his arm and said, "You're sure about this? I can't change your mind?"

Malcolm covered her hand with his. "I'm going through with this."

Malcolm cooked pancakes and bacon on the Saturday morning. This was his usual contribution to weekend breakfasts. He served heaping plates to Danielle and Gerta.

Once all three had finished eating, Malcolm explained his revenge project to Danielle. He did not minimize the risks to himself and to Gerta and the possible consequences to Danielle's life. She listened attentively without interrupting. Malcolm concluded with the backup plan, a new identity for Danielle.

Silence loomed over the table.

After a few minutes, Danielle raised her head, faced both parents and said, "I want in on this revenge project."

Malcolm and Gerta stiffened.

"You can't be serious, honey," Gerta said. "You don't want to risk becoming a fugitive, or worse. You're entitled to a normal life, a good life."

"If you guys get caught, I'll suffer the consequences as well. How normal will my life be then?" She let her parents reflect on this before adding, "I loved grandpa. He never missed one of my basketball tournaments and he even stood outside for hours during my high school marathon run. And

I loved uncle Eddie. He brought me a gift every time he came for a visit. He showed interest in my schoolwork and my hobbies." She frowned, then added, "I want revenge for them as much as you do, Dad. I have two years of military training. I can help."

Malcolm and Gerta turned to look at each other.

Malcolm sat facing Danielle, took her hands in his, and said, "Okay. You can join us, but not on our first raid. We need to test our plan first, before I let you participate."

Danielle nodded.

CHAPTER 6

CEO CARL TILLMAN

Carl Tillman stared out the window of his country estate. A red clover field stretched before him. A security guard walked by, conducting a round of the property.

Tillman ruminated over the glory days of his defunct company, Grenadiers Military Resources, or GMR. The former CEO of the defence contractor was not prone to dwelling in the past. Forward thinking had been the hallmark of his tenure as head of the company he'd founded in Kitchener, Ontario. But those days were now behind him. He was sixty-five years of age.

The phone rang. The call display announced his lawyers, Meyer Levin Brodie.

"Carl? Everett Meyer here."

"Hi, Everett. You bring good news or bad news?"

Meyer represented Tillman in a class action suit for the wrongful death of four contract soldiers in Fallujah, during the Iraq invasion. The families of the dead soldiers were suing GMR for negligence when sending their sons on an escort mission and not providing adequate backup.

"I bring some good news. The class action suit by the families of those soldiers has closed in our favour."

"Thank God. What a nightmare. I thought it would never end."

"I will admit that you impressed me when you fabricated those risk assessments, predated them, and inserted them in the files before the prosecutor subpoenaed all documents. When I presented the judge with the risk assessment, he concluded GMR had done its due diligence, and he ruled in our favour. You saved GMR a lot of money."

"I was desperate. I was negotiating the sale of the company. Besides, those families should be suing the U.S. military. It was pressuring us to reduce our costs."

Meyer paused before adding, "I have some not so good news as well."

"Why am I not surprised. Go ahead. I'm listening."

"It's about the criminal lawsuit accusing you of accepting kickbacks during the sale of GMR."

Tillman was fighting a criminal lawsuit for corruption. The case hinged on the testimony of his former executive secretary who had turned whistle-blower.

"Did you follow my suggestion?"

"Yes. I offered her a small fortune to be deposited overseas, out of sight of the authorities, if she would recant, but she refused. Is there a history between the two of you I need to know about?"

"I had promised I'd leave my wife to marry her, but I changed my mind. She's being vindictive. What happens now?"

"She has turned incriminating documents over to the prosecution. Recordings of meetings between you and the buyers. We can't stop that train now. It has left the station. We're in for a rough ride."

"Shit." Tillman mulled something over in his mind. "Am I looking at jail time?"

"Whoa. No, no. For one thing, I've talked to the buyers and they will deny having paid any kickbacks. I'm digging into your secretary's past. I will find dirt and use it to discredit her testimony. We'll delay the trial for as long as we can, and then we'll file an appeal. We can drag this process out for years. All the while, we'll push for an out-of-court settlement. We're talking years before that court case is settled. Who knows what will happen in the meantime? Leave this with us, Carl. Enjoy your retirement."

"Hmm. Easier said than done. I receive regular death threats from malcontents who've been laid off following the closure of GMR."

"Have you informed the police?"

"Yes. An inspector has met with me, taken copies of the letters, emails, and records of phone conversation, and promised to follow up. He said he would assign a patrol cruiser to drive by regularly, but they've been short of resources since the resurgence of this damn pandemic."

"Don't you have a private security team protecting the house and escorting you and your family during your outings?"

"Yes, but it's hard to relax when crackpots with a grudge are threatening to strike at me or my family. I fear kidnappings for ransom, or worse: assassinations."

"Have you considered hiring professionals? There's a new law on the books allowing private police contracting. These firms have the same powers of investigation and arrest as regular police services."

"I've read about this new law. Is there a firm you would recommend for my situation?"

"Certainly. I recommend The Reliant Detective Agency in Ann Arbor, Michigan. They are legendary in the investigating and protection field and licensed to work in Canada. They recruit from the Marine Corps Intelligence."

"Thanks, Everett. I'll look them up." Tillman ended the conversation.

There was a recent email that particularly unsettled Tillman. The email urged reparation for the death of those contract soldiers in Iraq, the unnecessary sale of GMR that resulted in hundreds of worker layoffs, and the misappropriation of company funds. It even mentioned his hidden overseas accounts. How the hell did they know about those? Some damn accountant must have talked. Tillman had not shown this email to the police.

Equally troubling was the murder of CEO Jamie Stonely some two months ago. The murderers had lynched Stonely in his own apartment, for God's sake. Tillman had researched the crime, and learned that Stonely had also received a threatening email before being attacked. Both emails, his and Stonely's, had been signed "The Confessors." Was he threatened by the same vigilante group? And these criminals were still at large.

Tillman walked to his den, opened his laptop and brought up the website of The Reliant Detective Agency. He studied their capabilities, reviewed their references, and placed the call.

"The Reliant Detective Agency. How may I direct your call?"

"I'd like to speak with Chief Chuck Harrington, manager of the Criminal Investigation Division, please."

"Who may I say is calling?"

Tillman gave his name and former position at GMR.

"One moment, please."

After a few electronic clicks, a voice came on the line. "This is Chuck Harrington. How may we be of help, Mr. Tillman?"

Tillman gave Harrington a general history of GMR, and he described the threatening emails and letters he had been receiving since the closure of the company. He put special emphasis on the recent email signed "The Confessors". After a back-and-forth of questions and answers, Tillman asked, "How would you go about finding and arresting these criminals?"

"Those criminals are very tech savvy, so I suggest a team of four veterans from Marine Corps Intelligence. One team member will be a cyber expert able to locate anybody who has left a trace on the web. The team will be equipped with weapons and a purpose-built vehicle, and ready to pursue and arrest the criminals. We call this type of assignment a search-and-delete operation."

"How much money are we talking about?"

"Reliant will charge four thousand dollars a day, plus expenses," Harrington said. "I estimate that two to three weeks will be required. We will issue daily updates and weekly invoices. Should I send you a contract to review?"

"Yes, please. I'll read it and let you know."

Tillman and Harrington exchanged coordinates. Tillman ended the conversation.

Tillman's mind turned to his schedule for the day, to a forthcoming interview with a reporter from *Defence Business Magazine*. The highly respected business and military publication had survived the internet revolution. They wanted to produce a series on famous defence business CEOs, past and present, the reporter had said, and he, Carl Tillman, had made the list. The interview and photo shoot would take two hours at most, the reporter had promised. Tillman had scheduled the interview on a day his family was out shopping. He did not want his family photographed and appearing in a magazine.

The security guard interrupted his musings by announcing the reporter's arrival. Tillman opened the door to a smartly dressed woman in her mid-thirties with shiny close-cropped black hair, brilliant brown eyes, and an engaging smile. She shook Tillman's hand and introduced herself. "Hello, Mr. Tillman. I'm Deborah Miner from *Defence Business Magazine*. Please call me Debbie. How are you?"

"Hello, Debbie. I'm well, thank you. Please call me Carl. Please come in."

Deborah crossed the threshold and brushed lightly against Tillman as she walked past. A whiff of peppery rose scent caressed Tillman's nose. His wife wore a similar perfume, a Givenchy fragrance.

Deborah was about five foot nine. She wore a hip-length suede jacket, a knee-length black pencil dress, and low-heeled black leather shoes. She carried a notepad tucked under her right arm, and a Leica camera hung from her shoulder. Tillman felt appropriately dressed in a loose cashmere pullover, jeans, and penny loafers. Feeling relaxed and comfortable, he wanted his guest to feel at ease, as well.

"Our photographer cancelled at the last minute, but he lent me his camera. Don't worry, I've been a photographer on past assignments. I promise not to botch up the pictures." Deborah smiled.

"It's not the photos I'm worried about; it's the misquotes. They make me sound heartless, or worse, dishonest." Tillman smiled, but his eyes showed sadness.

Tillman guided Deborah to the family room and motioned for her to sit on the white leather sofa. He chose the side chair.

Deborah turned to admire paintings on the walls. "That's a Thomas Thomson, and that one is a Norval Morrisseau. Nice. You have excellent taste, Carl." She placed her notepad and camera on the coffee table, retrieved a compact recording device from her jacket, turned it on, and placed it on the table. Deborah crossed her legs slowly, showing smooth, shapely legs. She interlaced her fingers over her knees, and bent forward, showing cleavage. She looked Tillman in the eyes and smiled.

"How would you like to conduct the interview?" Tillman asked.

"Let's start with you sharing your experience and accomplishments at GMR, and then we'll talk about your family and your life. But don't worry, nothing too personal. We'll finish with me shooting some photographs of you in your study. I'll be recording our conversation. Will that be alright?"

"That should be fine."

Tillman described how he and a few colleagues developed an advanced electronic camera for high-altitude military surveillance missions and drone operations. The manufacture and sale of the cameras to the American and Canadian military was very successful, and Tillman added a contracting business that provided soldiers as well as cameras. He renamed the company Grenadiers Military Resources. He concluded on a sad note: The profits and share value dropped when the war in Afghanistan ended, and he and the board of directors decided to sell the company's technology, and to close its doors.

Deborah had listened attentively, asked for clarifications, and took notes. She leaned forward and asked in a serious tone, "Carl, there's a delicate subject I must discuss with you. My editor insists that I touch on it."

The change in tone stunned Tillman. Deborah allowed him to switch gears. After a few moments, she said, "I need your response to the present criminal lawsuit, which claims you have accepted a thirty-million-dollar kickback from the buyers of GMR."

Tillman struggled to contain his anger. Tillman summoned the discipline and self-control he'd had to develop in order to face an adversarial board or a hostile press. "The matter is before the courts and, as instructed by my lawyers, I will not discuss this with anyone. However, I will state this: I'm innocent, and the courts will exonerate me completely."

"But you admit that selling the company at a price some experts estimate was below market value looks suspicious."

Tillman, now red-faced, stared at the reporter.

Deborah offered an olive branch. "I apologize for having been so blunt, but I had to record your response." She paused before adding, "I appreciate your professional attitude."

Tillman stared at Deborah. Although flushed with anger, he resisted the urge to throw her out unceremoniously. He admired her courage.

Deborah relieved the tension by saying, "Can I take photographs of you and your beautiful house?"

"Sure, please lead the way."

Deborah laced her arm under Tillman's, and walked with him to the study. She shot photographs of Tillman with varying backdrops. Once finished, she smiled at him and said in a playful tone, "I've learned you have German heritage. Do you own a lederhosen costume?"

"I do. I wear it at Oktoberfest," Tillman said. His facial muscles relaxed.

"Would you mind putting it on? It would make for beautiful pictures. Add colour to the article." She placed a hand on Tillman's forearm and smiled up at him.

Tillman considered the request. "Yes, I can do that. Give me a few minutes to change."

"Great!' Deborah said.

"I'll be back in five minutes."

Tillman did not worry about leaving a reporter unsupervised in his house. All sensitive documents were under lock and key. He climbed the stairs and headed for his closet and retrieved his lederhosen costume. He slipped into a slim-fit white box embroidered shirt and dark brown knee length leather pants and suspenders. He slipped on his bundhosen off-white socks and dark brown shoes. He shrugged into a sleeveless red vest with embroidered black stand-up collar, fitted a brown Bavarian felt hat, adorned with a feather, on top of his head at a rakish angle, and admired his image in the full-length mirror.

Deborah watched Tillman descend the stairs. Her eyes sparkled. "My, my. You cut a fine figure, Mr. Tillman."

Tillman wondered at the return to the formal address, but he savoured the compliment about his figure. His following a daily exercise regimen and a balanced diet had paid off. He relaxed.

Deborah approached Tillman. A spark of mischief glinted in her eyes. "These Oktoberfest parties can get quite lively, I hear."

"Well, the beer drinking does loosen inhibitions."

"Men wearing lederhosen and women wearing those sexy dirndl costumes must liven things up.?"

Without waiting for a reply, Deborah leaned forward, put a hand on Tillman's chest, and kissed him on the lips.

Tillman stood, stunned. His member rose to a full erection. He returned the kiss.

The two groped and caressed each other, moaning with pleasure. Deborah led Tillman to the coffee table. She turned, climbed on all fours on the table, lifted her skirt and lowered her panties to her knees. Tillman grabbed her with both hands and penetrated her from behind.

After both had climaxed, they moved to the couch. They sat panting, leaning against each other. Tillman was pleased he had not needed his Viagra pills, but he regretted the weak ejaculation and loss of pleasure caused by the medication he took for his enlarged prostate.

They rose and straightened their clothes. Deborah retrieved her recorder, her notepad, and slipped the strap of her camera over her shoulder. Tillman escorted her to the door.

"Mr. Tillman, that was wonderful, but business being business, I must broach a delicate matter with you." Tillman stared, perplexed. Deborah continued. "Your former executive secretary has agreed to an interview with me and to provide details of the kickbacks she claims you negotiated during the sale of GMR." Deborah faced Tillman. "I could leave out the interview from my article in exchange for some compensation."

After the initial shock, Tillman clenched his jaw. "I advise you to think twice before blackmailing me. Once the court has rejected the accusations against me, I will sue you and your magazine for damages, and your reputation as a serious business journalist will be toast."

Deborah smiled at him. "Mr. Tillman, let's not dramatize the situation. You and I can agree amicably on a fair compensation for not printing the interview, without involving expensive lawyers. Please think it over. You have a few days. I'll contact you before going to press. Au revoir." She walked to her Audi, climbed in, waved, and drove off.

Tillman fumed. That interview appearing in a prestigious business magazine would be embarrassing to him and his family. He considered how best to deal with the little blackmailer.

CHAPTER 7

THE HOMESTEAD

The village of New Hamburg lies twenty-five kilometres west of the city of Kitchener in the province of Ontario. Bucolic farmlands surround the village, an ideal location for the Jennings to vacation before their next job.

Robert Cole owned the newly opened Homestead Airbnb, a five-bedroom century farmhouse. He had accepted his first booking from Jennings Electric Inc. from Chicago—four people in three bedrooms for two consecutive nights. Robert had granted permission for his guests to set up a fire pit in the yard.

Robert, a widower in his mid-fifties, with a full head of brown hair, blue eyes, a fit five-foot-ten physique, enjoyed country life. He had quit his engineering job two years earlier and purchased a hobby farm north of New Hamburg. He raised a few animals, planted cash crops, and opened an Airbnb to supplement his income. Robert was born and raised on a dairy farm, and had enjoyed the farming life.

Tom, his twenty-two-year-old son with black hair and brown eyes, just like his late mother's, lived with him. Tom helped with the farm chores and would help run the Airbnb.

Robert owned a house in Waterloo, a sister city to Kitchener. He had tried to sell it without success. The property values had plummeted following the latest deadly variant to the influenza pandemic. He listed the house to rent with a rental agency, but it remained without tenants.

Robert felt anxious about opening an Airbnb and becoming a host to tourists and visitors. The learning curve would be steep. His first customers would arrive tomorrow.

Robert and Tom had enjoyed a quick break on the porch before tackling the afternoon chores. "Let's go feed the troops." Robert said as he stepped off the porch and walked toward the barn.

Tom rose, lifted Mac—a black, short-haired tomcat—from his lap, placed him on the porch, and caught up with his father. Mac meowed in protest and followed the men.

Weathered, grey wooden planks covered the old barn. The traditional gambrel sheet metal roof kept the rain out. "They built them to last in those days" was a common saying in the countryside.

They entered the barn and walked down an aisle made of smooth concrete covered with strands of straw and bordered by animal stalls. Diffuse sunrays pierced through the cobweb-covered windows.

A whiff of ammonia pressed at their nostrils as they approached the stall of Wilma the sow and her twelve piglets. Wilma was of the Lacombe breed with pinkish-white skin and large droopy ears. She was the pride of the barn. Wilma's priority in life was caring for her litter. A close second was eating.

Sensing her keepers arriving, Wilma rushed to her feeding trough, climbed on it with her front hooves, raised her head above the enclosure, and grunted in anticipation.

Robert dumped potato peels, fallen apples, and grain feed in her trough, and Tom replenished the water basin. The piglets picked up on their mother's excitement and they raced around the stall, squealing and jostling each other.

"How are you today, Wilma?" Robert asked his favourite boarder. She grunted her appreciation.

Mac the tomcat was stepping daintily down the aisle, avoiding anything wet or sticky. He kept a safe distance between him and the pail of water Tom was carrying.

The men had converted some stalls into a chicken coop and a rabbit hutch. Robert enjoyed picking the eggs, but his favourite task was milking Snowball, a sturdy Holstein well adapted to Canada's climate. He milked her twice a day while humming Beatles tunes. He saved a dish of fresh milk for Mac.

The men completed the chores, looked at their menagerie one last time, and headed back to the house. Robert carried the pail of milk, and Tom, a basket of eggs.

"I'd like to get a dog," Tom said. "I'm thinking of a Chocolate Lab. Uncle Bill knows where we could get a pup."

"Hmm . . . I'd prefer a five- or six-year-old dog with a quiet temperament. I don't have the energy for a young pup."

"Okay. That's better than not having one, I guess. I'll ask Uncle Bill to look around for a mature dog."

Robert placed a hand on Tom's shoulder, and the men walked side by side.

Tom stopped by his marijuana patch. He handed the basket of eggs to his dad, and leaned to inspect the leaves for any insect infestation. Ladybugs were roaming the plants and eating aphids and other pests.

"A gardener's best friend," Tom said. He picked a few choice leaves. "For drying and smoking later." Tom looked up at Robert. "It's a great pastime and de-stressor. Healthier than your cigars." Robert chuckled and said, "To each generation his own."

Tom was the better cook, and for dinner he sautéed two chicken breasts and potato slices in a cast iron pan. He added tomato slices sprinkled with chives, then brought the two plates to the kitchen table.

Mac jumped on Tom's lap and surveyed the plates, impatient for leftovers.

Once finished their meals, the men laid their plates on the floor for Mac to lick. They had been careful to remove any bones.

After apple pie and ice cream, the men washed and dried the dishes. When they were finished, they moved to the porch and sat on rocking chairs. Robert lit a cigar and passed the box of matches to Tom, who lit a joint. Mac jumped on Tom's lap, curled up, and set to purring.

A reddish tinge covered the evening sky, and white cumulus clouds floated lazily from the northwest. The weather was unseasonably warm and humid for September, but didn't portend a thunderstorm. The storms had been violent in recent years.

They watched a doe in the orchard stretch her neck to grab red apples from a McIntosh tree. A family of wild turkeys pecked at the fallen apples. The male gobbler stood guard, feathers so puffed up he could hardly walk.

"I miss Mom," Tom said.

"I do, too. I wish she were still here with us," Robert said with a sigh.

Tom's mother had died during the resurgence of the 2020 influenza pandemic. A vaccine targeting the mutation became available and it marked the end of the pandemic, but a widespread shortage of manpower was prevalent in all occupations.

"You're not attending your NA meetings anymore?" Robert asked.

"I got into an argument with my sponsor. I'm clean of cocaine, but he wants me to quit marijuana, as well. No mood-altering drugs of any kind, he said. I'm not giving up grass. It helps me relax and control my anger."

"Well, I noted you're much calmer and free of those angry outbursts. But don't go too long without attending meetings. Get a new sponsor." Robert paused, then added, "Isn't there a medical marijuana that doesn't make you high?"

"Yes, I should give that a try. If that works for me, I'll grow some." Tom paused, then said, "There might be a market for it. I'll ask the Cannabis Shop managers on my next delivery."

Robert reflected, then said, "I wouldn't dream of doing without my AA meetings. They bring me peace and serenity, something alcohol promised but never delivered."

After finishing his cigar, Robert returned inside and checked the bedrooms to make sure they were ready for his first guests. Satisfied, he sat at the kitchen table and reviewed for the umpteenth time the instructions on hosting an Airbnb.

CHAPTER 8

THE JENNINGS AT THE HOMESTEAD

Robert spotted a black SUV approaching. The municipality had neglected road maintenance in the past years. The vehicle was kicking up a cloud of dust.

This must be my Airbnb booking, Robert thought. The driver of the SUV, a black Jeep Wrangler, braked, cranked the steering wheel, and swung into the driveway. The jeep skidded to a stop. The vehicle's plate read U.S. Marine Corps.

A tall, lean man, fiftyish, jumped out of the jeep. A Chicago Cubs baseball cap partly shaded his face. He was wearing jeans and a blue cotton shirt under an unzipped denim jacket. His walk revealed a slight limp. The visitor approached the porch. "Good day. You must be the owner of this Airbnb? I'm Malcolm Jennings."

Robert descended the steps and extended a hand to shake. "Welcome. I'm Robert Cole, the owner." The men shook hands. Robert turned and extended his arm in Tom's direction. "This is my son, Tom." Tom nodded at Malcolm.

Two women and a man had climbed out of the jeep and were walking over. One woman was fiftyish, with clear amber eyes, and auburn hair with gray strands. The other woman, clearly her daughter, had the same eyes and amiable smile. She had tied her blonde, curly hair in a ponytail. Both women were slim, dressed in jeans and checkered shirts. The man that followed close behind, was tall and slim, with auburn hair, in his late forties.

Malcolm turned and introduced his companions. "Robert, this is Gerta, my wife, and our daughter, Danielle. They look like sisters, don't they?" Gerta elbowed him in the ribs and smiled. "And this is Larry, my right-hand man. A fine soldier and now a fine electrician."

They shook hands.

"Gerta is our financial manager, bookkeeper, and researcher. She prints our advertising materials. She'll set her portable printing equipment in the house, if that's okay?"

"No problem," Robert said. "One bedroom has a former nursery attached to it. There's a table and a chair in it. You can set up an office in there."

"That will work fine," Gerta said.

"You folks must be tired," Robert said. "Can I offer you some water or soft drinks?"

"That would be swell," Malcolm said.

Robert turned and nodded to Tom, who headed back into the house.

"Your reservation said four people, three bedrooms, for two nights. Is that right?" Malcolm nodded.

"It gave Chicago as your home address?"

"Yes, we're all from Chicago."

"What brings you to these parts?"

"I'm an electrical contractor, and I plan to bid on residential and commercial projects in the Kitchener area. I'll be looking over some of these projects in the next few days." Malcolm noticed Robert's questioning look. "I'm licensed to work in Ontario. I'm aware of the paperwork that's involved. If I'm successful, I'll be returning with a full crew."

"You'll need more permanent accommodations in that case. I have a house in Waterloo for rent. It has five bedrooms, a finished basement, and a three-car garage. Three-car garages are rare in the city. But you won't have any trouble finding houses to rent. The last wave of the pandemic has changed things. There are a lot of properties for sale or rent."

"It's the same all over," Malcolm said. "I'll keep your offer in mind. But the initial crew will be small and I'd like to treat them to a few nights in the countryside first, at a place like this one." Malcolm looked around the yard.

"Sure. I have four bedrooms to rent with two double beds each. That will sleep up to eight people comfortably."

Tom had returned with a pitcher of water and glasses. The group moved to the porch and found seats. Tom served everyone a glass of ice-cold water.

Robert turned to Tom. "Why don't you show Danielle around? Have her meet Wilma and Snowball." He turned to the others. "They're our favourite animals."

Danielle smiled at Tom. "I'd like that." The two walked away toward the barn. The parents watched the young adults walk away, chatting and laughing.

Gerta spoke first. "It's a nice farmhouse you have here, Robert. It's even prettier than the photos on your website."

"It's called Victorian style," Robert said. "That and Ontario Gothic are common styles in our countryside."

All four walked down to the front of the house and stood admiring the red brick, the white quaintly ornamented gables, and the wrap-around porch.

"Please come in and I'll show you around." Robert extended an arm toward the front entrance.

Malcolm climbed the three steps, then stopped and grimaced. Robert looked on and waited.

Malcolm looked up at Robert. "A bullet to the hip. I served at the Bagram Air Base in Kabul." He resumed climbing the porch steps. "You Canadians were there, as well, I recall."

"Yes. Canada joined the NATO contingent in Kandahar."

Robert led the group up the stairs and showed them the guest bedrooms. "Guests can use the main bathroom upstairs and the powder room downstairs. Tom and I share the master bedroom. We have our own en suite bathroom."

Gerta inspected the bedroom with an adjoining nursery that Robert had mentioned.

"This will be ideal for us. I'll set up my printing equipment in the nursery," she said.

Robert led the group to the first-floor kitchen and showed them which appliances and dishes they could use. "You're welcome to eat all your meals here. The rental does not include food and beverages, but you can help yourselves to the staples."

"That'll be perfect!" Gerta said.

Malcolm turned to Gerta and Larry. "Let's unload our luggage and drive to the city for dinner."

"And we need to stop for groceries," Gerta said.

Malcolm turned to Robert. "Can you recommend a restaurant for us?"

"This region has a strong German heritage. Do you enjoy German cuisine?"

"We sure do," Gerta said.

"Then I recommend the Shenke restaurant in Kitchener. It's a Bavarian style country inn."

"Excellent. We'll check it out," Malcolm said.

The team unloaded the jeep and set up in their rooms.

Tom and Danielle returned from the barn tour and helped with the unloading. Malcolm informed Danielle of their plan for dinner. "Great. Can I invite a guest?" Danielle said as she looked up at him. Malcolm looked at Tom and smiled. "Absolutely."

Tom turned to his father with raised eyebrows. Robert smiled and nodded.

After settling in, Malcolm's team climbed into the jeep. Danielle waved Tom over and he climbed aboard. Robert waved from the porch as the troop headed toward the city.

CHAPTER 9

MALCOLM RECRUITS MORENO

At 6:00 a.m. the next morning, Malcolm woke to the sound of Robert and Tom leaving for the barn. He got up, slipped on a pair of jogging pants and a t-shirt, and walked downstairs to the living room. He moved the coffee table aside to make room for doing his exercises.

Danielle came down the stairs, quietly. She wore a jogging suit. She smiled at her father, pointed at the door leading outside, and walked out, closing the door softly behind her.

Malcolm began with stretching motions before moving to muscle strengthening exercises. He went through the motions, but couldn't concentrate. Last night's dream haunted him. He relived the recovery of his brother Eddie's body from the underside of the bridge that arched over the Euphrates river. The air stank of burned flesh and gasoline. Malcolm had awakened dripping with sweat.

Once he completed his exercise routine, Malcolm returned upstairs, showered, and dressed. He gently nudged Gerta awake, then walked over to the bedroom where Larry slept, and tapped on the door. "Rise and shine. I'll put the coffee on."

Danielle had returned from her run and she climbed the stairs. She joined her mother in the newly renovated bathroom with a double sink.

Malcolm listened to mother and daughter chatting and laughing together. He smiled, then headed downstairs. He walked to the kitchen and prepared a pot of coffee.

Larry, with his toiletry bag cradled under one arm, walked past, headed for the powder room.

Ten minutes later, Gerta and Danielle walked down the stairs and followed the smell of coffee to the kitchen counter. They grabbed a bun with jam that Malcolm had prepared, a mug of coffee, and sat at the large kitchen table. Larry soon joined them.

Gerta looked around. "Are the owners up?"

"They're at the barn," Malcolm said.

"Good, let's review our plan for today," Gerta said.

Malcolm faced her. "I've booked the appointment with Tillman's private security chief, Luis Moreno, for ten o'clock. We'll wear our technician's uniforms. You, Larry, and I will meet with him in his office. He'll have looked over the website Gerta has set up and expecting to be shown hi-tech security equipment. We'll follow the plan we have rehearsed." Malcolm looked intently at Gerta and Larry. "We'll only get one shot at this."

Gerta and Larry nodded.

Malcolm turned to Danielle. "You'll stay behind, keep watch over our things, and observe our hosts. Learn as much as you can about them, but discreetly."

Malcolm drank from his mug, then said, "After we've recruited Moreno, we'll drive over to Robert's rental property in the city and see if it's a good hideout for after the raid." He drank another mouthful of coffee. "Afterward, I want to do a dry run of our escape route out of the city. We'll drive the part up to the city of London for today. We'll dry run the rest of the escape route when we return home tomorrow."

As Malcolm drove the jeep along Huron Road, he recognized the Tillman estate in the distance from the pictures Gerta had downloaded from the internet. The residence, a large two-storey house, sat on higher ground some distance from the road. A meandering laneway, bordered by trees and bushes, led to the residence. A large guardhouse, more like a security team's residence, sat near the entrance to the property. Malcolm parked the jeep by the guardhouse door.

A separate guard booth with a gate arm controlled the entrance to the laneway that led to the Tillman residence. A man in a dark-blue uniform left the guard booth and walked over.

Malcolm lowered his window. "Is this Mr. Tillman's residence?"

"Yes, it is. Do you have an appointment? There's no entry on the visitors' log."

"No, not with Mr. Tillman, but with Security Chief Moreno. He's expecting us, Jennings Electric, at ten o'clock."

"He's doing the rounds now, but I can reach him by radio. Your firm, again? And what is it regarding?"

"Jennings Electric. Security products and services."

The guard unclipped his portable radio, and after a brief back-and-forth conversation, he turned to Malcolm. "Mr. Moreno will be here shortly. If you could wait in your car, please?"

Moreno drove up in a black Toyota Camry. He parked by the guardhouse, and walked over to Malcolm's open window.

"Hi. I'm Luis Moreno. You wanted to show me some new security equipment?"

"Hi, Mr. Moreno. I'm Malcolm Jennings. Yes, we'd like to show you some samples of our latest equipment."

"Good. Let's go inside."

The four entered the guardhouse. The building housed a meeting room with a workstation, a kitchen counter with cupboards, a door leading to a washroom, and one leading to sleeping quarters. Moreno sat on the far side of the small conference table, his back to his work desk. From his seat, he could look through the picture window and observe the entrance to the property and the guard booth. Malcolm and Gerta sat facing Moreno. Larry placed an equipment case on the table and stood by the door.

"Thank you for agreeing to meet with us, Mr. Moreno." Malcolm introduced Gerta as the company's electronics specialist, and Larry as the weapons specialist. Malcolm handed over a business card and a brochure of Jennings Electric.

"Thanks for coming. Your timing is opportune. As you already know, Mr. Tillman was the CEO of a supplier of military equipment and personnel to the Canadian and U.S. armies. Since the company folded, disgruntled former employees have been sending threatening letters and emails to Mr. Tillman. Some included death threats. Mr. Tillman especially fears possible kidnapping of family members for ransom. I'm looking forward to what you've got to show me?" Moreno eyed the equipment case. "Samples? Brochures?"

"Before we show you samples of our products, we'd like to learn more about your existing setup," Malcolm said.

Moreno straightened, then said, "Okay. Ask away."

"How much property do you have to protect?"

"There's the principal residence where the Tillman family lives. It's a two-storey house with five bedrooms and a three-car garage. Mr. Tillman's family includes his wife, a son, and a live-in girlfriend. We escort them when they leave the property. Mr. Tillman and his son, Paul, each own a car. A housekeeper lives with the family. There's a small horse barn with two riding horses, and a hangar with a light aircraft. The property covers over fifty acres. A rancher drops in daily to care for the horses, and a landscaping contractor visits once a week to care for the flowers, trees, and ornamental bushes."

"How large a security team have you assigned to protect the property?"

"We run two guards per shift, three shifts a day, seven days a week. I supervise the daytime shift, but I'm on call twenty-four seven."

"Do you have camera surveillance? Electronic or closed circuit?"

"We have cameras at some key locations, entrance to the property, entrances to the house. We've installed closed-circuit cameras."

Malcolm turned to Gerta and nodded. This information matched what Gerta had discovered during her research.

"Has Mr. Tillman been a good employer to work with? Have you become personal friends?"

Moreno frowned. "Our relationship is strictly professional, but what does that have to do with your product line?"

"Mr. Moreno, we would like to discuss a proposition with you."

Moreno looked on with furrowed eyebrows.

Malcolm leaned forward. "We know of your financial difficulties, your gambling debts. We know your creditors are dangerous people and they are threatening you unless you settle what you owe promptly."

Moreno straightened in his seat. "How would you know anything about my financial situation?"

"Gerta has read your phone conversations and your emails."

Moreno's eyes narrowed. His face was flushed. He glanced out the window. The guard stationed at the guard booth was too far to hear someone shouting for help. "What kind of proposition?"

"A proposition that will make you a lot of money. And this money couldn't come at a better time, right?"

Moreno sat red-faced.

Malcolm continued, "Mr. Tillman has overseas accounts containing over thirty million dollars. If you can arrange for us to meet with him privately in his residence, we will convince him to give us access to those accounts. We'll share the take with you." Moreno sat speechless. Malcolm continued, "Then we'll be on our way, never to be seen again. Your share will be large enough for you to do the same."

Moreno straightened in his chair. "I want no part of this. You guys had better leave now before I call the police."

"Easy now, Mr. Moreno. You haven't heard all the details yet. Just give me a few more minutes of your time. You won't regret it."

Moreno stared at Malcolm, his expression growing darker.

"We'll give you twenty percent of the take, six million dollars." Malcolm paused, then added, "It's fraud money, so Tillman won't go to the police with this."

Moreno blinked and swallowed hard. "I don't see how you could carry that out without getting caught. I can't ask my guards to stand down and look the other way while you rob the place."

"We have a plan. You'll clear the schedule for the evening shift. You'll phone each guard individually, and at the last minute, so they won't discuss it amongst themselves and get suspicious. We'll post our man at the gate."

Moreno raised his eyebrows at that. "Assuming I go along with this plan, what's preventing the police from arresting me?"

"Let's review your present arrangements," Malcolm said. "You're renting an apartment, and you live alone, so there's no real estate property to dispose of and no wife or children to worry about. We'll provide you with new identity papers and one hundred thousand dollars in cash up front so you can prepare your escape. You can make a fresh start in the country of your choosing, one with no extradition treaty with Canada. The police and your creditors will never find you."

Moreno sat, pensive.

Malcolm continued, "Once we've accessed Tillman's funds, Gerta will transfer your share to an account of your choosing, anywhere in the world, right there on the spot."

Moreno sat upright in his chair, his face impassive. Malcolm thought, *He's trying to appear bigger than he is. He must be a bluffer at poker.*

Moreno stared at Malcolm, then said, "Okay, let's say I'm interested. When can you get me those new identification papers?"

Gerta answered, "We'll take a photograph of your passport or your driver's licence, and we'll prepare a new passport, driver's licence, social security number, and credit card. We'll have those ready for you on the night of the raid."

"How do I know they'll be any good?"

Malcolm retrieved a passport from his jacket pocket and handed it over to Moreno. "This is one of my passports. Note the different name."

Moreno leafed through the document from cover to cover, then stopped at the data page. "It looks real, but will it pass a scan at the border?"

Gerta leaned forward and pointed at the code on the passport's data page. "This code must match the one in the government's database. I can access that database. I will select the code of a person with a clean record. I will then program the microchip that is embedded in the cover page to match the information on the data page." Gerta showed Moreno where the microchip was located on the cover page. Moreno rubbed the microchip with his fingers.

Malcolm asked Moreno to find a visa page with an entry stamp on it. "I've used this passport to cross the border already. See the stamp?"

Moreno stared at the stamped visa page. He returned the passport to Malcolm. "When did you want to do this?"

"In a month's time. On an evening when Tillman is home, alone."

"First, explain to me how you'll go about this."

Malcolm nodded to Larry, who came forward and opened the equipment case. It contained two M16s and two semi-automatic pistols.

Malcolm looked directly at Moreno. "We're former soldiers, ready for the unexpected. One of us was an enhanced interrogation officer." This last part was not true, but Malcolm felt he needed the lie to convince Moreno.

Moreno examined the weapons on the table. "If you fire those weapons, the noise will alert the neighbours."

"We'll only fire those weapons when the police have already arrived," Malcolm said.

Seeing that Moreno was hesitant, Malcolm added, "We saw a military gun range a mile down the road. Your neighbours will think any gunfire is coming from the gun range."

Moreno looked reassured.

Malcolm summarized the plan he and Gerta had devised. "One man will guard the entrance to the property, one will guard the front of the house, and a team will enter the house and subdue Tillman. Gerta will transfer the funds. The entire operation will be over inside one hour, two maximum."

Moreno kept blinking and rubbing his hands together.

Malcolm rose. "I'll call you in three weeks' time, and we'll pick an evening when Tillman will be alone."

Moreno considered, then said, "That can work. Mr. Tillman and I schedule their comings and goings a week in advance."

"Can you make sure the live-in housekeeper is away on that night?"

Moreno mulled the question over. "I guess I could invent a reason to get her out of the residence for the night."

"Good!" Malcolm said.

Gerta looked at Moreno. "I'll need your passport or your driver's licence."

Moreno handed over his driver's licence. She photographed it and handed back the document. "Any preference for your new name?"

Moreno thought for a moment. "Just make it a Latino name."

Gerta nodded.

Larry closed the equipment case and waited by the door.

Gerta retrieved a cell phone from her satchel, and handed it to Moreno. "This is a burner. We'll call you on this phone."

Moreno picked up the phone and slipped it in his pocket.

Malcolm climbed behind the wheel, fired up the engine, and turned to his team. "Let's drive the side roads that border on the property and firm up our emergency escape plan."

Moreno leaned over his desk and wiped his forehead with a Kleenex and threw it in the garbage can. His phone rang. The display read 'caller unknown'. He picked up.

"Yes."

"Moreno. This is Marcos."

Moreno straightened. "I told you not to call me at work."

"I'll call you when and where I choose to."

"Why are you calling?" Moreno bit his lips.

"Your monthly payment is late."

"I've had a streak of bad luck. I need more time." Moreno wiped his forehead. "Christ. I already gave you my house and my Range Rover."

"You collected insurance on the Range Rover, so, no sympathy for that one." Marcos let a moment pass, then continued. "Your balance owing is two hundred and fifty thousand. Your employer is a multimillionaire. He owns luxury cars, and there must be a safe in his house. Figure something out."

"I'll win back the money. Just give me a bit more time for Christ's sake."

"Come back to me with a solid plan or I send Miguel with his baseball bat. He'll start on your left arm."

"Hold on, for God's sake. Okay. I'll come up with a plan. But I'll need some time to put it together."

"How much time?"

"Give me six weeks."

"You have three weeks."

Marcos hung up.

CHAPTER 10

TOM AND DANIELLE

Tom and his father returned from the barn, washed up, and sat down for breakfast. Mac the tomcat had climbed on Tom's knees and was sniffing at the food on the plate.

Danielle was sitting in the living room, reading.

"Come join us at the table, Danielle," Tom said. He then looked over at his father, who smiled and nodded.

"Thanks for the invitation," Danielle said. "'I would enjoy the company." She rose, walked to the kitchen counter, filled a mug with coffee, and took a place at the table.

"How was the room? Did you have a comfortable sleep?" Robert asked.

"Great. The bed was firm, which I like." She smiled, then added, "It was so quiet. Not like in the city."

"First time sleeping in the country?" Robert asked.

"First time on a farm."

"This is a hobby farm," Robert said. "It's nothing like the dairy farm of my childhood, but I love having a few animals around."

"Tell us about your training with the Marines," Tom said.

"Dad was a Marine, and so was Uncle Eddie. I followed in their footsteps, I guess. The training was like you'd have seen on TV and in the movies. It's a lot of hard physical training at first, but I attended university courses, as well, in the general science program. I left the army six months ago to work with Mom and Dad."

"Are you an electrician, as well?" Tom asked.

"Apprentice electrician, and I help Mom with the accounting and the paperwork. I enjoy it."

Robert looked pleased with that statement. "I was an engineer. I liked it a lot, but I enjoy the challenge of running a hobby farm and an Airbnb. I still do the odd engineering project."

Danielle looked up at Tom. "When you showed me around the barn yesterday, I could tell you love animals, especially the sow and her piglets. Wilma, you called her? Are you planning to be a farmer?"

"No, no. I enjoy caring for animals and helping dad with the hobby farm, but I want to learn a trade and work on different projects. I'd like to learn electrical work."

Mac jumped off Tom's lap and climbed on Danielle's. He poked his head over the edge of the table.

"He's fun," Danielle said as she petted him.

Tom mulled over something before saying, "We'll be driving over to a friend's farm shortly to help with the barn chores. She lives alone. Would you like to come?"

"Yes, if you think I won't be in the way. I know nothing about farm work."

"You won't be in the way. Right, Dad?"

Robert smiled back. "You two go ahead without me. I have plenty of work to do here." He looked up at Tom. "Take the pickup. Say hi to Sharon for me. Leave the dishes. I'll clean up."

Sharon Doyle's farm lay southwest of New Hamburg, some twenty kilometres from Robert's Airbnb. During the drive, Danielle asked, "You said Sharon lives alone?"

"Yes. Her husband died during the last year of the epidemic. The same year my mom died, also from COVID."

"I'm sorry."

"I really like Sharon. She takes good care of her animals. She doesn't work in the fields. She leases her three hundred acres to local farmers for income. Her two sons, a few years older than me, live and work in Toronto, but they come and visit regularly. Dad and I drive over every other day to help out and check in on her."

Since the death of their spouses, Sharon's and Robert's two families had stayed close. Tom looked to Sharon as a surrogate mother, and he confided in her about his problems, his romantic relationships, and his dreams.

Tom parked the pickup in Sharon's driveway. He and Danielle walked to the front door. Tom knocked, but there was no answer. "She must be in the barn."

The barn stood about a hundred metres from the house. It boasted a peaked roof common to country barns. The animals occupied the ground floor. Hay and straw were stored on the second storey, or loft. Tom and Danielle entered and walked along the main aisle.

Tom spotted Sharon, who was feeding the rabbits at the far end of the aisle. Rabbit hutches stood waist-high against the barn wall. As the young couple approached, Sharon put down the pail of feed pellets, and walked over to greet her visitors.

Sharon was in her early fifties, with brown hair, clear brown eyes, and a slim figure. She smiled, bright-eyed, and smothered Tom in a hug. "Hi, Tom. I see you've brought a friend over?" She extended her hand for Danielle to shake. "Hi. I'm Sharon."

"I'm Danielle. Pleased to meet you, Sharon."

"As you can see, I run a small hobby farm much like Tom and his father do. But I couldn't do it without their help."

"I'm glad I got here before you'd finished all the chores," Tom said. "Let me water the animals and clean their litter while you show Danielle around."

"Thanks. You're a sweetheart."

Sharon guided Danielle to meet the animals. They stopped first at the two milking cows who had been milked and were eating silage before returning to the fields. Next, they watched the four pigs who were eagerly slurping the whey from their feed trough. Then they petted the rabbits, and finally, they visited the six laying hens.

"Can I pick the eggs?" Danielle asked as they approached the laying boxes.

"Sure." Sharon handed Danielle a basket. "But don't let Charlotte scare you." Sharon pointed at a White Leghorn sitting a laying box. "She's a broody hen, and she'll peck your hand to protect her egg. But don't worry. She won't draw blood."

"Danielle slipped her hand underneath Charlotte, who pecked it immediately.

"Ouch." Danielle pulled her hand out in shock. A red dot marked the spot where Charlotte had struck.

"You forgot to retrieve the egg," Sharon said with a chuckle.

Danielle bit her lips, stuck her hand quickly underneath the hen, and retrieved a white egg. Charlotte pecked Danielle's hand again. Danielle laughed this time. "Thank you, Ms. Charlotte." Danielle finished picking the rest of the freshly laid eggs.

"Forgive me for prying, but is it not lonely living by yourself?" Danielle asked.

"It is at times, for sure. It's worst during power, telephone, or Wi-Fi outages. Since the last wave of the pandemic, utilities have been short of maintenance personnel, and interruptions are more frequent. But Tom or Robert drive over and visit often."

The women walked over to join Tom, who was spreading fresh litter under the cows.

A grey cat came forward and rubbed herself against Danielle's leg.

"Meet Bella," Sharon said. "Her kittens have become rambunctious, and Bella wants to introduce them to us in the hope we'll adopt them."

Bella, as if on cue, ran back to her nest in the hay where four two-month-old kittens tumbled and play-fought with each other.

"They're so cute," Danielle said as she kneeled and picked up a kitten, petted him, while whispering endearments.

Tom appeared, lugging two full pails of milk. "I think the chores are done."

"Thank you so much, Tom," Sharon said as she put a hand on his shoulder. "Let's have coffee and muffins in the house."

Danielle brought the basket with the eggs, and Tom brought the pails of milk. Sharon let out the two cows, and closed the heavy barn door behind them.

BAD KARMA

On the drive back to the Homestead, Tom asked Danielle, "Will your dad hire local help if he wins some electrical contracts? I'd like to apply as apprentice electrician."

CHAPTER 11

THE RELIANT DETECTIVE AGENCY

Chief Chuck Harrington managed the Criminal Investigation Division of The Reliant Detective Agency in Ann Arbor. He summoned his team leader. "Captain Morris! In my office, please!"

Team captain James Morris was nicknamed Popeye by his team following a successful drug bust. He'd accepted the nickname with pride. He walked over to his supervisor's office and entered, leaving the door ajar. Glossy movie posters adorned the walls. Popeye never tired of looking at them. His favourite, *The French Connection*, hung on the wall to his left. Next to it hung *Silence of the Lambs*. Next to that, *The Pink Panther*, and the last, *Steve Jobs*. Chief Harrington had posted this last one in honour of the team's cyber expert, Agent Louise Jackson. The team had floated the nickname "Jobs" for Agent Jackson, but it never stuck.

"Yes, Chief?" Popeye said as he faced Harrington, who was sitting behind a grey metal desk covered with file folders that lay in a half circle, like coliseum seats.

"We've clinched a good-paying contract," the chief said. "We're to identify, locate, and arrest the assassins who've murdered a prominent CEO some three months ago. Our client has received a threatening email like the one the murdered CEO received before he was attacked. Our client fears he may be next in line." Chief Harrington let Popeye catch up.

Popeye wrinkled his forehead. "You're referring to CEO Jamie Stonely of Stonely Holdings in New York City?"

"Yes."

Popeye rubbed his chin. "The criminals robbed and murdered Stonely."

"They had more than money on their mind. It smells of revenge," Harrington said.

"Why do you say that?"

"They hanged the man."

"Yes. Your deduction makes sense. Who's our client?"

"Carl Tillman, former CEO of Grenadiers Military Resources, or GMR, in Kitchener, Canada. He received the untraceable email a few weeks ago. He's reported it to the Canadian authorities, the RCMP. The FBI has been investigating the Stonely murder, but they haven't arrested anyone yet. Tillman's turning to us to find the murderers, fast."

Harrington picked a document from his desk and thumbed through the front pages. "We'll be operating under the new private policing bill. It's in effect in the U.S., Canada, and Mexico." He closed the document. "It's been rushed into law with little consultation. I see conflicts of jurisdiction between the different law enforcement bodies and private policing contractors like us. Our legal team has produced a protocol for us to follow. Make sure you read this document and follow it." He handed it to Popeye.

"What's our timetable?"

"Urgent," Chief Harrington answered. "I promised results in two weeks, three at the most." He looked at Popeye with raised eyebrows.

"That's doable if I drop everything else."

"Put the entire team on it today. This contract could lead to many more in the future."

"I'm on it."

Popeye walked to Agent Louise Jackson's cubicle. "Hi, Louise. Did you overhear my conversation with Chief Harrington?"

Louise Jackson, mid-forties, with ebony skin and dreadlocks down to the shoulders, was an IT specialist recruited from Marine Corps Intelligence. Louise had graduated from Stanford and completed a contract assignment for NSA. She sat facing her two laptop screens. She raised her eyes. "Yes, I heard everything, and I'm on it. Give me a few hours and I'll have the details of Stonely's murder on our internal website. Remind everyone to be discreet about what they see. I'll post crime lab results that some of the FBI boys and girls haven't seen yet." She winked at Popeye.

"Wow. I love that self-confidence, but hey, you produce results." Popeye smiled and winked back.

Louise used research-level search engines that fell into uncharted legal territory. She could search and read highly sensitive documents and communications using a similar program to those she had worked on while employed by NSA. Reliant's legal team had prepared legal defence scenarios in the event of leaks, accidental or deliberate, that would originate from their agency. Such a leak would bring on government scrutiny, destroy Reliant's business model, and possibly close the firm down.

Popeye walked over to his team members, who sat at open-concept workstations.

"Did you guys overhear my conversation with Chief Harrington?"

Agents Ashley Hurd and Pierre Chamberlain nodded.

"We're on it already, O Great Leader," Ashley said.

"Good! So, you're already contacting everyone you know, friend or foe—anyone who may know something about this murder? I expect you'll search as far back as your primary school buddies?"

Everyone looked at him with raised eyebrows.

"We'll convene tomorrow at one p.m. and share what we've learned." Popeye returned to his office.

Every team member turned to their phone and laptop and began contacting colleagues, as well as personal and professional acquaintances. They kept an eye on the in-house website where Louise was posting details of the FBI's investigation of Stonely's murder. They posted all the relevant info they discovered.

Popeye held his team's abilities in high regard. Chief Harrington had recruited each one from the military intelligence community, and all had served in either Iraq, Afghanistan, or Syria. All were in their mid-forties.

Within the first hour, Louise had accessed FBI files and posted crime scene investigation reports, forensics lab reports, and police interviews concerning Stonely's murder. She was now digging for the FBI's list of suspects.

CHAPTER 12

THE TILLMAN HOUSEHOLD

Carl Tillman and his wife, Amanda, sat at the dinner table waiting for their son, Paul, and his live-in girlfriend, Linda, to join them. Amanda sat upright on her Regency mahogany dining chair, her dark-brown eyes fixed straight ahead, her pupils narrowed. "What in heaven's name is keeping them? They're always late. We sit here like idiots and the food gets cold. It's disrespectful. Carl, go talk to them."

Carl was reading a magazine, a behaviour Amanda frowned upon. He raised his head. "I've told them a hundred times already. You spoiled Paul. He's thirty years old and he doesn't have a job yet."

"Could you at least go upstairs and see what's keeping them? And please don't shout from the foot of the stairs. That's so crude." She looked up at their housekeeper. "Anita, could you please put our plates in the oven?"

"Yes, madam." Anita removed the plates of chicken breasts, golden sauce, mashed potatoes, and sweet peas.

Carl sprinted up the curved stairs. He was impressed by his energy level. From the landing, he overheard a heated discussion between Paul and Linda. He disliked Linda, didn't approve of her. A gold digger, in his opinion, but Amanda liked her, so he kept his opinion to himself.

Linda was berating Paul. "When will we get out of this prison camp and do something fun for a change?"

"What do you expect me to do? Dad has these bodyguards escorting us everywhere. We can't go anywhere without a pre-approved destination and a security escort tagging along."

"Show some balls and make some frigging arrangements. I want to go somewhere interesting without these toy soldiers following us around."

"Where do you want to go, anyway? The clubs sit half empty like raided tombs. Suggest something instead of complaining all the time." Paul paused before saying, "What happened with horse riding? Dad purchased two quarter horses for us, and you haven't ridden in months."

"I'm having serious regrets about teaming up with you," Linda said. "Derek Meyer had the hots for me, but I chose you instead. Now I hear he's flying all over the place, to casinos, to beach resorts, while I languish in this dungeon. Your father has this airplane, a Witchcraft or some such name, and you have a pilot's license, so why don't we fly somewhere fun for a few weeks?"

"It's a Beechcraft. But okay, I'll ask Dad if I can borrow it, and we'll fly somewhere for a few weeks, a month even." Paul mulled over an idea, then said, "My friend, Brandon, he's living in his parents' luxury condo in the Caymans. He's invited us over. The condo's in a fully guarded compound on a beach. That should satisfy Dad's obsession with security."

"Why do you need his permission? Don't you have enough money for us to leave whenever we feel like it?"

"You know very well I'm on a weekly allowance, so I don't have savings to draw from."

Linda whispered, "What about the vault in the basement? Ask your mother for the combination. She'll give it to you. We will borrow what we need for the trip, and you pay it back later."

Linda had lowered her voice. Carl could no longer hear the conversation, so he knocked on the door of the suite. "Guys, we're waiting for you at the dinner table. Hurry up and come down to dinner."

Paul and Linda followed Tillman downstairs and took their places at the table.

"Sorry, Mom. We forgot about the time," Paul said.

Amanda looked at her son, let out an exasperated sigh, and motioned to Anita to bring back their dinners. The matriarch unfolded her white cotton napkin on her lap, while Carl escaped to a dream world inhabited by more congenial company. He caught Paul and Linda exchanging furtive looks with each other, no doubt working mentally at their newly hatched plan.

After dinner, Amanda retired to the living room, sat in her favourite armchair, and leafed through a fashion magazine.

Paul drew up a chair next to his mother, leaned over and whispered, "Mom, Linda and I need to go on a trip before we go mad from acute cabin fever." He then segued into his plan to fly the Beechcraft to the Caymans and spend a month at his friend Brandon's family resort. His mother bit her lips, wrung her hands, and stared at Paul with sad eyes.

"I need to borrow an advance on my allowance. I'll pay you back later," Paul said.

"I'm okay with your borrowing what you need for a trip, but you know your father won't go along with this," she said. "He's extra worried about security these days." She let out a deep breath and rose. "Let's go talk to him. He's in a good—well, neutral mood tonight."

Mother and son approached Carl, who was working at his laptop in the den. Paul presented his plan, stressing the safety of Brandon's guarded compound.

"I know Brandon's father," Carl said. "A good business executive. I've had dealings with him during my GMR days."

Paul's face lit up.

"I'm sorry, but the Beechcraft must remain here in case of an emergency," Carl said. "Besides, jet fuel is cripplingly expensive, and the airports you'll be refuelling at will be crawling with criminals. I'm paying a small fortune for a security team to keep us safe and you're planning to fly cross-country without security backup?"

Paul and his mother looked at each other and lowered their gaze. Carl had defaulted to his martinet persona, as Amanda called it.

"Why don't you and Linda go to the bars that are still open, or to parties at your friends' houses? I'll pitch in for a limo to drive you and your friends to the hot spots, as you young people call them." Carl paused for a moment to mull over some ideas in his head. "Or why don't you and Linda invite friends to a garden party in the backyard? I'll pitch in for a DJ and a caterer. How about that?"

"I'll think about it," Paul said. He looked up at Linda standing by the kitchen counter. Linda shook her head at his beaten-puppy face. She walked toward the stairs, and Paul followed her. They returned to their suite.

Amanda put a hand on her husband's knee and said, "Why don't we let them leave for a brief trip of their choosing without an escort? They can call us daily, let us know how they're doing. They feel cooped up, and I understand them."

"Let's give some more time for things to calm down. Maybe next year?" He looked at his wife with tired eyes. "Don't you like the suggestions I made? They're young and fickle. That's the problem. At their request, I bought them two riding horses, and I've been paying a stable hand to care for the horses. Paul and Linda haven't ridden in months! I've sold the animals. A rancher will come and pick them up tomorrow afternoon."

Carl sat, wringing his hands, then said, "This isn't a good time to let them ride around without an escort. I'm still receiving death threats. Since the last wave of this damn pandemic, police surveillance is sparse, and criminals are multiplying like cockroaches."

Tillman stared at Amanda. "I'm worried for our safety. I've placed a contract with a detective agency. I don't trust our security team, or the police, to protect us."

"Surely it's not that serious? What detective agency? You never consult me about these matters."

"Well, I consulted Everett. He recommended the Reliant Detective Agency in the States. I've talked with them. They explained that with this new private policing law, they'll have the same powers to investigate and arrest criminals as the police do."

"How much will that cost?"

"I've released an initial hundred and fifty thousand dollars. They'll be here tomorrow night, after the rancher has picked up the horses, and they'll lay out their plan of action."

"I think you're overreacting, Carl." Amanda sighed and said, "Explain this to Paul? He looked so depressed when you turned his idea down."

Tillman climbed the stairs. He stopped on the landing when he heard the children shouting.

Linda had lost it. "Where were your frigging balls? Didn't you tell Father Führer that you're extending him a courtesy by informing him of our plans, and if he doesn't approve of them, that's just too bad? We're adults, and we make our own plans!"

"Keep your voice down, for Christ's sake! Mom's on our side and she has savings. She'll help us." Paul added, "Tell you what. I'm so confident of success, let's pack right now."

Carl heard the thud of suitcases being thrown on the bed. He cursed, turned around, and returned downstairs.

CHAPTER 13

THE JENNINGS DRIVE TO CANADA

Malcolm sat at the wheel of his Jeep Wrangler, with Gerta and Danielle onboard, heading toward Detroit. Steve drove close behind in a cargo van with Duke riding shotgun. Larry followed in a second cargo van with newly recruited Jim Burke onboard.

Duke had performed well during their first heist, which had earned him this second assignment. Gerta had expressed reservations about Duke's character from the very first interview. His having been dishonourably discharged for exchanging food for sex in Afghan villages was a red flag to her. She felt that a man who seeks immediate gratification, and who is prone to short-term thinking, could not be trusted.

Malcolm had agreed that Duke was none too smart and very impulsive.

"I feel sorry for the guy. He's an orphan who has bounced from one foster home to another before he was old enough to join the Marines. The man is looking for a family to join. I need his physical strength — brains and ethics are optional."

Jim was a veteran of the Afghanistan war. Disillusioned with the business side of war, he had requested a discharge. He had floated since, pursuing high-risk, high-paying security assignments with military contractors.

Malcolm knew him from Afghanistan and trusted him. Jim had joined the team for the action and the money, and Malcolm was fine with that.

The caravan approached the St. Clair River, which marked the border between Detroit and Canada. One could cross into Canada via the Detroit-Windsor Tunnel or the Ambassador Bridge. Completion of the proposed Gordie Howe International Bridge had been delayed by the latest resurgence of the pandemic. Malcolm crossed over the Ambassador bridge, and the two cargo vans followed. They lined up behind a file of cars and transport trucks that carried people and goods to America's largest market.

Malcolm advanced to the Canadian border inspection booth, lowered his window, and handed over the passports.

The border agent asked for everyone's nationality, and he scanned the passports. A flag must have come up on his screen because he stared at it intently, then turned to Malcolm and Gerta. "Care to comment about those previous arrests for the two of you?"

Malcolm answered. "It was a public demonstration against corporate excesses that got out of hand. You may remember the Occupy movement?"

"Before my time, but I've heard about it." The agent reread his computer screen, paused, bit his lips, then turned to Malcolm. "What's the purpose of your trip?"

"We'll be attending bid review meetings in Kitchener for electrical projects. I have the paperwork for working in Ontario. The two vans behind me are part of my crew."

The agent eyed the two vans. "An officer will come over and guide you and your crew to secondary inspection." The agent kept the passports.

A second agent appeared. He guided Malcolm, Steve, and Larry to secondary inspection. The agent instructed Malcolm and the team to wait inside the station while agents combed through the contents of the vehicles. Gerta handed over a folder that contained the licenses and the work permits.

Thirty minutes had passed when a voice on the speaker system called Malcolm to the counter. An agent was waiting for him. "Your electrical contracting paperwork is in order, and so are your weapons trading and debt collection licences." The agent paused, then said, "Why do you carry so much weaponry? You have enough weapons to hold the entire city of Kitchener hostage."

"Our legal advisor said Canada has dropped the restrictions on gun ownership, and of the import and trading of firearms. That Canada now allows the free flow of firearms and ammunition across your border? Is that correct?"

"Yes. That's now the case, but you didn't answer my question."

"There's a pent-up demand for weapons in Canada. That side business keeps the electrical business afloat through lean times."

The agent handed over the file with the documents, the passports, and the key fobs. "You're clear to go."

Malcolm and his crew headed toward Robert's Airbnb in New Hamburg. Danielle leaned forward between the front seats and asked, "Dad, can we stop at Sharon's place to say hi? It's on the way."

Malcolm turned to Gerta, who nodded. "Sure, honey. You point the way."

CHAPTER 14

THE STOP AT SHARON'S HOME

Malcolm's jeep and the two cargo vans rode into Sharon's driveway. He and Danielle climbed out and walked toward the house. Danielle rapped on the door.

Sharon opened the door. "Danielle. What a pleasant surprise."

"Hi, Sharon. It's so nice to see you." The women hugged. "Did Tom tell you we'll be staying at the Homestead for two nights?"

"Yes, he did." Sharon released Danielle and turned to Malcolm. "You must be Danielle's father. I can see the resemblance."

"Yes. This is my dad," Danielle said.

"Pleased to meet you, Sharon. I'm Malcolm." He stretched his hand for Sharon to shake. "I hope we didn't scare you, barging into your driveway like an invading army?"

"Not at all. It's still common, in the countryside, for travellers to stop and ask for directions. Did you drive directly from Chicago?"

"Yes. We left this morning," Danielle answered. "I'm so excited. I couldn't wait to see you, Tom, and the barn animals again."

"You must be tired from travelling all this way? Bring everyone inside. I can offer you cold lemonade. How many of you are there?"

"There are seven of us," Malcolm said. "Is it okay if we sit under the big maple tree in your front yard? It's so nice out."

"Absolutely. I'll bring out the lemonade."

"Let me help you," Danielle said.

The women walked to the kitchen while Malcolm returned to the vehicles.

Sharon retrieved the large plastic canister of water and three lemons from the fridge. She placed everything on the kitchen counter. "I'll let you crush some ice cubes while I slice and squeeze the lemons," Sharon said to Danielle.

There was a knock on the front door, and a woman entered. "Sharon? Danielle?"

"Oh. It's Mom," Danielle said.

Gerta walked over to the kitchen. "Hi. I'm Gerta. You must be Sharon. I came to help with the lemonade."

"Hi, Gerta. It's nice of you to offer." Sharon shook hands with her visitor. "Yes. If you and Danielle could bring over the pitchers and the glasses, I'll bring over some muffins."

Gerta grabbed the two pitchers, Danielle, the glasses. Sharon followed with a basket full of freshly baked apple muffins.

The men were already sitting in the shade of the giant silver maple tree. After Malcolm had introduced everyone to Sharon, the women served the assembly, then took a seat in the shade. Everyone sighed with pleasure as they savoured the lemonade and the muffins.

Sharon spoke first. "So, you've landed some electrical projects in the region?"

"Not yet, but we will carry out bid review meetings on several projects and hopefully win one or two contracts."

"I hear there's a lot of construction work in Kitchener, but there's a shortage of labour?" Sharon said.

"Yes, ever since the last wave of the pandemic, we contractors are short of trained personnel."

"Tom is interested in working for you, Dad," Danielle said.

"Let's see if we land some of these projects first."

Duke turned to Sharon. "Is there any coffee or tea, by any chance?"

"No, I'm sorry. I'm out of both," Sharon said. "I need to go grocery shopping."

Malcolm looked at Duke. "That wasn't polite, Duke." He turned to Sharon. "Please forgive our poor manners. We're simple construction workers lacking in social graces."

The awkwardness evaporated quickly. Everyone relaxed and enjoyed the shade from the giant tree. Malcolm turned to Sharon. "That was very hospitable to let us relax in your yard and to serve us refreshments. Danielle mentioned you manage your farm by yourself."

"I couldn't do it without help from Robert and Tom."

"Do you have animals in the barn?" Duke asked.

"I have two milking cows, a few pigs, chickens, and some rabbits," Sharon said.

"I like animals. Can I go visit the barn?" Duke got up and started toward the barn.

Sharon frowned.

"Hold on, Duke," Malcolm called out. "We can't impose on Sharon's hospitality."

Duke stopped, looked back at Malcolm. Everyone looked at Sharon. She hesitated. "If more of you are interested, I can give you a tour of the barn?"

"No, no. We have to get going," Malcolm said. "Thank you for offering."

Danielle spoke. "Duke. You can join me and Tom when we return to help with chores. Tomorrow, maybe?"

"That's a good idea," Sharon said.

Malcolm looked up at Duke. "And you'll be able to put those muscles of yours to good use."

Duke frowned, muttered something under his breath, then sat with the others.

Malcolm surveyed his team, then said, "Let's help with cleaning up before we leave."

Gerta, Danielle, Sharon, and Malcolm gathered and carried everything into the house.

Malcolm shook Sharon's hand. "Thank you for your hospitality, Sharon."

"It was a pleasure meeting you, Malcolm. Good luck with the projects."

Danielle came forward and hugged Sharon.

Duke was standing by Steve's van, his eyes surveying the barn, the house, then Sharon. He climbed aboard.

With everyone back in the vehicles, Malcolm led the caravan toward The Homestead.

CHAPTER 15

RELIANT ZOOMS IN ON THE JENNINGS

The clock showed 1 p.m. Popeye gathered his team in the meeting room. He had arranged for the cafeteria to deliver coffee, tea, and pastries.

Popeye opened with, "Okay, guys. I want everyone's report. Pierre, you go first."

Pierre consulted his notes, then said, "I've called my university buddy, Harry, at the FBI field office in Chicago, and he confirmed the DNA and fingerprints collected at the Stonely crime scene led nowhere. I asked him for a copy of the FBI's short list of suspects, but he refused. Then I saw Louise had posted a copy on our site."

Popeye gave a thumbs-up to Louise.

Pierre continued, "Following your suggestion, I pursued the antiestablishment angle of the crime. I agree with you. Why go to the trouble of hanging their victim? I asked Louise for a copy of the FBI's watch list of antiestablishment troublemakers. She found and posted the list." Everyone turned to Louise and shook their heads in amazement.

Pierre continued, "One name caught my attention: Malcolm Jennings. He and his wife were arrested at an antiestablishment rally. I know him from Afghanistan. We served in the same platoon. He wasn't a captain yet, but he was a natural leader. We looked up to him."

Popeye interrupted, "It's a big jump from protesting at an antiestablishment rally and robbing and murdering a CEO. Why are you so interested in this guy?"

"It's because of his adventures in Iraq, which he shared with us in his platoon. I'll never forget the story where he and his teammates recovered the body of his brother, Eddie, and three other contract soldiers in Fallujah. The insurgents had tortured, burned, and hanged the four men from a bridge."

Everyone shook their heads in sympathy.

Pierre continued, "And when Louise posted the crime scene photos of Stonely hanging from a rope in his apartment, it reminded me of Malcolm Jennings' story."

Pierre looked at his notes. "I followed up on Malcolm Jennings. He received a medical discharge five years ago, a bullet wound. He now runs an electrical contracting business in Chicago."

Popeye interrupted again. "Pierre, don't over focus on this Jennings fellow. Post what you have on our website, and move to the other names on the FBI's list of antiestablishment troublemakers. Any progress on those?"

"The few I've investigated so far do not match the profile for the violence and tech expertise on display during Stonely's robbery. So, nothing promising so far."

"Thanks, Pierre. Keep at it," Popeye said. "Ashley, your turn."

Ashley cleared her throat, then spoke. "I've called some friends—Nicky at the *Chicago Tribune*, and Susie at *The New York Times*, but they knew nothing more than what Louise had already posted on our internal site." She looked up at Popeye. "I've concentrated on the first five names on the FBI's list of suspects, but I've nothing worth reporting so far."

"Thanks, Ashley." Popeye turned to Louise.

She scrunched her eyebrows. "My spidey senses tingled at seeing the Jennings' names on the FBI watch list of antiestablishment troublemakers. Not Malcolm's name, but that of his wife, Gerta. I know her. I worked alongside her at the NSA. We did programming for the Prism project and the Mystic program—the programs that collect and store all the phone and internet communications in North America. Gerta later moved to the FBI and did programming on their data banks."

"And that is significant why?" Popeye said.

Louise paused, then said, "When looking at the IP addresses of the threatening emails the criminals sent to Stonely and Tillman, I couldn't identify their sources, but I can tell they both came from Chicago. Gerta Jennings lives in Chicago and she has the skills to send untraceable emails and transfer funds to untraceable accounts, as the criminals did during Stonely's robbery."

"That's hardly enough to suspect her," Popeye said. "What's her background, anyway?"

"Gerta, nee Mueller, was born and raised in a working-class neighbourhood of Chicago. She attended Caltech on a combination of scholarship, grants, and loans, and graduated with honours in computer science. Her first employment out of college was with the NSA."

"Lots of people have computer science degrees," Popeye said.

"For sure, but get this: Gerta shared with me that her late father, Albert, worked for the Security Printers Group, the people who produced passports and security documents for many countries. Albert's employer fired him with cause for refusing to get vaccinated against COVID-19, and they refused to pay him a severance package and extended health benefits."

"That's a sad story, but is it relevant?" Popeye said.

"It gets more interesting," Louise said. "The courts were accusing Albert Mueller of masterminding the robbery of printing equipment and software from his employer. He died of cancer six months later, penniless, having sold his house and drained his savings to pay for the treatment and his legal defence. The authorities have never recovered the security printing equipment."

"I think I know where this is going," Popeye said. "Gerta's access to security printing equipment, and her cyber expertise, would help the murderers travel under false identities and avoid getting caught. This is too big a coincidence to be ignored. Where is Gerta now, do you know?"

"She no longer works for the FBI. She's co-owner of Jennings Electric Inc. in Chicago, along with husband, Malcolm. The two have a child, a girl, who must be twenty years old."

"Do you have any evidence that ties the Jennings to Stonely's murder?" Popeye asked.

"No. I need more time to research their comings and goings at the time of Stonely's murder."

Popeye mulled this over, then said, "Louise, you keep digging on the Jennings. Ashley, you keep looking at the suspects on the FBI's list, and Pierre, you return to the list of antiestablishment troublemakers. Let's meet again tomorrow at one p.m."

CHAPTER 16

THE JENNINGS ARRIVE AT THE HOMESTEAD

Robert was returning from the barn when he heard the low hum of engines. A black SUV followed by two white cargo vans took form down the road. *This must be the Jennings,* Robert thought.

The Jeep Wrangler slowed and turned into the driveway, and the two Chevy cargo vans followed behind. The labels on the side of the vans read "Jennings Electric Inc."

Malcolm climbed out of the Jeep and walked over. He called out, "Good day, Robert. Glad to see you again. It's been a month, hasn't it?"

Robert extended a hand to shake. "Welcome back, Malcolm. I see you brought the full crew along this time."

Gerta and Danielle jumped out of the jeep and joined Malcolm. Robert shook hands with them.

"Is Tom around?" Danielle asked with raised eyebrows.

Robert pointed at the barn. Tom appeared and raced over. Danielle jumped into Tom's arms and they hugged. Gerta nudged Malcolm in the side, and smiled up at him.

"Did you drive up directly from Chicago?" Robert asked.

"Yes, we did, except for a brief stop at your friend Sharon's house. Danielle was eager to see her again."

"I'm sure Sharon was glad to see her. I told her you'd be visiting for a few days."

"Sharon was most hospitable," Gerta said.

Malcolm looked up at Robert. "Let me introduce you to my crew." He turned toward his men, who had climbed out of the vans and were walking over. "Larry you've met before, but please meet Steve, Duke, and Jim, all former Marines, but now fine electricians."

The men shook hands with Robert and Tom.

"You've only booked two nights. What are your plans for the longer term?"

"We'll be looking for rental housing," Malcolm said.

"Don't forget about my rental house in Waterloo: five bedrooms, a finished basement, and a three-car garage. It's still sitting empty."

"Yes, I remember, and I'll keep it in mind. But for the next few days, Gerta and I want to treat the crew to a few nights in the countryside. We'd like to set up a fire pit and eat outdoors, picnic-style. That's still okay with you?" Malcolm asked.

"Yes, I'm okay with it as long as you follow the basic fire safety practices."

"Great." Malcolm turned to the men. "We've received the okay to set up, boys."

The troop started setting up an impromptu camp in the yard.

"You folks must be tired and thirsty. Do you want to come in for some lemonade, soft drinks, or cold water?"

"That would be super. Can we take it on the porch? It's so nice out."

"Certainly." Robert turned to Tom. "Could you bring out some refreshments and glasses for everybody?"

"Sure." Tom walked toward the house.

"I'll help you with that," Danielle said as she followed behind him.

Larry approached Robert. "Can we use some of your field stones for a fire pit?" Larry pointed at a stone pile at the far end of the yard.

"Sure. As long as you put them back before you leave."

"Thanks. And can we borrow some of the Adirondack deck chairs from the patio behind the house?"

"Yes, you can. And you can borrow some boards and logs from the woodshed to erect makeshift benches. But the same condition applies. You put everything back before you leave."

"Understood," Larry said as he raised a scout's salute.

"You can use the water in the well to cook and to put out your fire. It's cold and safe to drink. I have it tested regularly." Robert pointed to a well in the yard. "You'll have to use the hand pump."

"That'll be swell."

Malcolm approached Robert, and with a bashful tone said, "I apologize for imposing on you so much, but an open campfire is a real treat for us city folks."

"That's quite alright."

Duke approached Malcolm. "I've lost my cell phone. It must have fallen out of my pocket when I laid under the tree at the lady's farm."

Robert, who overheard, said, "Let me give Sharon a call. She may have seen it." He placed the call, but the line was dead. "There must be a service interruption. They are still common in the countryside since the pandemic."

Duke looked at Malcolm. "Can I borrow a van? I'll drive over and get it."

"Yes. That'll be alright," Malcolm said.

Duke walked to a van, climbed in, and left.

Tom and Danielle came out of the house with pitchers of lemonade, soft drinks, and drinking glasses. They set everything down on the porch.

"Refreshments are served on the porch!" Malcolm shouted to the men. They dropped their activities and walked over.

After they had refreshed themselves, the men returned to put the finishing touches to the fire pit and the improvised benches.

Gerta climbed into the van they had nicknamed the "Chuckwagon," and she backed it up close to the fire pit. She pulled a small foldable table from the back of the van and set it up. She returned to Malcolm's side. "We need to do some serious grocery shopping."

Robert overheard. He said, "The smokehouse is full of goodies." He pointed to the small structure beside the garage.

"Is it still in use?" Gerta asked.

"Yes, it is," Robert said. "I have venison and smoked ham curing in there."

"Venison! Smoked ham! I'll pay you a king's ransom for some of that," Malcolm said. "Can you spare some? The troops would surely appreciate it."

"Yes, I can spare some. Follow me."

Malcolm and Gerta followed Robert to the smokehouse. When Robert opened the wooden door, the salty, smoky aroma of curing ham and venison wafted out and made everyone's mouth water. "I can part with half of the venison and the smoked ham," Robert said. The men agreed on a price. Gerta left to fetch a carving knife and plates from the Chuckwagon.

"I remember you saying you don't stock any beer or wine in your residence?" Malcolm said. "I've a good supply of beer, but it's lukewarm."

"I've got plenty of ice cubes in the freezer compartment of the fridge. I'll fill a small cooler with ice cubes for you."

Robert paused, then said, "Tom grows and sells marijuana as a sideline. He may have some to sell you."

"That's great. I'm sure the guys will want to buy some from Tom."

At that moment, Duke returned with the van. He climbed out and walked over to the fire pit, and sat on a bench. He looked preoccupied. Robert walked over. "Did you find your cell phone?"

Duke gave a jolt and looked up at Robert. "Oh. Yes. It was right there, lying in the grass underneath the maple tree."

"That's good."

Duke returned to watching Steve struggling to set the logs on fire. Steve rose, walked to a van, retrieved a soldering torch, returned, set the torch ablaze, and laid it on its side, pointing at the logs. The logs caught fire and crackled. Steve spread his arms wide like a magician, and said, "Voila!"

Robert smiled at Steve's antics. He then turned his attention to Duke sitting quietly and pensively as if something was troubling him.

CHAPTER 17

DUKE IN TROUBLE

Tom helped his father to fill a cooler with ice cubes, and the men carried it to the Chuckwagon.

The crew had gathered around the fire pit. Malcolm stood up. "We have to dig into our emergency supplies of beer and wine tonight, so make it last." Guffaws spread across the assembly. Malcolm continued, "Our host has kindly supplied a cooler with ice cubes to chill the beer."

Vigorous clapping followed.

"I'll go visit the barn animals," Duke said as he rose and turned toward the barn.

"If you find anything we can roast on a spit, bring it over," Steve said. The group laughed aloud.

Expecting trouble, Tom headed toward the barn, as well.

Duke swung the barn door open and strode in. Tom heard the commotion created by the sudden entrance of a stranger in the barn. The hens squawked, Snowball the cow mooed, and Wilma the sow grunted excitedly. Tom rushed to catch up with Duke.

"Wow, there's a mama pig with cute piglets in here," Duke said. "We could have ourselves juicy piglets to roast over the fire tonight." Duke swung a leg over the enclosure, jumped in, chased, and grabbed two piglets.

Tom shouted, "Duke! Put down those piglets quick, and get out of there!"

Duke turned around, holding two squiggly piglets in his hands. "What's the problem?"

Wilma lunged and clamped her jaws on Duke's leg. The searing pain stunned Duke at first, then he howled. The sow held on to Duke's leg, vise-like. She swung Duke's body left to right, as she would a giant puppet. Duke grabbed the sow by the ears and twisted them, but to no effect. He tried to gouge her eyes out with his thumbs, but Wilma didn't release her hold. She dragged Duke to the far corner of the pen, away from the piglets.

Duke stuck a hand into his pant pocket, reaching for his handgun, but before he could point the pistol at Wilma, she released Duke's thigh and clamped her jaws on his arm. A bone cracked. Duke dropped his pistol and passed out. Wilma dropped Duke's body on the floor. She nudged it with her snout and grunted.

Robert had entered the barn and caught up to Tom. He handed over a shovel. Tom grabbed it and climbed into the pen. He placed the shovel between the sow and Duke. Wilma snorted and rejoined her piglets. The trembling and squealing piglets huddled around their mother. Wilma emitted a comforting grunt and laid on her side. The piglets latched on to a teat and suckled.

Duke lay unconscious on the straw, with blood leaking from the gash on his left thigh. A fractured bone had pierced the skin of his left arm.

The assembly at the fire pit heard Duke's howls of distress, and rushed to the barn. Malcolm arrived first. "What the hell is happening here?" He saw Duke lying unconscious in the pen, and he jumped inside. Tom stood guard with his shovel.

Malcolm inspected Duke's injuries. "Jesus Christ!" He turned to Larry, who stood outside the pen. "Help me get him out of here." Larry climbed into the pen, and both men lifted Duke over the enclosure. Robert and

Steve received Duke's body and laid him down. Malcolm, Larry, and Tom climbed out of the pen.

Malcolm kneeled and confirmed that Duke was breathing. He turned to Larry and Steve. "Get the stretcher."

They ran off.

Malcolm stood, stared at the sow, and said through gritted teeth, "This animal is a menace. We need to put it down."

"No," Tom said. "It's not the animal's fault. Duke was grabbing the piglets. She was just defending her litter."

Robert weighed in. "Forget about the sow. Let's get Duke to a hospital, fast." He looked up at Malcolm. "I've got a first aid kit in the house."

Malcolm raised a hand. "We've got one, and Gerta will know what to do."

Larry and Steve returned with the stretcher. They placed Duke on it and rushed out of the barn.

Tom looked into the pen and saw Duke's gun in the straw. He turned to Robert and pointed to the pistol.

Robert looked over and said, "Can you retrieve it?"

Tom nodded.

When Robert reached the Chuckwagon, Gerta had prepared the first aid kit, and she was examining Duke's injuries. Danielle arrived with a bowl of warm water, soap, and washcloths from the house. Mother and daughter cleaned, disinfected, and dressed Duke's wounds. Larry and Steve emptied the cargo area of one van. They laid Duke and the stretcher in the back of the van.

Malcolm said, "I'll drive. Larry and Steve, you'll ride with me. Robert, you'll ride up front and navigate. You know the way best."

Malcolm climbed behind the wheel. Robert got in.

Duke was coming around and groaning. Malcolm floored the accelerator and pointed the van toward Kitchener.

Cracks and potholes marred the pavement, but Malcolm maintained a speed of 120 kilometres per hour. Duke groaned every time they hit a pothole. Robert called the hospital to alert them of Duke's injuries and of their estimated arrival time.

Robert guided Malcolm to the hospital's ambulance drive-in entrance. Two attendants raced to the van, pulling a stretcher carriage. They transported Duke inside, with Malcolm on their heels. Larry, Steve, and Robert stayed behind.

Larry parked the van while Robert and Steve walked to the emergency room.

Robert wrinkled his nose at the smell of antiseptic and cleaning fluids as he passed the entrance door. Steve secured three free seats. Robert walked to the triage nurse and introduced himself.

"Yes. You're the man who phoned in the patient's injuries. We need you to register the patient." She pointed at the registration desk.

Robert went looking for Duke in order to get the information he would need. He located Duke. Medical staff surrounded his gurney. Malcolm stood nearby, holding Duke's belongings in a plastic bag.

The resident doctor was inspecting the wounds. "Cripes! What happened here?"

"A pig attacked him," Malcolm said. The staff stared at him with raised eyebrows. Duke groaned, half-conscious.

After examining the wounds, the doctor instructed the nurse to set up an IV dispenser with painkiller and antibiotics. "Wheel him to the X-ray room. We need pictures of the leg and the arm. Afterward, take him to the pre-op room. I'll go schedule the surgery." The doctor left.

Robert rummaged through Duke's clothing and retrieved his wallet, and returned the bag to Malcolm, who rushed to catch up to Duke and the nurse.

Robert completed the registration for Duke and returned to Steve's and Larry's side in the ER. Robert surveyed the waiting room full of men, women, and children, all in different stages of distress. Many slept in their chairs, while others nursed an arm, a leg, or whatever hurt.

Two hours had passed when Robert walked to the triage nurse to ask for an update. "We'll let you know as soon as your friend comes out of surgery," the nurse said.

Robert returned to his seat. Shortly after, Malcolm showed up. "They'll save Duke's leg and they can fix his arm, but he will never run a marathon.

The hospital will keep him for a few days. They have him on antibiotics. The rehab for his leg will take months, but the arm will heal faster."

The men nodded in sympathy.

Malcolm turned to Robert. "Is it normal for a pig to attack a man?"

"If a stranger jumps into the pen of a sow with a litter and picks up a piglet, the sow will attack, guaranteed. What Duke did was ignorant and dangerous. I cannot accept that kind of behaviour at my Airbnb. I need to ask you and your crew to leave the Airbnb, tonight. You'll have no trouble finding alternate lodging in the region."

Malcolm remained silent for a moment. "That's rather harsh. I mean, I agree. Duke behaved in a rash, irresponsible way, but he's a recent hire, on a temporary employment contract. I will fire him immediately." Malcolm mulled something over. "We'll vacate your place tonight, but I must point out, the rest of the crew has been respectful and disciplined. I ask you to reconsider, to give us a second chance."

Robert remained silent. He looked at Malcolm. "Let me discuss this with Tom when we gat back to the Homestead, and I'll let you know my decision."

"That's all I ask. Thank you," Malcolm said.

CHAPTER 18

RETURN FROM THE HOSPITAL

When Malcolm and the men returned from the hospital, it was evening. They joined the others at the fire pit. Gerta, Danielle, Jim, and Tom looked up expectantly. Robert signalled for Tom to follow him into the house.

Malcolm updated his crew on Duke's condition. He shared with them his decision to end Duke's employment contract. He told them about Robert and Tom deliberating about whether they can stay at the Airbnb.

"I really want to stay here," Danielle said.

"The decision is out of our hands," Malcolm said. He looked at Gerta. "We may have to move to a motel tonight. Can you look at some options?" Gerta nodded.

Robert and Tom returned from the house. Everyone looked up at them. Robert approached Malcolm. "You can stay on for the two nights you have booked." He hesitated before adding, "I have your word there'll be no inappropriate behaviour?"

Malcolm nodded. "You have my word. Thank you."

Danielle rose and walked over to Tom, and they hugged.

Malcolm turned to his crew. "Let's eat."

Gerta, Danielle, and Tom had prepared dishes of venison and ham. They had kept everything warm, wrapped in aluminum foil. They served everyone. The salty, smoky aroma of cured meat filled the air. The venison was a big hit, and everyone asked for seconds.

Malcolm turned to Robert. "Thanks for sharing your bounty with us." He turned to his men. "Guys, we all pitch in with cleaning up."

All heads nodded.

The lights in the yard flickered. The rotating power outage for the Hamburg region took effect, and the yard and the barn turned dark, but the moonlight was strong and one could see reasonably well. Danielle whispered to Tom, "What was that?"

"Since the pandemic, the utilities have been short of maintenance personnel and they've instituted rotating power blackouts for crews to schedule repairs and upgrades."

"Will there be electricity and hot water in the house tonight?"

"Don't worry. Dad had battery backup installed in the house, and he had an extra-large hot water tank installed. We won't run out of hot water."

Danielle turned to Gerta. "Let's shower first, while the men smoke, drink, and talk." They hurried into the house.

Robert listened to the banter of the men as they sat around the fire.

Gerta and Danielle returned from the house, their gypsy dresses swaying as if to music. Their wet hair glowing in the firelight.

"My, my. Look at those pretty lasses!" Steve said. "In the mood for a romantic evening, ladies?"

"Not with you ruffians," Gerta teased. "My beau is here, so you best keep your horns in check, guys." She winked at Malcolm and returned her gaze to the men. "I suggest you guys line up for the showers. The barn smells sweeter than you do." Laughter floated around the assembly.

Danielle approached Tom. "Thanks for helping with the dinner. That was sweet of you." She took his hand and looked into his eyes. Tom blushed. She said, "Why don't we check up on Wilma and her litter. The poor gal must be freaked out." The two headed for the barn, holding hands.

Malcolm and Gerta began gathering the plates, and the men rose and did likewise. Everyone headed toward the kitchen with arms full.

Robert stayed behind. He seized the opportunity to peek inside the vehicles. The Chuckwagon's cargo area and seats were jam-packed with equipment. Larry and Steve had thrown everything in there when they emptied the other van for the trip to the hospital.

Robert turned on his flashlight. He recognized tools for electrical work, but spotted military-grade weapons, bulletproof vests, and night vision goggles. He resolved to discuss this with Malcolm, and inform the police.

When Malcolm returned from the house, Robert walked over to him. "I've peeked inside the Chuckwagon and I saw a pile of weapons in there. Why do you carry those with you?"

Malcolm looked at Robert with raised eyebrows. "Well. They're all legal, if that's what you're worried about."

"But why so many? And I saw bulletproof vests?"

"I run two sidelines: firearms trading, and debt collection. Firearms trading is big business in Canada since your country has relaxed its gun laws."

Robert remained silent.

"Where's Danielle?" Malcolm asked.

"I saw Danielle and Tom walk to the barn," Robert said. "I'll go find them."

Robert reached the barn entrance and proceeded down the central aisle. Wilma must have smelled him because she grunted excitedly, hoping for food. Snowball was chewing cud, and she turned a large black eye in his direction.

Robert heard giggling from the far end of the aisle. He called out, "Are you guys alright?"

Tom answered, "Yes, we're alright, Dad. We're coming."

The young people appeared out of the dark, holding hands. The three filed out of the barn. Mac the cat followed behind them.

When Robert reached the yard, Larry, Steve, and Jim were moving equipment from the Chuckwagon back to the cargo van. Robert inspected the fire pit. Someone had poured water on the embers and it looked safe.

Robert entered the house and walked into the kitchen. Dishes lay neatly stacked to dry on the counter. Robert sat at the table and observed his guests settling for the night.

Robert saw Tom come out of their master bedroom and look down the hallway. Danielle came out of her bedroom and walked over to Tom. They kissed, whispered to each other, giggled, and parted.

Once the house was quiet, Robert retired to the master bedroom, which he shared with his son. Tom lied on his bed, hands behind his head, staring at the ceiling, a smile on his face.

Robert looked down at him. "I see a romance developing between you and Danielle, but remember we are Airbnb hosts and Danielle is a guest."

"Danielle and I like each other and we want to be an item."

"Fine, but wait till their stay is over, and then you two can date all you want."

Tom frowned.

Robert changed the subject. "I'm relieved that this idiot, Duke, did not lose his leg and his arm. We have liability insurance, but still, I don't want anyone hurt."

Tom said, "What a fool. He's lucky to be alive."

Both men shook their heads, baffled.

"I'm driving to the city tomorrow morning," Robert said. "Do you mind staying here while I'm out?"

"Sure. I've no deliveries planned for tomorrow."

"Good. I want to check on our house in Waterloo. It's been over two months since I last stopped by." Robert paused before adding, "I'll stop by the police station and report about the firearms and combat gear I saw in the vans. That has me worried."

"These guys were soldiers. They may think it normal to carry weapons along."

"Malcolm says he has a licence to trade in firearms, but I want to inform the police, just in case."

Father and son settled for the night. Mac climbed into Tom's bed, curled up near his head. Robert forgot to check in on Sharon before turning in.

CHAPTER 19

MALCOLM GIVES MORENO HIS ADVANCE

Malcolm rose at 6:30 a.m. after a night filled with nightmares about the upcoming job going sideways, and everything going wrong that could. He walked down to the living room and began his stretching and strengthening exercises. Once his routine completed, he put the coffee on.

Robert and Tom had already headed to the barn to care for the animals, and Danielle was out on a run on the country road.

The rest of Malcolm's team rose, did their ablutions, and assembled in the kitchen. Everyone grabbed a bun with jam, and a mug of coffee, before sitting at the table. Danielle returned from her run, climbed upstairs, showered, dressed, and joined the group.

Malcolm addressed his team. "I want to drive to Tillman's residence this morning and confirm with Moreno he's ready for tomorrow night. Gerta, Larry, and Steve, you'll be coming with me." Malcolm drank from his mug before continuing. "Afterward, I need to drop by the hospital and talk to Duke. We'll do some shopping on our way back." He drank another mouthful of coffee. He turned to Danielle. "You and Jim will stay here. We should be back by noon."

Everyone rose and left the table except for Gerta and Malcolm. Gerta leaned over and whispered, "I see the beginnings of a romance between Danielle and Tom."

Malcolm searched Gerta's eyes. "How do you feel about it?"

"I like him. He reminds me of you at that age. A handsome lad." She nudged Malcolm on the shoulder. Malcolm smiled and finished his coffee.

Malcolm parked the jeep by the guardhouse at the Tillman residence. He and his teammates entered the guardhouse. Moreno was sitting at his desk. He turned around. His left arm was in a cast. He had been expecting them. Malcolm had called first on the burner phone.

Malcolm offered his hand to shake, but Moreno did not return the gesture. Unperturbed, Malcolm sat facing him. Gerta and Steve sat beside Malcolm. Larry stood by the door.

"Are we all set for tomorrow night?" Malcolm asked.

"Yes. Tillman will be home alone. His wife, his son, Paul, and the live-in girlfriend will be having dinner with relatives in town at seven p.m. I have an escort booked to pick them up at six-thirty p.m."

"What about the housekeeper?"

"She'll be babysitting a friend's children."

Malcolm rubbed his chin. "That's good. What are your plans for the guards on the evening shift?"

"I'll call them individually tomorrow afternoon and give each one the evening shift off, with pay. The coast will be clear."

"Great, we'll be here at eight-thirty p.m.," Malcolm said.

"How many men and how many vehicles did you say?"

"There'll be seven of us, one SUV, and two cargo vans."

Moreno stared at Malcolm. "Where's my advance?"

Larry placed a shipping box on the table and pushed it toward Moreno.

Moreno looked toward the picture window, then reached for the box. He opened it, counted the five stacks of hundred-dollar bills, looked up, and nodded. After storing the box in his desk, he turned toward Malcolm. "And the new identity papers?"

"We'll have them tomorrow night," Gerta said.

Malcolm looked Moreno in the eye. "If you do not pull your end of the deal, start running, and never stop."

Moreno swallowed hard and nodded.

Malcolm rose and walked toward the door. Gerta, Steve, and Larry followed behind him.

Once back in the jeep, Malcolm considered for a moment, then said, "I need to stop at the hospital and fire Duke." He floored the accelerator.

CHAPTER 20

ROBERT AIDS SHARON

Robert's mind was elsewhere when he and Tom did the morning barn chores. He felt uneasy about his guests. The men carrying a gun on their person and lugging around an arsenal in their cargo vans troubled him. Equally worrisome was Tom's attraction to Danielle.

Tom leaned on his pitchfork and turned to his father. "I tried calling Sharon yesterday evening, and I tried again ten minutes ago, but she's not answering her phone."

"Oh, damn. I haven't checked on her in a few days. You have me worried. I'll drive over now and let you finish here."

Robert raced to his car, unplugged it, climbed in, and peeled down the road toward Sharon's farm.

As Robert entered Sharon's driveway, everything was quiet. He climbed out of the car and noticed the trampled grass in the front yard below the large silver maple. As he approached the front door, he heard cows mooing and pigs squealing. He raced to the barn and looked everywhere for Sharon. The animals grew excited and noisy by his arrival, but Sharon was nowhere to be found. He raced back to the house and knocked on the front door. Getting no reply, he tried the doorknob. The door opened, and he entered.

He called out Sharon's name. No reply. He climbed the stairs and walked to the master bedroom. The door was open. He saw a person lying under the blankets, facing away.

He approached and whispered Sharon's name. He recognized Sharon's hair. Leaning forward, he froze at the sight of large purplish bruises on Sharon's neck and shoulder. Sharon moaned.

"Sharon, this is Robert. Are you alright?"

Sharon turned around, winced from the pain, and opened her eyes. She took a few breaths. "Robert?"

"What happened to your neck and shoulders?"

"It hurts so much when I move my neck."

"What happened? Who did this to you?"

"It was that giant man, Duke. He works in Malcolm's crew. He showed up yesterday, late afternoon. I was at the barn. He raped me." Sharon moved one hand to her shoulder with difficulty. "He squeezed my neck and shoulders so hard I'm sure he tore some muscles."

"The bastard." Robert looked at Sharon's injuries and his face flushed with anger. "I'm going to kill that son of a bitch." Robert tried to calm down and think logically. "We've got to get you to the ER right away. I'll call nine-one-one."

Robert pulled out his cell phone. He stared at the screen. "It reads 'no service.' There must be a service outage. I'll try your landline."

Robert ran down to the kitchen and grabbed the wall phone. The line was dead. "Damn," he cursed, and he returned to Sharon's bedroom.

"The phone lines are dead. I'll help you down the stairs and get you to my car somehow."

"Wait, hold on, Robert," Sharon said as she took shallow breaths. "I don't think we'll make it down those stairs safely. And I don't want to ride in a car seat. I'll wait for an ambulance." She took a few more breaths. "What time is it?"

"It's nine o'clock. In the morning."

"Nine o'clock in the morning? I came to, lying on the floor in the barn. It was last night. I limped back to the house and tried calling for help, but the wall phone was dead, and I couldn't find my cell phone."

Sharon sobbed. "I swallowed some painkillers, climbed into bed, and fell asleep." She lifted the blankets a few inches, peeked, and wrinkled her nose. "I've wet the bed."

Robert made calculations in his head. "You've been here alone and in pain since yesterday."

"God! The animals. Nobody has fed or watered them since yesterday afternoon!" Sharon said.

"I'll go look in on them. Can I get something now? A glass of water? Some painkillers?"

"Yes, water and painkillers, please. Bring the bottle of Tylenol that's in the bathroom cabinet."

Robert walked to the bathroom, spotted a glass, rinsed it, and filled it with water. He grabbed the bottle of Tylenol.

He helped Sharon prop herself on the pillows. She winced and groaned. Robert held the glass to her lips. Once she had drank water and swallowed the pills, she rested her head against the headboard.

Robert looked at her. "Can I bring you something to eat?"

"Yes, my stomach's growling. A glass of milk? Bread with peanut butter? That'll keep me while you're feeding the animals?"

Robert rushed to the kitchen and returned with the food on a tray. He placed the tray on Sharon's lap. "Do you need help with drinking the milk?"

"I'll manage. Run and see to the animals, please."

As Robert walked to the barn, he tried his cell phone again. Still no service. He swore.

The animals seemed to sense that relief was at hand when Robert entered the barn, for they intensified their mooing, squealing, and clucking. Robert filled the water troughs first, then the feed troughs. He pulled up a stool and milked the two dairy cows. He gathered the eggs in a basket.

Robert surveyed the animals one last time. He walked back to the house carrying a pail of milk in one hand and the basket of eggs in the other. He stored the milk in the fridge and placed the eggs on the kitchen counter.

Robert tried his cell phone again. The service was back. He called 911, reported the rape, and requested an ambulance.

The dispatcher said the first responders would be at Sharon's farm in about two hours."

"Why so long?"

"I'm sorry, but your situation is not an emergency. Please stay on the line." Robert cursed under his breath. The dispatcher transferred Robert to a police officer. The officer instructed him to collect all the clothing the victim wore during the assault, and to turn it over to the first responders. "Make sure the victim doesn't wash, shower, or comb herself until the hospital has carried out a sexual assault forensic exam. A detective will meet the victim at the hospital and take her statement."

After hanging up, Robert returned to Sharon's room. Colour had returned to Sharon's face.

"I've reached nine-one-one, but the ambulance won't be here for another two hours. Are you sure you want to wait that long? I'll call Tom. The two of us can help you down the stairs and out to my car."

"Thanks, Robert, but I prefer to wait for the ambulance." She stared at her blankets. "Can you help me to the bathroom? I want to get cleaned up, and my crotch is very sore."

"I'm sorry, Sharon, but the police said you mustn't wash yourself or comb your hair before the hospital carries out a rape kit." Robert bit his lips. "They even want me to collect the bedsheets."

Sharon looked despondent. "I was so looking forward to getting cleaned up. This is so humiliating." Tears ran down her face.

Robert moved a chair close to her bed, sat, and reached for her hand.

Robert's cell phone rang. It was Tom, asking for news. After Robert had explained the situation, Tom said he was coming over right away to lend a hand.

After Sharon had regained some composure, she said, "I'd better bring clean clothes and toiletries with me to the hospital." She instructed Robert on what essentials to put in a tote bag.

They heard a vehicle drive onto the property, a car door slamming, the front door opening, and footsteps racing up the stairs. It was Tom.

He approached the bed and stared in horror at the dark bruises on Sharon's neck and shoulders. Robert freed his chair for Tom to sit.

Tom peppered Sharon with questions. He swore he would hang Duke from a tree branch and skin him alive.

BAD KARMA

Robert rested a hand on Tom's shoulder. "Slow down, Tom. Sharon needs a rest from all our questioning."

Tom rose, took the tray from Sharon's lap, and left. He returned with a tray containing a chicken sandwich with cheese, lettuce, and mayo, and a glass of apple juice. He placed the tray on Sharon's bedside table.

"Oh, thank you, Tom. You're a sweetheart," Sharon said.

Meanwhile, Robert had called and reached Sharon's oldest son at his workplace. He handed the cell phone over to Sharon.

"Patrick. It's Mom. I was attacked yesterday afternoon. . . . Yes. . . . he raped me. . . . My neck and shoulders are hurting. Robert is here. He called an ambulance. They'll be here shortly. . . . No. No. Don't rush over. Robert is here, and so is Tom. They're looking after me. Come this weekend, as usual. That'll be fine. . . . Yes. Robert called the police. . . . The man is a member of a crew of electricians that are staying at Robert's Airbnb. . . . No. He was not a complete stranger. I had seen him earlier in the day. Young Danielle, her parents, and the crew had stopped over on their way to Robert's place. He returned later, alone. I was in the barn. That's where he attacked me. . . . No. Patrick. Do nothing rash. Let Robert and the police deal with that man. . . . Don't worry. I'm in excellent hands. Come Friday after work and stay the weekend. . . . No. I'll be fine until then. . . . Promise me again, Patrick, that you won't do anything rash. . . . Good. I trust you, honey. See you Friday."

After Sharon had hung up, Robert reached Sharon's youngest son, Danny. Again, Sharon convinced Danny not to rush over to her side. Danny promised to come after work on Friday and spend the weekend with her.

The ambulance eventually arrived. The paramedics placed Sharon on a stretcher, carried her downstairs, and secured her in the ambulance. Robert handed over a plastic bag containing Sharon's bedding. After confirming they had gathered all clothing and articles related to the assault, the paramedics departed for Grand River Hospital.

Robert turned to Tom. "I'll follow Sharon to the hospital. I'll want to meet with the police and the hospital security, and tell them that Duke is being treated at the hospital and that he needs watching. Can you return to the homestead and monitor things?"

"Do you think Malcolm and the others knew about this?" Tom asked.

"I don't know. I remember the bastard saying to Malcolm he had lost his cell phone back here and was returning to find it. The son of a bitch may have hidden his crime from his teammates, but regardless, I'm kicking them out of our Airbnb."

CHAPTER 21

SHARON AT THE HOSPITAL

The paramedics wheeled Sharon into the emergency area, and Robert raced to catch up with the stretcher.

The doctor examined Sharon's bruises. "What happened here? A car accident?"

"A sexual assault," the nurse said.

"I see." He nodded to the nurse, who carefully pulled down Sharon's pants and panties. He leaned over for a better look at the bruises around Sharon's genitals. He turned to the nurse. "Have the sexual assault nurse carry out a sexual assault forensic exam. When that's done, take the patient to the MRI station and have a scan of her neck and shoulders carried out." He turned to Sharon. "Would you like an emergency contraception pill?"

Sharon hesitated, then said, "Yes." The doctor nodded to the nurse, who wheeled the stretcher toward the enclosed cubicles in the emergency ward.

Robert made to follow, but the doctor stopped him. "Please report to the triage nurse. You'll need to fill out paperwork. The rape kit exam will take two to three hours."

Robert walked to the triage nurse and introduced himself as the emergency contact for Sharon Doyle, the sexual assault victim.

The nurse pointed to the registration counter.

"Is someone calling the police about her arrival?" Robert asked.

"The first responders have called already. A police detective will be here shortly."

"I need the police and the hospital security to know that the rapist is being treated here at this hospital. His name's Douglas Ferguson. You admitted him yesterday evening."

The nurse looked on with raised eyebrows. "Let me look at his file." She punched keystrokes on her computer. "Mr. Ferguson is being treated for severe trauma to one leg and one arm. He's hooked to an IV machine." She looked up at Robert. "I don't think you have anything to worry about until the detective gets here." Seeing that Robert did not look reassured, she added, "I'll notify security, and have them keep an eye on Mr. Ferguson's room until the police take over."

Robert completed the registration, then walked over to the cafeteria. He pulled out his cell phone and called Malcolm.

"Malcolm here."

"Hi, Malcolm. This is Robert Cole calling." Robert told Malcolm what Sharon had told him about Duke raping her the previous day, under the guise of retrieving his lost cell phone.

Malcolm was silent for a moment, then said, "I can't believe Duke would do a thing like that." Malcolm paused, then added, "I can assure you I and the crew did not know anything about that."

Robert paused before saying, "You should see the bruises on Sharon's neck and shoulders. We're talking about violent sexual assault here. The police will arrive shortly, and I'm sure they'll arrest Duke. I hope the bastard does maximum jail time." Robert was red-faced by now.

Malcolm remained silent for a moment, then said, "I don't know what to say. Yes. The man deserves serious jail time. I fired him because of the incident with the piglets, but now I have even more reason to have done so."

A moment passed, then Robert said, "I want you and your crew to vacate the Airbnb immediately."

Malcolm considered, then said, "I understand your position. I would do the same, if I was in your shoes. We'll clear out of the Homestead within a few hours." He paused, then said, "Hiring that man was a grave error in judgement on my part. Gerta had reservations because of his character. I should have listened to her. I regret taking him along to Sharon's home. This news will devastate Danielle. She is fond of Sharon. I apologize to you now, and I'll apologize to Sharon directly."

"I don't want you, nor anyone in your crew, to visit or talk to Sharon. I will pass on your apology for what good that will do."

Malcolm let out a deep breath. "I understand how you feel." The line was quiet, then he added, "If there's anything I can help with, please let me know."

Robert hung up.

After two hours had passed, Robert went looking for Sharon's enclosed cubicle. The nurse had completed the rape kit exam and Sharon was resting in bed. She smiled when she saw Robert. He pulled up a chair and placed a hand on hers.

A doctor and a nurse walked in. "I'm Dr. Ross," the doctor said. "How are you feeling, Ms. Doyle?"

"More comfortable, thanks to the painkillers."

"The anti-inflammatory medication will help with the pain, as well." The doctor leaned over and examined the bruising on Sharon's neck and shoulder, then he leafed through the MRI images in his hands. After a moment, he said, "I see a hairline fracture to the right clavicle, tears to the ligaments and the tendon of the right shoulder, and soft-tissue damage to the cervical spine."

Sharon and Robert listened, wide-eyed.

The doctor turned to the nurse. "Fit a cervical collar on Ms. Doyle and apply cold packs over the bruises."

"When can I return home?" Sharon asked.

"Will there be someone at home to care for you?"

Robert raised his hand. "I'll check in on her regularly."

"She'll need twenty-four-hour supervision for the first day."

Robert nodded.

"If all signs are normal, you can return home later today," the doctor said before leaving.

A police officer had been waiting outside Sharon's cubicle. He intercepted the doctor and questioned him for a few minutes. After the interview was over, the officer entered the cubicle and introduced himself. "Ms. Doyle? I'm Inspector Walter Weber. How are you doing?"

"Hi, Inspector." Sharon smiled. "I feel groggy. Thank you for asking."

Robert rose, introduced himself, and said, "We're expecting one of your detectives any minute now."

"I'll be covering this case myself," Inspector Weber said. "I'll be taking Ms. Doyle's statement. We'll need privacy for this."

"Of course." Robert turned to Sharon. "I'll check in on you later. Can I bring you anything from the cafeteria?"

Sharon shook her head. Robert left, then reconsidered and sat by the nurses' station.

After half an hour, Robert saw Weber leave Sharon's cubicle. Weber walked by the nurse's station, noticed Robert, and stopped. "I need to speak with you. Let's move to a place more private." He pointed to a small alcove.

Weber spoke first. "Ms. Doyle's assailant has the nickname Duke, and she mentioned he and his companions are lodging at your Airbnb."

"That's right. His name is Douglas Ferguson. He and his companions were staying at my Airbnb, but I've ordered them off my property. That man, Duke, is being treated in this hospital right now."

"Oh. What for?"

"My pig mauled him yesterday. The idiot had jumped into the sow's pen and picked up two piglets."

"Do you have the address of this man? And that of the rest of the crew?"

"I have the name and address of his employer, Jennings Electric Inc., from Chicago. The booking is under the employer's name. I know very little about these people."

"I'll have the man placed under arrest and assign an officer to guard his room round the clock while I get a warrant for his DNA and fingerprints."

"I'm glad to hear that. I want to talk to you about the Jennings crew and things I've observed."

"What sort of things?"

"They're carrying military-grade weapons in their vehicles. The owner, Malcolm Jennings, an electrical contractor, is supposedly bidding on local projects, and he claims to have licences for trading in firearms, and for conducting debt collection, in Ontario. Is it legal for them to be carrying around military-grade weapons in their vehicles?"

"I'm afraid so. The federal government has repealed the laws controlling ownership, sale, and transportation of firearms in Canada and across the border." He looked at Robert's facial expression. "I don't like this any more than you do. I blame the widespread looting during this last wave of the pandemic. The politicians caved in to pressure groups, lobbying for the right to protect themselves." The inspector stared in the distance with furrowed brows for a moment, then said, "Anything in their behaviour that seemed strange to you?"

"They sure don't act like the electricians I've worked with. They've built a fire pit in my yard—with my permission, mind you—and eat outside, picnic-style. This guy, Duke, he faked having lost his cell phone at my friend Sharon's place, drove over and raped her. He returns to my place, jumps into the pig pen, grabs two piglets, intending to roast them over the fire pit." Robert paused, then said, "I'm sure most of them carry weapons on their person. Duke dropped his pistol in the pigpen."

The inspector was digesting what Robert had said. "We'll run checks on these men and their businesses. I'll interview them and have a look at those weapons."

"You'll have to hurry. They've promised to vacate within two hours' time, and that was an hour ago."

"I'll drive over now. If you'll give me this guy Malcolm's number, I'll call him and tell him to wait for me." Robert passed on the information, and the inspector shook Robert's hand and left.

Robert walked to Sharon's bedside. She lay with a cervical collar around her neck, eyes closed. Robert stood, observing her face. Light freckles covered her nose and cheeks. The red tinge in her hair gave her a handsome look.

Sharon opened her eyes and smiled. "Thank you for being here. Those painkillers are strong. I feel like I'm floating on a cotton cloud."

"Your priority is to rest." Robert leaned to kiss her but stopped himself. "I'll ask the hospital to call me when they discharge you. I'll meet the ambulance at your home. And don't worry about the farm and the animals. Tom and I will look after them."

"Thank you, Robert." Sharon closed her eyes.

Robert marched to the nurses' station. "The room number of Mr. Douglas Ferguson, please."

"Are you family?" the attendant asked.

"No, but he lodges at my Airbnb. I'm Robert Cole. I'd like to check in on him and see if there's anything I can bring him while he's recuperating."

"Mr. Cole? The attendant looked at her screen. "You're the primary contact for Ms. Doyle?"

"Yes, that would be me."

"Mr. Ferguson is in room 214."

Robert proceeded to the second floor and looked for room 214. He found it. He entered, leaving the door open.

Duke laid on the bed, propped up, his left leg and left arm bandaged, an IV tube hooked to his right arm. He recognized Robert, and a sour expression moved over his face. "What do you want? Have you put down that crazy pig yet?"

"Hi, Duke. I'm pleased to see you, too." Robert approached the bed. "I hope you're in pain and feeling miserable."

Duke gritted his teeth. "Fuck you, too! When I get out, I'll sue you for every penny you've got."

"Is that so?" Robert looked Duke in the eyes. "For my part, I'll make it my priority to shorten your lifespan, but I haven't figured out how to do it without getting caught. Nobody should spend a day in jail for killing you. The avenging angel will have to remain anonymous, his service to society going unrecognized. Bye for now."

"Fuck you!" Duke spat in Robert's direction.

Robert turned to leave, but a police officer was standing in the doorway, staring wide-eyed. The officer said, "You can't be in here. I need to take your name and details before you leave."

CHAPTER 22

ROBERT'S HOUSE IN WATERLOO

Robert left the hospital and drove north toward the adjoining city of Waterloo. He wanted to check on his rental house. He followed King Street, then wound his way through side streets and reached Green Acres Crescent.

To his surprise, a boy and a girl, about seven and five years of age, were playing on the front lawn. Robert parked and walked over. "Hi, guys! Do you live here?"

The children stopped their play. The boy spoke. "Mom's home." He pointed to the front entrance.

"What's your name?" Robert asked.

"I'm Dev, and this is my sister, Sabita."

"I'm Robert. I'll go talk to your mom. See you guys later."

Robert searched his memory. Had he missed a communication from his realtor about him renting the house?

He rang the doorbell. A woman with jet-black hair and almond skin tone answered the door. She wore a sari with blue and rose design.

"Yes?" she said.

"Hi. My name is Robert Cole. Did you move in recently?"

"Yes. Last week. Are you a neighbour?"

"No. I'm the owner of this house."

The woman looked puzzled, then alarmed. "You cannot be the owner. We're renting from Mr. Chopra."

Robert frowned. "Chopra? Who is that?"

"Mr. Chopra sponsored our immigration to Canada. He owns a property management company and he rents this house to us. You must have the wrong house."

"This is the correct house. You are Ms. . . . ?"

"I've never seen you before. How could you be the owner?" Her eyes betrayed confusion and distrust. She called to her children. They stopped their play and ran into the house.

Robert stepped aside to let the children pass.

Noticing the fear in the woman's face, Robert took a step back. "I've listed this house with Elmira Real Estate to rent for me. My agent is Paul Noonan. Has Mr. Chopra ever mentioned those names?"

The woman shook her head. "No. I've never heard those names before."

"That's strange. Could you give me the phone number of this man, Chopra?"

The woman stood wide-eyed. "You should talk to my husband about this."

"Can you give me your husband's phone number? I'll call him right now."

"No, sorry, I don't know you. Leave me your name and number, and my husband will call you back."

Robert handed her a business card with the Homestead's number on it. The woman took the card, backed into the house, closed the door, and set the lock.

Robert considered what to do next. He reached into the mailbox on the wall by the door. He pulled out the mail. The address on one envelope read, Mr. Ramesh Sharma, P. Eng. The sender was TMMC. Robert knew that was the Toyota Motor Manufacturing Company, who operated a car assembly plant in the nearby city of Cambridge. He had worked on engineering projects at that car plant.

Robert returned the mail to the mailbox and walked to his car. He looked back at his property. Everything was tidy. That comforted him. He called his real estate agent.

"Elmira Real Estate. How may I help you?" a man's voice answered.

"Hi. I'd like to speak with Paul Noonan, please?"

The man paused before answering. "I'm sorry, but Mr. Noonan is no longer with us. Can someone else help you?"

"Whoever took over Paul's client list. My name is Robert Cole. I have a property listed with him."

"Hmm, let me see here, Mr. Cole." The line went quiet for a moment. "Mr. Cole. We haven't assigned another agent to take over Mr. Noonan's client list yet. I'll transfer you to our office manager, Mr. Taylor. Please hold."

After the clicking of telephone lines, a voice came on. "Hello, Mr. Cole. I'm James Taylor, manager of Elmira Real Estate. You're asking about Paul Noonan?"

"Yes. Paul was handling my property at 210 Green Acres Crescent in Waterloo. A family moved in a week ago, and Paul never informed me of this. The tenants say they are paying rent to a Mr. Chopra."

"Oh, my. This is embarrassing." Taylor was silent for a moment, then he said, "I'm sorry to inform you agent Paul Noonan left abruptly a month ago, leaving no forwarding address. I'm looking at your file, and I see we haven't assigned an agent to your property yet. It's inexcusable, I know, but we're desperately short of qualified personnel. I realize this doesn't answer your questions."

"Are you saying a family has moved into my property without your knowledge, and a stranger is collecting the rent?"

"I don't know what to say, Mr. Cole. I can promise you I'll assign one of our senior agents to your account, and he or she will sort this out."

"I'm very pissed off about this. Please have your agent call me as soon as possible." Robert hung up and cursed under his breath.

Robert called Lawyer Rick, his real estate attorney. Rick came on the line. "Robert. Good to hear from you. How is your Airbnb business going?"

"Hi, Rick. I'm calling about my house in Waterloo. Something really odd is going on."

"Oh? Why are you saying that?"

"I had the house listed with Elmira Real Estate, and agent Paul Noonan was looking into renting it."

"Yes. I remember you listing with them. What's happened?"

"A family moved into the house a week ago, without me or Elmira knowing anything about it. Noonan has left town without leaving a forwarding address, and a man called Chopra is collecting the rent."

"Wow. That's weird."

"I need your help to straighten that out. The tenant said that Chopra owned a property management company."

"They're new in town. I've never dealt with them yet."

"Should I go to the police with this?"

"I think we need more information first. Leave this with me."

"Oh. The tenant is Ramesh Sharma, an engineer who works at the Toyota plant. I've met his wife and two young children."

"Good to know. I'll sort this out."

"Thanks, Rick."

Not satisfied with waiting while Rick sorted this out, Robert drove over to the Toyota plant to talk to the tenant, Ramesh Sharma. The plant was twenty minutes away.

Robert entered the plant's lobby, approached the reception counter, and asked for Ramesh Sharma. The receptionist called his name on the plant speaker system, and pointed to a telephone on the counter. The telephone rang and Robert picked it up. "Hello, Mr. Sharma?"

"Yes. That's me. Who's calling, please?"

"My name is Robert Cole, and I'm calling about the house you're renting on Green Acres Crescent. Can you meet me in the lobby?"

Ramesh hesitated. "Can it wait till noon hour? What is this about?"

"It's best to discuss this in person. It'll take less than twenty minutes of your time, and it's urgent."

"Are you with Immigration Canada?"

"No, but it's an urgent matter."

"Okay. I will come now, but I'm at the far end of the plant. I'll be there in fifteen minutes."

Fifteen minutes later, a man wearing a white hard hat and a light blue shirt with the TMMC logo entered the lobby from the plant side. He searched the room, which was packed with salespeople, and he spotted Robert, the only person in casual attire. "Mr. Cole?"

Robert rose, extending a hand to shake. "Mr. Sharma?" Ramesh nodded nervously and guided Robert to a tiny visitor meeting room. The room barely accommodated a tiny table and three narrow aluminum chairs.

"You said this was urgent?" Ramesh said. "My wife just called. She's frantic. She said a man showed up who claimed to own the house."

"Yes. That was me, and I own that house. Your wife said you pay rent to a man called Chopra. He doesn't represent me or the firm I hired to rent the house." Robert let Ramesh digest that information, then continued, "How did you come to rent from him?"

"Now, hold on. Are we talking about the correct house, 210 Green Acres Crescent?"

"Yes, we are."

"I know Mr. Chopra's family. We come from the same village in Punjab. He immigrated to Canada some ten years ago. He sponsored me and my family with Immigration Canada. Mr. Chopra owns a property management company, and he provided lodging for us. My part was to find employment, which I did. I'm paying back the sponsorship fee Mr. Chopra is charging us as fast as I can." Ramesh caught his breath. "Immigration Canada would not have approved Mr. Chopra's sponsorship if he was not an honest man. How could you be the owner?"

"That's easy to prove. Let's go to city hall and you'll see my name on the deed of the property. Can you leave the plant for a few hours?"

"No, no, I can't leave my work just like that. I can't make heads or tails of what you're saying. If there's a mistake, I didn't cause it." Ramesh was close to hyperventilating.

"Can you give me Mr. Chopra's address and phone number?"

"No. I'm not getting involved in a dispute between you and Mr. Chopra." Ramesh rose. "I need to return to work." He left without shaking hands.

Robert returned to his car. He mulled over the situation. Should he wait until Rick got back to him? Regardless, he would need a copy of the deed to his property as proof he owns it. He drove to city hall.

Robert stood at the property records counter while the city clerk searched in his computer for a copy of the deed for 210 Green Acres Crescent. The clerk located the document and printed a copy.

"I see here that this property changed hands a month ago," the clerk said. "Chopra Properties Inc. bought it. They have been buying a lot of properties in the Waterloo Region lately."

"That's not possible," Robert said. "Are you sure you have the correct address? I haven't sold that property!"

"I see your name as the previous owner, Mr. Cole, and the transfer documents are in order. Agent Paul Noonan of Elmira Real Estate signed on your behalf. There's a copy of his power of attorney in the file. I'll print copies of both documents for you."

Robert looked closely at the copies. "My signature on the power of attorney document is a forgery. It's close, but it's not my signature. I don't recognize the law firm that filed the transfer documents. And I see they've issued a bank order to Paul Noonan for five hundred thousand dollars. That's less than half what the property is worth."

The clerk stared in disbelief. "We had no reason to suspect foul play. Mr. Noonan is a recognized real estate agent, and the law firm is licensed in Ontario." The clerk considered for a moment. "If someone committed fraud, as you claim, it's a criminal matter for the courts. I don't see there's anything I can do to help."

The clerk stared at the documents. "I hadn't noticed this before, but the law firm shares the same address as Chopra Properties."

Robert rose, and through clenched jaws, said, "I'll go talk with these guys."

"Please wait, Mr. Cole. Let me prepare a package for you."

The clerk printed an extra copy of the documents, slipped them inside a large envelope, and handed the package over to Robert. "I'm very sorry, Mr. Cole. I wish I could do more. The retrieval and printing charges are on us."

Robert thanked him and left. He sat in his car and called Lawyer Rick.

"Rick. I've just been to city hall and I've discovered that this guy Chopra has purchased my property. Paul Noonan forged my signature on a power of attorney document and signed the transfer documents in my name. Noonan sold my property for half its value. He, the law firm, and Chopra must be in cahoots."

"You have been busy."

"I'm driving over to speak with Chopra."

"I advise against that, Robert. Let me put a case together. We'll sue Noonan and Chopra for committing fraud. This will be a long process, but we'll win in the end and you'll recover possession of your property. Be patient."

"I'll leave you to put the case together, Rick, but I need to confront this man and let him know he won't get away with this."

"Okay, if you must, but call me after you've talked to him."

"Will do. Goodbye, Rick."

Robert drove toward the address he had for Chopra Properties in old Kitchener. The address took him to a grimy red brick building that testified to a harsh industrial past. The landlord had converted the multi-storey industrial building into offices, on the cheap. Tattered venetian blinds hung behind dirty windowpanes. Patches of grey paint had peeled off the concrete steps that led to the front entrance.

Robert entered a small vestibule where mailboxes filled one wall. He saw Chopra Properties Inc. listed on the call box. He pushed the button.

A man's dulcet voice answered, "Chopra Properties. How may I help you?"

"Hello. I'd like to meet with Mr. Chopra?"

"Who's asking, please?"

"My name is Robert Cole. I'm here to discuss a property at 210 Green Acres Crescent."

There was silence for a few seconds. "Someone has rented that property. I'm sorry, but I have other houses. Are you looking to rent or to buy?" the man asked.

"To rent."

"Please wait downstairs. Someone will come down to greet you."

Shoes thumped down the stairs. A man appeared. He was in his thirties, six foot four, bearded, with a dark complexion. He wore a long, white cotton shirt with long sleeves over white, baggy pants. The man nodded at Robert, leaned past him to look outdoors, then said, "Are you the man looking to rent a house?"

"Yes."

The man pointed toward the stairs. "Third floor." He stood aside to let Robert go first.

At every landing, a lamp with a dusty yellowed globe hung from the ceiling.

Once they reached the third-floor landing, Robert let the large man pass ahead. The man knocked twice on the dark oak door, as if in code, and walked in.

Once inside the room, Robert faced a large oak desk, behind which sat a man in his late fifties, with a brown complexion and a well-trimmed light grey beard. He wore a black sleeveless jacket over a white shirt. The man rose, walked around the desk, and extended his hand to shake. "Mr. Cole, is it? I'm Ajeet Chopra. Please call me Ajeet."

Robert recognized the voice from the intercom. He declined the handshake, but noticed a missing index finger on the man's right hand.

Taken aback, Chopra's eyes narrowed. "Have we met before?"

"No, but my name should ring a bell. I'm the owner of the house on 210 Green Acres Crescent."

Chopra stared at Robert, sizing up his visitor. "Yes, I purchased that house a month ago. Paul Noonan from Elmira Real Estate signed the papers on your behalf." He kept staring at Robert. "You had assigned power of attorney to Mr. Noonan. Do you have seller's remorse? Have you changed your mind?"

"Paul Noonan forged my signature," Robert said as he stared back at Chopra. "Noonan left town after the sale. Do you have contact with him?"

"No. Why would I?"

"I will sue Noonan for fraud, and I will regain ownership of my property. The process will go a lot smoother if you join forces with me. We bring Noonan to justice. You get your money back, and I my property."

"Oh, no! That won't be possible! I have clear ownership of that property. I've no further business with agent Noonan, or with you." Chopra put on a stern face and returned to sit behind his desk. "If Mr. Noonan has committed fraud, as you claim, then that's for you to take up with the authorities. I've purchased a property that had been sitting empty for two years, and I've rented it to a deserving immigrant family. I've been a model citizen."

"You've purchased that property for half its market value. That smells of complicity to commit fraud."

"One third of the houses in this city are sitting empty. Since the pandemic, the market has crashed. The city approved the purchase and sale. I had no reason to suspect that anything was amiss."

"You were clearly in cahoots with Noonan to defraud me. I'm sure the courts will see it that way, as well."

Chopra leaned back in his chair and placed steepled hands in front of his mouth. In a voice that feigned sympathy, he said, "I understand why you're angered with Mr. Noonan. I'll admit I benefited from this transaction, but I did not plan it. Let me offer a solution." Chopra rubbed his chin. "Let's look at this from a practical point of view. The courts are slow at ruling on matters of fraud, and the legal fees will be crippling. I think I can salvage this situation to your satisfaction, and with less risk and cost." Chopra paused, then continued, "I'll purchase a property that is being seized for unpaid taxes and put the property in your name. I'll pay the closing costs, and I'll find a tenant for the property. I'll collect the rent until I've recovered my investment. You will own a property comparable to the one you had, maybe nicer, and you won't have to disburse a penny."

Robert looked Chopra in the eye. "I will take my chances with the courts. I will enjoy bringing down a small-time crook."

Chopra shook his head. "Mr. Cole, life can be unfair, but it's better to adapt than to fight. I speak from experience." Chopra rose. "I immigrated to Vancouver ten years ago from the Punjab, educated but penniless. My dream was to start a real estate business in the booming Vancouver market, but the banks refused to lend me money. So, I borrowed from loan sharks." Chopra raised his right hand, showing a missing index finger. "The first time I missed a payment, they left me this reminder. I didn't give up and run. I worked harder than before, paid back the loans, and my business succeeded."

Robert remained unmoved.

Chopra stared at Robert. "I see you are not interested in my offer. I know you and your son have moved to a hobby farm in New Hamburg. The police cannot provide round-the-clock surveillance to a small country property."

"My business here is done." Robert turned to leave, but Chopra's strongman stood in his way.

"Don't make a rash decision, Mr. Cole. Sleep on it," Chopra said. "My offer expires in five days." He signalled for his enforcer to let Robert leave.

The goon escorted Robert down the stairs and into the street. He photographed Robert and his car with his iPhone.

Robert climbed into his car. He steered the Nissan Leaf north on King Street, in the direction of the Mt. Hope Cemetery. He stopped at a flower shop along the way and purchased a bouquet of fall mums.

Robert entered the cemetery from Braun Street. He parked, and walked to the columbarium wall. A construction crew was extending the structure.

Robert placed the fresh mums in the pot attached to the niche of his late wife, Paulette. He sat on a concrete bench. "I miss you, Paulette, and Tom misses you badly. I wish you were here to help us." Robert informed her of their friend Sharon's rape by one of his Airbnb guests, and him expulsing all the guests. He described Noonan and Chopra stealing his house in Waterloo.

When finished with unburdening his sorrows, Robert gazed at the clouds floating lazily in the sky from the northwest. A flock of Canada Geese flew overhead, honking, heading south. "That's it for now, Paulette. Rest in peace, my love."

Robert returned to his car. It was already 3 p.m. Many chores awaited. He steered the car toward home. Hopefully, Malcolm's crew had vacated the Airbnb.

CHAPTER 23

THE JENNINGS VACATE THE AIRBNB

Malcolm drove into the Homestead. The team climbed out of the jeep and joined Danielle and Jim around the fire pit. Danielle had prepared sandwiches for lunch and she and Jim served everyone.

Malcolm addressed the team. "I have bad news." Everyone looked up at him with raised eyebrows.

"Robert called me from the hospital to tell me Duke raped Sharon yesterday. She's in the hospital. Robert is there with her."

Danielle bit her lips. "We knew already. Tom told us when he returned from Sharon's farm an hour ago. He gave us all the sordid details." She paused, then added, "Tom is superpissed. He is very close to Sharon."

"I can't say that I blame him," Malcolm said. "I ended Duke's employment this morning before I knew about the rape." He looked at Gerta. "I should have listened to you and never hired him."

Gerta shook her head, then asked, "How is Sharon? Did Robert say?"

"Robert didn't say. He doesn't want me to talk to Sharon. So I don't know." Malcolm let a moment pass, then added, "There's more bad news. Robert wants us to vacate the Airbnb immediately. I told him we would. We'll pack our gear and belongings after lunch and move to new lodgings."

Murmurs travelled through the assembly.

Gerta looked up at him." It shouldn't be a problem. There are lots of vacancies in the region."

"Good." Malcolm looked around. "Where is Tom?"

"He's doing chores in the barn," Danielle said.

"Good. I have some good news. We are on for the assignment tomorrow night." The men looked at each other and nodded.

"What's the estimated take this time around?" Jim asked.

Malcolm looked toward the barn, and seeing no sign of Tom, he said, "Gerta has identified thirty million dollars hidden in foreign accounts." He raised a hand. "Let's not count our chickens yet. We'll go over the plan tonight."

As no more questions came, Malcolm said, "Enjoy your lunch."

Steve had lugged two one-gallon jugs of wine from the back of the jeep. "We picked these up in town." Everyone cheered. Steve twisted the cap off, cradled one jug under an arm, walked around the assembly, and filled everyone's glass.

Malcolm turned to Gerta. "Will you have Moreno's identification papers ready for tomorrow night?"

"Yes. I have them with me."

"Thanks, Gerta." Malcolm reached over and hugged her tightly. He kept her in his arms for a long time, enjoying her warmth. "You're a precious companion, in life and in business." Gerta kissed him.

After everyone had been served, Danielle took her father aside. "Tom would like to join the crew as an apprentice electrician. But after what Duke did to Sharon, I don't think he'll want to have anything to do with us anymore."

Malcolm put a hand on Danielle's arm. "You have strong feelings for Tom?"

"I like him very much."

"Have you explained to him we knew nothing of what Duke was planning?"

"Yes, I did."

"That's all you can do. He must decide for himself if he believes you." Malcolm looked into Danielle's eyes. "Do you think we can trust him with our debt collection work?"

"I don't know. He's gutsy, and he'll pull his weight, no question about it."

"I could use the extra help. But let's see how things develop."

Danielle kissed her father on the cheek. "Thanks, Dad." They returned to the fire pit.

Steve returned from the house with a plate heaped with meat slices. "I've nothing against ham and cheese sandwiches, but I've warmed up some venison for myself. But there's too much for me, so I was thinking of sharing some with you guys."

"If you value your life, you will," Jim said. Guffaws arose from the group.

As the crew sat eating their lunch, Mac the tomcat jumped in Malcolm's lap and sniffed at Malcolm's sandwich. Malcolm picked up the cat, cuddled him, then put him back on the ground. Mac meowed in protest, walked over to Gerta, jumped on her lap, poked his head between her elbows, and sniffed at her plate. Gerta picked up the furry animal, walked toward Danielle, and put him gently in her lap. "Can you look after this guy?"

Danielle petted the cat. "Okay, big boy, I'll share my grub with you."

When everyone had finished eating, each took their dishes to the kitchen.

A police cruiser turned into the driveway. Inspector Weber climbed out of the passenger side. He noticed Malcolm and his crew assembled around the fire pit. He walked over. His driver, Constable Kidnie, followed one step behind.

"Good afternoon, folks," Weber said.

Malcolm rose. "Good afternoon, officer. I'm Malcolm Jennings."

Weber shook hands with Malcolm. "I'm Inspector Weber. Pleased to meet you. As I mentioned over the phone, I need to take your statement, and that of your crew members, concerning the sexual assault of Mrs. Doyle at her farm yesterday."

"Yes. I understand."

Weber looked around and spotted the two cargo vans. "These are your vehicles? Mind if I have a closer look?"

"Why the interest?" Malcolm asked.

"The Airbnb owner mentioned you carried weapons in your vehicles. I'd like to see them."

"Okay."

Malcolm and the inspector walked to the nearest van. He swung the rear doors open. Weber surveyed the cargo area and noted electrical tools, rolled tarps, duffel bags, and equipment cases.

"What's in the equipment bags and the cases?"

Malcolm retrieved one bag and opened it. It contained assault rifles. He opened a case. It contained handguns.

"Wow! But I thought you were electricians?"

"We trade in firearms and debt collection as side businesses. We're licensed."

Weber examined the weapons, but knew of no correlation with recent crimes committed in the region. "Can I see your licences?"

"Certainly. We have shown all these licences to the Canadian Border agents already."

"It's just a formality. For our records," Weber said.

"Not a problem. Our office manager, Gerta, will bring over the file with all the paperwork."

"Please hand the file over to Constable Kidnie. He'll photograph the documents, and he'll hand the file back to you."

Malcolm nodded, then said, "The other van has our personal effects, cooking and camping gear, even a stretcher. Do you want to have a look?"

"No, that's fine." Weber stepped back to allow Malcolm to close the rear doors of the van.

"Let me introduce you to the crew," Malcolm said. He led Weber to the group that was assembled around the fire pit.

Gerta handed over the file with the licences to Constable Kidnie.

"You're leaving the Airbnb today, I'm told," Weber said to Malcolm. "Where are you moving to?"

"We don't know yet. We'll book motel rooms for now, but if we clinch an electrical project, we'll rent a house."

The inspector nodded, then switched subjects. "Douglas Ferguson is one of your employees?"

"Was. I fired him this morning. Have you charged him yet?"

"Yes, for aggravated sexual assault." Weber looked at the crew. "I need to take down everyone's statement, one at a time. I'll carry out the interviews in the kitchen."

Weber had completed the interviews and had moved to the porch when Robert drove into the yard. Robert walked over and joined the inspector.

"Inspector Weber. I see you've caught everyone before they left."

"Yes. I've interviewed the entire crew."

The two men sat down.

"You were right," Weber said. "These guys are carrying quite the arsenal in those vans. We've run some checks, and confirmed Jennings Electric holds a temporary licence to work in Ontario, and they have bid on local electrical projects." He paused before adding, "They also carry licences to trade in weapons and to conduct debt collection in Canada." Weber rubbed his chin. "Malcolm and Gerta Jennings have criminal records. The Chicago police arrested them for disturbing the peace at a protest rally some years ago, but nothing more serious than that."

"I'll be relieved when they leave," Robert said. "I hope the bastard who raped Sharon goes to prison for a long time."

CHAPTER 24

MALCOLM LAYS OUT THE PLAN

The Jennings' crew moved into the newly renovated historic New Hamburg Inn. Gerta rented the entire establishment of five guest rooms for two nights. The innkeeper agreed for them to park their vans inside an old carriage barn that had been converted into a garage.

Malcolm called a meeting in his master suite. The group rounded up chairs and sat in a circle around a worktable. Malcolm posted Jim as watch outside the suite's entrance. Jim left the door partly open so he could hear the discussions.

Malcolm unfolded a road map and a satellite view on the table. The satellite view showed the Tillman residence, the surrounding fields, and side roads. The road map showed the cities of Kitchener-Waterloo and the surrounding countryside.

"I'll explain the plan Gerta and I prepared for this operation, but I welcome your suggestions," Malcolm said. Everyone nodded.

"We'll move on the property at eight-thirty p.m. tomorrow, in two teams. Larry, Steve, and I will drive to the guardhouse and meet with Moreno. The others will park on the side road." Malcolm circled a spot on the document. "Moreno will have given the security personnel the evening shift off. Tillman will be at home alone. We need to complete our business and clear out by ten-thirty p.m."

After a pause, Malcolm continued. "Steve will man the guard booth, and Jim will cover the front of the residence. The rest of us, we'll go inside the house. I'll hold Tillman in the living room while Gerta clears the second floor, Larry the main floor, and Danielle the basement." Malcolm looked around the table. "Everyone good with this so far?"

Everyone nodded.

Malcolm addressed Larry, Gerta, and Danielle. "Keep your eyes open for a safe. There's bound to be one." All three returned a nod. "Once we've cleared the house, Gerta and I will work on Tillman at his computer, most likely in his den."

"What about landlines and closed-circuit cameras?" Larry asked.

"Moreno will have disabled the cameras, and he'll show us where to cut the landlines."

Gerta interjected, "I'll bring two signal scramblers. One I'll bring in the house; the other is for Steve to place in the guard booth."

Danielle asked, "Why park the vans on the side road? That's quite a long walk to the house, through fields, in the dark."

"That's our contingency plan. If police cruisers show up, Steve will call me on his portable radio, and I'll send Jim to support him. Steve and Jim must keep the police from reaching the house until we're finished with Tillman. Then we all fall back to the side road."

"What weapons do I prepare?" Larry asked.

"For the guys stationed outdoors, an M16, a handgun, spare ammo, a knife, and night vision goggles." Malcolm turned to look at Steve. "You let Larry know what more you'll need at the guard booth." Steve nodded. Malcolm continued. "For those of us indoors, each will carry a handgun, a silencer, and a knife. We'll bring a tote bag with four M16s and eight magazines in case we have to shoot our way out."

Malcolm sat back and waited for questions. Everyone was exchanging comments with one another. During a lull in the conversations, Malcolm said, "Gerta will issue a portable radio to each one of you. Keep it turned on. Oh, everyone will wear a bulletproof vest."

"Inside the house?" Gerta said. "They're heavy and uncomfortable."

"Yes, even inside the house. This is non-negotiable."

Gerta bit her lips but nodded.

"Are we returning here after the job is done?" Steve asked.

"We're booked here for two nights for appearances, but we're not returning here after the raid. This is too risky. We'll break into Robert's empty house in Waterloo, and spent the night there." Everyone looked on with raised eyebrows.

"Larry and I drove by the place earlier. It'll be perfect. It's a thirty-minute drive from the Tillman residence." Malcolm brought out the road map and circled the location of the house on it. "There's a tall hedge on three sides. There's a three-car garage where we can hide the vans, and switch the plates and logos without being seen. We'll leave early the next morning."

"What's the plan for returning home?" Larry asked.

"We'll cross in Detroit. We already test-drove the side roads on our previous trip. The police forces are thin on the ground, and they cannot set up roadblocks on all the side roads." Malcolm looked around the table. "Questions?"

"I don't trust this guy, Moreno," Larry said.

"We can't run this job without him. He's drowning in gambling debts, and he needs money badly. And he asked for identification papers, so he plans to run." Malcolm looked around the table. "He's smart enough to know retaliation will be harsh and swift if he double-crosses us. Gerta is monitoring his phone calls and his emails."

The men nodded.

Gerta leaned over and pointed a finger at the satellite view. "Tillman owns a small plane. I see an aircraft hangar and a short take-off and landing strip in the field. Should we worry about that?"

Malcolm shook his head. "We'll have our eyes on Tillman the whole time. I'm not worried about it."

Malcolm broached a new subject. "I'm considering adding Tom to our team. I'd like to start him off as a wheelman tomorrow night. He'd keep watch from the side road during the operation."

Larry raised his eyebrows. "I'm not comfortable adding a rookie to a job like this. What if he talks to his father?"

Malcolm considered. "The kid's no greenhorn. Gerta researched him. He's done time for aggravated assault." Malcolm let everyone to consider this news. "I'll vet him, and if he's unsuited to our line of work, I'll drop him. Is that acceptable?"

No one seemed convinced.

"Okay, let's drop the subject for now. We'll talk after I've interviewed him."

Everyone nodded except Larry, who shook his head. Gerta put a hand on Larry's arm and gave him a reassuring look.

"Oh, what about Duke?" Larry said.

"Duke is under arrest for aggravated sexual assault. What he did was unforgivable. He's no longer our concern."

Everyone looked somber.

Malcolm rose. "Okay, guys. Let's huddle tomorrow morning during breakfast." The crew members rose and returned to their rooms.

Malcolm walked over to Jim. "Could you help Gerta with plugging in all the electronics, the scramblers, the burner phones, the walkie-talkies?" Jim nodded.

Malcolm walked outdoors and saw Tom driving into the entrance to the inn.

CHAPTER 25

MALCOLM INTERVIEWS TOM

Malcolm watched Tom park and climb out of his pickup truck. Danielle ran past Malcolm, reached Tom, and hugged him. The two kissed and chatted together.

Malcolm walked over. "Hi, Tom. How are you?"

"Hi, Mr. Jennings. Danielle told me she and your crew were staying here. I came to see you."

"After what Duke did, I'm surprised you would want to have anything to do with us."

"Danielle explained everything to me—that you did not know what the bastard was up to, that he's a recent hire and not a friend of your family."

"That's right. His crime was a surprise to all of us. I fired Duke. The police will deal with him."

Tom considered, then said, "Danielle must have told you that I'd like to join your crew as an apprentice electrician."

"Yes. Danielle has mentioned it. I could use the extra help, but I'm sure your father will not approve of this."

"Dad is furious at what Duke did to Sharon, but he knows you had nothing to do with it. He'll come around, eventually."

Danielle slipped her arm underneath Tom's. She looked up at him with sadness in her eyes.

"I understand your father's feelings," Malcolm said. "We brought this man into your life. I'm sorry about what happened to your friend, Sharon." Malcolm let a moment pass, then added, "Come in. Let's sit down and talk."

Danielle held onto Tom's arm, and said, "I need to talk to Tom for a minute. It won't take long."

Malcolm nodded, then walked indoors.

Danielle looked up at Tom. "Are you sure about this? Some of the work we do, the debt collection business. It's very dangerous."

"*You're* doing it."

"I'm following the lead of my parents. And I have two years of military training. Promise me you'll listen carefully to what Dad says. It's critical you don't mention anything you discuss with him, to anybody—not even to your father."

"Cripes. You make it sound like a secret society."

"The debt collection business is like that. It's for our safety, my safety. If you have any doubts about that kind of work, don't join our crew. I'll understand."

Tom mulled this over, then said, "*You* accept doing that work. That's good enough for me."

Tom walked up to Malcolm's suite. He approached Malcolm's worktable and sat.

Malcolm spoke first. "Danielle speaks highly of you. I'm impressed by how you and your father are looking after your friend Sharon and her animals." Without waiting for an answer, Malcolm tapped Tom on the shoulder. "You're a good friend to have."

Malcolm adopted a serious tone. "Tom, this is a preliminary interview. If we both agree that you're a good fit for the team, I'll recommend to the crew that we hire you, but they'll have to agree, as well."

"I want the team to approve of me."

"Good." Malcolm considered, then said, "Are you a discrete person?"

"If the situation demands it."

"In our debt collection business, discretion is essential. This discussion must remain confidential. What you see and what you do during a job assignment must stay between you and your team. There can be no exceptions. It's a code that ensures everyone's safety. If you break the code, there will be severe consequences. Do you think you can live by that code?"

Tom paused, then said, "Yes, I can live by that code."

Malcolm smiled. "But first, I need to ask you some personal questions." He turned in his chair and faced Tom. "Why do you want to work with us, despite Duke's assault on your friend, let alone your father's misgivings?"

"The decision is mine to make. I want to learn a trade and make money while doing so. There's not enough work at the Homestead for two men. I want to move into an apartment and build a life for myself. Oh, and I have dual citizenship. Mom was American. I could follow the crew to the States when your projects here are done." Tom hesitated, then said, "And I want to follow Danielle."

Malcolm smiled. "Those are excellent reasons. And I think Danielle will agree with the last one." He paused, then said, "Do you have a criminal record?"

Tom hesitated before answering. "Yes, for cocaine possession, but the sentence was commuted to counselling and community service. I'm clean now." Tom paused, then added, "I served three months in jail for aggravated assault, but the bastard had it coming."

"Aggravated assault! What weapon was involved?"

"A baseball bat."

"Thanks for your honesty, Tom. How about electrical experience?"

"I do electrical repairs around the house and on the farm: hundred and ten volt circuits, photovoltaic panels, and small electrical motors."

"What schooling have you completed?"

"Community college for two years. I've a diploma in sound engineering. I create music on my synthesizer and sell the tunes on the internet. It's a small income but fun."

"What kind of vehicles have you driven?"

"Pickup trucks, cars, minivans, and tractors, of course."

"Good." Malcolm leaned back in his chair. "Tomorrow night's assignment will involve driving one of the cargo vans. You'd stay by the vehicle while the crew does a debt collection job." Malcolm looked squarely at Tom. "Debt collecting can be violent and messy."

"How violent?" Tom asked.

"You remember what I said about our code?" Malcolm said. Tom nodded. "These assignments would qualify as aggravated assaults and worse."

"Are you saying I'll be an accessory to a crime and could end up in jail?"

Malcolm paused before answering. "We plan the assignments carefully so that no one gets arrested. But it could happen." After a moment of reflection, Malcolm added, "We've got two debt collection jobs to complete. Then we're back to electrical work. I could use your help now, but if you're not comfortable with what I said, you can reapply later, when our last collection job is done."

"When is that likely to happen?"

"In three to six months' time."

"To be clear. Tomorrow night, I would stay with the van? Nothing more?"

"That's right."

"Danielle said she's taking part in the operation?"

"Yes."

"Who are you collecting from?"

"Not your average honest hard-working citizen. We're dealing with a man who has committed major fraud."

"If the man deserves what's coming to him, I'm okay with it."

"That's an excellent answer, Tom." Malcolm then asked in a neutral tone, "Have you ever handled a firearm?"

"I've hunted deer with Dad's Winchester, but I've never used a handgun." Tom thought of something. "I'll be back in a minute." He stood and left. He returned and handed a pistol over to Malcolm. "This is Duke's gun. He dropped it in the pigpen."

"Thanks!" Malcolm took the pistol and turned it over in his hands. "You've cleaned it. I'm impressed." He looked at Tom. "If you're hired, I'll show you how to handle a handgun, and you'll get to keep it. It's an excellent skill to learn." He noticed the anxious look on Tom's face. "Don't worry. You won't need to carry tomorrow night. The crew will, of course." He paused, but when no questions came, he continued, "Your wage would be a thousand dollars per week."

"That's great. I'm happy with that. Will you recommend me to the crew, Mr. Jennings?"

"I'll give you an answer by noon tomorrow. How's that?"

"That'll be fine."

The two men rose and walked outside. Danielle had been sitting on a chair on the porch. She ran over, took Tom's hands in hers, and asked, "How'd it go?"

"I'll know by noon tomorrow."

Tom and Danielle walked to the pickup truck. Danielle ran back to Malcolm. "I'd like to help Tom with the chores at Sharon's farm."

"Sure."

Danielle ran back to Tom's side. The two climbed into the pickup and left.

Malcolm rubbed his chin and thought, I hope I'm not making another error in judgement.

CHAPTER 26

DUKE MEETS HIS MAKER

It was early morning, a cool September breeze blew over the fields, and a light mist covered the fields. A doe and her yearling were picking red McIntosh apples from a tree branch in the orchard at the Homestead. A flock of wild turkeys pecked at fallen apples.

Tom and Robert were feeding and watering the barn animals. When the chores were completed, the men returned to the house. Robert carried a pail of fresh milk, and Tom, a basket of eggs. Mac the tomcat followed the procession. The men climbed upstairs to their bedroom en suite to wash and shave. The guest rooms stood empty.

Robert opened the windows on the first floor. The weather reporter called for a warm, clear day.

Tom cooked a breakfast of bacon and eggs. "What are your plans for today?" he asked his father.

"I'll drive over to Sharon's farm to check in on her and feed her animals. I've nobody booked for the Airbnb, and frankly, I welcome the rest. How about you?"

"I need to deliver some marijuana to the cannabis shops in town. Then I'll drive over to see Danielle afterward." He gave his father a tentative look.

"If Malcolm agrees to hire me, I'll pack a travelling bag and stay with his crew for the next while."

Robert's eyes narrowed as he looked directly at Tom. "You can't be serious. These men are very likely criminals. One of them raped Sharon. I forbid you to join that outfit."

"Malcolm and his crew knew nothing about what Duke was up to. They would have stopped him if they'd known." Tom hesitated, then said, "I want to work on construction projects, learn a trade, and get paid while doing it." Tom did not divulge that his primary motivation was staying close to Danielle.

Robert took a swallow of coffee and added, "I worry they'll drag you into some dangerous operations."

"Malcolm said my first job will be to drive a cargo van. There's nothing dangerous about that."

Robert frowned. He took the empty plate to the kitchen sink. He turned to Tom. "I'll take the Leaf. You can use the pickup for your delivery."

"Thanks, Dad."

Robert left.

Tom waited for his father to drive off, then he loaded some packages of cannabis into the cargo bed of the pickup, climbed behind the wheel, and headed toward Kitchener.

Tom drove to the Grand River Hospital parking lot and walked to the main entrance. He found the stairs that led to the second floor, climbed them, and stopped at the landing. He peeked down the hallway and saw the police officer posted by Duke's room. The officer sat reclined in his chair, his head resting against the wall, reading a magazine.

Directly across from him, he saw a door labelled "Supply Room." On the wall to his left, he noticed the red handle of a fire alarm. Tom slipped into the supply room, closed the door behind him, and flipped on the light switch.

Bedding supplies and hospital garments lay stacked on shelves. Tom slipped a green gown over his head and fitted a mask over his face. He scrunched some sheets of bedding into a bundle and placed it on the floor. He pulled a butane lighter from his pocket and set fire to the pile of fabric.

He slipped out of the room, triggered the fire alarm, and disappeared down the stairs. An ear-splitting ringing resonated through the D wing.

Tom walked along the first-floor hallway to the next set of stairs. He climbed back to the second floor. He peeked to his left and saw the police officer assigned to Duke's room running down the hall in the direction of the supply room. Smoke was belching out from the bottom of the closet door.

A nurse had arrived first. She stood, uncertain what to do. An attendant appeared. He held a fire extinguisher. He nodded for the nurse to open the closet door and he doused the flames with retardant.

Tom entered Duke's room. The giant lay propped up on the pillows, wide-eyed with his mouth open.

"There's nothing to worry about, sir. The fire is under control," Tom said.

Tom walked to a small sink mounted on the wall. He pulled a small pouch from his pocket, retrieved a syringe, a needle, cotton swabs, and three tiny packets of rose-grey powder. He emptied the powder into a plastic glass, poured in an ounce of tap water, and stirred the solution.

The fire alarm was still blasting. Duke asked, "Shouldn't you wheel me out to the assembly point?"

"Everything is under control, sir. You're safe here."

After screwing on the needle, Tom filled the syringe with solution through a cotton swab. He turned, studied the IV tubing connected to Duke's arm. He inserted the needle into an available port and emptied the syringe with one firm push of his thumb.

Duke looked on. "What have you injected into the IV?" He looked up at Tom with scrunched eyebrows. "Your voice sounds familiar. I know you."

Tom stared at Duke. "Say hi to Satan for me."

"Fuck." Duke sat up in the bed and pulled at the IV tubing. He pulled the catheter from his arm, and cried for help at the top of his lungs. The fire alarm drowned his voice. He located the nurse's call button and pressed it.

Duke jumped out of bed and ran toward the door. Before he could reach it, his legs went rubbery, and he crashed face-first on the tiled floor. His nose broke with a crack, and a dark red halo formed around his head. An alligator clip still clung to a finger of his left hand.

Tom stuffed the drug paraphernalia back into the pouch. He looked around, making sure he was leaving nothing behind, and raced to the door.

The police officer and a group of staff were assembled in front of the supply room. Smoke filled the hallway. Tom rushed down the stairs and walked out of the hospital.

Alarms rang and lamps flashed at the second floor nurses' station. The patient in room 214 had pushed the call button and his heart rate had flatlined. The attending nurse activated Code Blue and raced toward Duke's room. Code Red, Code Blue, and the fire alarm blasted through the D wing. It was bedlam.

CHAPTER 27

THE JENNINGS PREPARE FOR THE RAID

The new residents of the New Hamburg Inn woke to a beautiful September morning. Malcolm completed his exercises, washed, and walked down to the kitchen. The Innkeeper had prepared a continental breakfast buffet. Malcolm returned with a pot of coffee, two mugs, cream, and sugar. He set everything on the table in his suite. Gerta woke up, greeted him, and walked to the washroom.

Malcolm sat and consulted his checklist for this evening's raid. The team knocked on the room's door at 8 a.m. and filed into the suite. All carried mugs of coffee and pastries. Jim took his post outside the door.

Once everyone had sat at the table, Malcolm said, "I want to go over everybody's tasks for tonight."

"Not again," Steve said.

"Yes, again," Malcolm said. He ran through the list of who would do what during the raid on the Tillman residence. Everyone listened intently. "Is everyone clear as to their duties?" Malcolm asked.

Affirmative nodding from everyone.

"Are we hiring Tom?" Danielle asked, her fists clenched.

Everyone turned to Malcolm.

"With Duke out of the picture, I need an extra hand to keep watch over our vehicles on the side road." Malcolm paused before adding, "I interviewed Tom yesterday. He knows basic machine and electrical repair. He's driven pickup trucks and cargo vans."

The men turned to their neighbours and murmured amongst themselves.

Malcolm waited for the exchanges to stop, then he said, "I trust Tom to perform well and be discreet. He'll carry a walkie-talkie but no cell phone. If he performs well tonight, I'll hire him."

"I still think it's too risky taking along a rookie on a job like this," Larry said.

Malcolm considered, then said, "I'm impressed with Tom's attitude. He wants to join our team, despite Duke's assault on his friend, despite his father's disapproval. I take responsibility for him. If his behaviour is not to par, I will deal with it." Malcolm looked at everyone around the table. "Is that acceptable to everyone?"

Everyone chatted heatedly with their neighbour. Danielle rested a hand on her mother's forearm. Gerta rubbed her daughter's hand. After a few minutes, everyone looked at Malcolm and nodded.

"Good," Malcolm said. "Hand over all cell phones and personal ID to Gerta. She'll issue walkie-talkies to everyone. We'll eat lunch and dinner here. We'll order takeout. Let's get to work."

Danielle clasped her hands and closed her eyes. Gerta rose and tapped Danielle on the shoulder. "Come on, honey."

Gerta collected everyone's cell phones and ID papers and distributed the walkie-talkies. She then inspected the signal scramblers, her laptop, and her iPad, confirming they had fully charged.

Danielle took everyone's orders for lunch and dinner.

Jim gathered the team's belongings and prepared them for loading into the cargo vans.

Malcolm walked over to Larry and Steve. "Drive the vans into the horse barn and paste on new labels and replace the licence plates. Use the 'Ontario Fibre Optics' labels. Inspect all the weapons and fill all the cartridge holders and magazines." He looked at Larry. "You've prepared a list of what equipment goes into what vehicle?"

Larry nodded. The men left.

At five minutes to noon, Malcolm's phone rang. He looked at the call display, then picked up. "Inspector Weber. How can I be of service?"

"Hi, Mr. Jennings. I'm calling about your employee, Douglas Ferguson."

"Duke's no longer my employee, but how can I help?"

"Someone murdered him this morning in his hospital room."

"How is that possible? You had a guard posted outside his room."

"We believe the murderer set fire to a supply room on that floor in order to draw the guard away. The killer then slipped into Ferguson's room, injected a fatal dose of opioid in his IV tubing, and escaped unseen."

"Have you arrested the murderer?"

"Not yet. We're investigating all possibilities. I need to talk to you about Mr. Ferguson. Can you come to the station?"

"Yes, I can. What's the address?"

"Come to the headquarters at 200 Maple Grove Road in Cambridge."

"I'll be there within the hour."

"Good. I'll be expecting you."

Malcolm assembled his crew in his suite. "The police just called. Someone murdered Duke this morning in his hospital room."

Everyone looked stunned. Malcolm repeated inspector Weber's theory, then added, "I'm driving over to police headquarters to answer their questions. I may learn more."

The air buzzed with everyone's theory about who could have murdered Duke and why.

Malcolm raised his hands to quiet the crew. "Everyone. We need time to sit and digest this news. It's noon. You guys have lunch." He nodded to Gerta and Danielle. The women brought out sandwiches on trays, and Jim distributed soft drinks.

Malcolm walked outside to his jeep.

A pickup drove into the driveway of the Inn and parked. Tom climbed out and walked over to Malcolm. Danielle raced out of the inn and ran over to hug Tom. "Someone murdered Duke," she said.

"How did that happen?" Tom looked at Danielle and Malcolm with raised eyebrows.

Malcolm repeated what he knew of the murder.

Tom shook his head. Danielle put a hand on his arm.

Malcolm paused, then added, "I've some good news. The team has agreed for you to join the operation tonight."

"That's great. Thank you, Mr. Jennings." Tom turned to Danielle and hugged her.

Malcolm looked at the young couple and smiled. He said to Tom, "You go and have lunch with your new team. I've got to go to town for a while, but when I return, I'll go over your assignment for tonight."

"Sure thing," Tom said.

Malcolm climbed into the jeep and left.

Danielle held Tom back before they returned indoors. "Tom, I'm happy, but I'm worried. You must follow Dad's instructions to the letter. The part about discretion. It's critical."

"Don't worry. It doesn't take a genius to realize what business I've signed up for. I can keep my mouth shut, and I'll pull my weight."

Danielle squeezed his arm and kissed him.

They both walked indoors. Danielle said, "Can you believe it? Someone killed Duke? Do you think your father or Sharon had anything to do with it?"

"I don't think so. But whoever killed Duke has rendered the world a service. And I hope he never gets caught."

Danielle looked at him with raised eyebrows.

CHAPTER 28

ROBERT BECOMES PRIME SUSPECT

After completing the morning chores at Sharon's farm, Robert climbed the stairs to her bedroom. He tiptoed to Sharon's bedside. She was resting on her back, eyes closed. He approached the bed and whispered, "Hi. How are you feeling?"

She opened her eyes and smiled.

"Fairly well, actually."

Her voice was groggy. She propped herself on the pillows.

"I have the oxycodone pills to thank for that." She looked up at Robert. "I visited the washroom without help last night, and I drank the glass of water you had left for me. Thanks for that. What time is it?"

"It's going on nine o'clock. I've fed and watered the animals, and everyone's litter is fresh. They've asked me to thank you for making those arrangements while you're recovering." Robert smiled at his joke.

"Thanks, Robert, and thank Tom, as well. Is he here?"

"No. He's delivering cannabis to some shops in town." Robert hesitated, then said, "He wants to work with Jennings Electric as an apprentice electrician. He's hoping to start today."

Sharon looked up at him. "Are you okay with him working with those people?"

"No, I'm not. But that's what he wants to do. I'll watch and support him as much as I can."

Sharon placed her hand on Robert's arm. "I feel embarrassed at the state I was in when you found me yesterday. It was a godsend you came over to look in on me." She looked up at Robert with a softness in her eyes.

"Your job now is to get your strength back. Let me prepare some breakfast. How about fried eggs, coffee, toast, and jam?"

"That would be wonderful, especially the coffee." Sharon looked around for her clothes. "Could you give me some help with getting dressed? I want to get up and join you downstairs."

Robert helped her pull off her nightshirt and slip into pants and a blouse.

"Could you help me get down the stairs?" Sharon asked.

"Absolutely!"

Sharon sat at the kitchen table. Robert placed a glass of water with ice cubes in front of her and prepared breakfast.

They sat across from each other, ate, and shared about how quickly children grow up and leave home. They talked about their animals, their crops and, of course, the weather.

An hour flew by. Sharon moved to the upholstered recliner in the living room and fell asleep. Robert placed a glass of water on a side table beside her. He sat on the sofa, watched her rest, leaned back, and fell asleep himself.

Robert woke a few hours later. Sharon was still sleeping. He rose, and walked to the kitchen. He retrieved cured ham, lettuce, and mayo from the fridge and made a sandwich. He placed it on a plate, added a few carrots and radishes. He brought the plate to Sharon's side table.

Robert returned to the fridge, crushed some ice cubes, filled half a pitcher with water, added lemon slices, and sugar. He brought the pitcher and a glass to the side table.

As Robert was leaving and about to close the door softly behind him, a police cruiser rolled into the driveway. Inspector Weber climbed out of the passenger side.

"Mr. Cole, glad to find you here. I stopped by your Airbnb, but you weren't home."

Weber signalled toward the door. "Can we go inside?"

Constable Kidnie followed behind the inspector.

The three men entering the living room. Sharon had awakened. "Good morning, Inspector."

"Good morning, Mrs. Doyle. How are you feeling?"

"Recuperating as best and as fast as I can. Thank you for asking."

Robert looked at Weber. "Do you have the results from the rape kit?"

"Yes." The inspector turned to Sharon. "Fingerprints lifted from your neck and shoulders match those of Douglas Ferguson. DNA results will come later, but we have enough to charge him with aggravated sexual assault."

"That's good news," Robert said.

"Yes, but it's now academic."

"Why do you say that, Inspector?" Sharon's voice trembled. "Did he escape from the hospital?"

"Someone murdered him this morning." The inspector studied Robert's face. "From first indications, someone injected a fatal dose of opioid in his IV system, but the autopsy will confirm this."

Robert and Sharon stared at each other with raised eyebrows.

"Wasn't there an officer guarding his room?" Robert asked.

"Yes, there was—that is until he left his post to attend to a fire someone had set in a supply room down the hallway. That's when the murderer must have entered Ferguson's room, unobserved."

Inspector Weber observed Robert's reactions. He added, "We're reviewing the hospital's cameras, and the forensics team is gathering fingerprints and DNA from Ferguson's room and the supply room."

The inspector asked, "At what time did you arrive here this morning, Mr. Cole?"

"Around eight o'clock. I went to the barn to feed the animals, and then I returned to the house to check in on Sharon."

"And what time was that?"

"Nine?"

Weber looked at Sharon. She nodded.

"And you've been here since then?"

"Yes," Robert said. "Sharon fell asleep on the reclining chair, and I rested on the couch."

Weber turned to Sharon. "Did you wake during that period?"

"No, I was zonked out."

Weber turned to Robert. "I need you to accompany me back to the station to take down your statement and to answer some questions. We'll need a set of your fingerprints and a DNA sample."

Robert looked confused. "Are you suspecting me? But I was here all morning."

"We'll go over all that at the station."

Sharon looked up at Robert, wide-eyed.

Robert followed the two officers to the police cruiser and climbed into the rear seat.

"Where to, Inspector?" Constable Kidnie asked.

"The Central Division on Frederick St. The Rural North Division's been closed."

Once at the station, Weber had Robert registered. He asked Constable Kidnie to walk Robert to be fingerprinted, photographed, and to have a DNA sample collected.

After they had completed those tasks, Constable Kidnie took Robert to an interview room. The constable set up the recording machine, verified the functioning of the ceiling-mounted camera, and stood by the door.

Weber entered, turned on the recorder, identified everyone present, and stated the purpose of the interview.

"Mr. Cole, please describe your actions, starting with the moment you rose this morning to the present."

Robert described his activities in detail.

Inspector Weber then looked squarely at Robert. "Yesterday, the officer posted to Mr. Ferguson's hospital room witnessed you threatening the victim's life. Is that correct?"

"Yes. I was angry, and I threatened him, but I couldn't think of a way to kill the bastard without getting caught, so I didn't do it."

"It strikes me you may have solved that problem," Weber said while staring at Robert. "There is a gap, unaccounted for, in your morning activities." The inspector paused and studied Robert's reaction. "We'll carry out a time analysis and determine if there was sufficient time for you to drive to the hospital and back while Ms. Doyle was sleeping."

"I'm glad someone killed Ferguson, but the honour is not mine," Robert said.

"You had motive and opportunity, which makes you a prime suspect." The inspector paused before adding, "We will hold you at the station until forensics' preliminary results are in—sometime before noon tomorrow, I expect."

"I'm surprised you can keep me here with no evidence," Robert said. "I want to call a lawyer for advice, and I need to arrange for someone to look after my farm animals, and those of Sharon."

"Certainly. You may make as many calls as you need to." Weber turned to Constable Kidnie. "Please take Mr. Cole to a quiet place where he can make phone calls." After a moment of reflection, he added, "And have the desk assign a cell for Mr. Cole, a comfortable one."

Robert's first call was to his friend, Lawyer Rick.

"Hi, Robert. Are you calling for a progress report on this guy Chopra?"

"No. I've got an even more urgent issue on my hands."

"Oh? What is that?"

"I've become a prime suspect in the murder of a member of the crew that was lodging at my Airbnb. This guy raped my friend Sharon Doyle the day before yesterday, and someone murdered him this morning. The police suspects I did it to avenge Sharon. I didn't, of course."

"Don't say anything to the police until I get there. Give me half an hour."

"Understood. Thanks."

Robert's second call was to Tom, but the line was dead. He couldn't leave a message.

Robert's third call was to his friend, Uncle Bill. The two helped each other with heavy chores around their respective farms. Uncle Bill agreed to look after Robert's and Sharon's animals. "Oh, don't forget to feed Mac the tomcat," Robert added before signing off.

Constable Kidnie escorted Robert to his cell for the night. It was clean and well lit. It contained a bed, a stainless steel sink, and a toilet with a privacy curtain. A desk, a chair, a table lamp, and a TV filled a corner of the cell. The officers on duty had ordered takeout pizzas, and they shared two large slices and a Coke with Robert.

Lawyer Rick arrived shortly afterward. Rick cut to the chase. "I called Inspector Weber from my car, and something he said troubled me."

"What did he say?"

"Jesus, Robert. You threatened to kill that man in the presence of a police officer. That was a very dumb thing to do, especially when someone murders the man the next morning."

"I spoke in anger. Surely, the police can't use that as proof I killed the bastard."

"It got their attention, and I can't blame them. The only thing we can do is wait for the forensics team to clear you, which should happen tomorrow before noon."

"Can you get me out on bail or something?"

"I can't do that until they charge you. They have twenty-four hours to do this. In the meantime, I'll line up a criminal lawyer, just in case." Rick looked Robert in the eye. "You job is to reflect on who could have done the murder. If they charge you, we'll need to divert the police's attention to a more probable suspect."

A worried looked crossed Robert's face.

CHAPTER 29

RELIANT DRIVES TO CANADA

As 1 p.m. approached, Popeye sat in Reliant's meeting room. He had arranged for coffee, tea, and pastries to be delivered. His team filed in. Everyone picked up a hot drink and a pastry, and sat.

Popeye opened the meeting. "Hi, guys. Let's hear the results of your research. Ashley, you go first."

Ashley placed a sheaf of paper on the table, then looked up at the team. "I've researched five more names on the FBI's list of suspects. They are a sorry bunch of criminals with records for attempted robbery of rich and famous people, but none with the technical skills to carry out an untraceable transfer of funds. Nothing in their background leads me to believe they would hang their victim."

"Hmm . . . okay," Popeye said. "Stay on your list." He turned to Pierre. "What about you, Pierre?"

Pierre did some throat clearing before saying, "I went through the next five on the FBI's list of violent antiestablishment activists. These guys have arts and political science degrees. Some are teachers; others are middle management types. I couldn't place any of them near New York City on the day Stonely was robbed and murdered." Pierre looked at Popeye. "I took a break from my list and helped Louise with her research on the

Jennings. I called their electrical contracting business in Chicago and got their answering machine. The recorded message said the shop was closed for the next two weeks."

"Do we know where they went?" Popeye asked.

Louise answered for Pierre. "They've blocked tracking on their cell phones, and they've disconnected the GPS tracking on all their vehicles."

"That's suspicious," Popeye said.

Louise continued, "I think I can place the Jennings near New York City on the day of Stonely's murder. My search engines flagged gas transactions, paid with a fake credit card, that traces a road trip from Chicago to New York City and back on that day."

"We may have a strong suspect here," Popeye said. "Did you find a connection between the Jennings, Stonely, and our client, Carl Tillman?"

"I've found a connection between Malcolm Jennings and Stonely," Louise said. "Malcolm's father worked his entire life for Windy City Machining in Chicago, a company owned by Stonely Holdings. The company went bankrupt under suspicious circumstances, and left the self-administered pension fund and medical benefits funds empty. Malcolm's father died of cancer shortly after, penniless."

"I can see a motive for revenge," Popeye said. "And what about Tillman?"

"Pierre knows of one. Tillman's former company, Grenadiers Military Resources, or GMR, was being sued by the parents of contract soldiers that were tortured and killed in Fallujah during the war in Iraq. GMR had supplied the contract soldiers."

Pierre interjected, "And one of them was Malcolm Jennings' younger brother, Eddie."

"Holy smokes. That's one big coincidence," Popeye said. "Does the threatening email to Tillman mention how much time he has to make restitution?"

Louise fixed Popeye. "No, but the criminals sent the email to Stonely four weeks before attacking him. The assassins could be moving in on Tillman as we speak."

Popeye mulled this over, then said, "I believe we have a solid lead and we need to act on it immediately." He paused, then said, "I'm calling

Tillman to set up an appointment for tomorrow. I want his agreement to set up a trap for the criminals."

"Tillman already has a local security firm protecting his residence," Louise said.

"I doubt they have the experience to handle what's coming their way," Popeye said.

He considered, then said, "We're leaving for Kitchener tomorrow morning. Louise; put together a travel itinerary for the next four days and book a hotel for us in the area."

Louise rushed to her workstation. The others looked at Popeye for further instructions.

"Pierre and Ashley, pack for three nights, minimum. Assemble all the gear we're going to need. Go heavy on the firepower and the protective gear. If we're dealing with the Jennings, some of them are veteran Marines. Load everything in one of the armoured Suburbans. I'll go update Chief Harrington and get his authorization for the trip."

The crew rushed to their tasks.

Popeye and his team sped eastbound along I-96, en route to Detroit in an armoured Chevy Suburban. He ignored the speed limit, as there were few patrol cars on the interstate highways since the pandemic.

Pierre leaned forward from the rear seat. "Can I drive for part of the way? I've never driven an armoured Suburban."

"There'll be an opportunity to switch drivers after we pass customs," Popeye said. "But wait. Did you take the armoured vehicle training course?"

"I haven't gotten around to it yet," Pierre said. "But how different can it be from driving a regular Suburban?"

"A big difference. It weighs fifteen hundred pounds more than the standard Suburban. This baby's a level ten armour-piercing-rated vehicle, a mini-tank. It handles nothing like what you've ever driven before. I'm not letting you sit at the wheel of this iron-clad mammoth until you've passed the driving course."

"I'm sure it's not as hard as you make it sound."

"Just take the course and find out."

Ashley, who sat shotgun, played with the GPS screen. "We're less than five hours away from Kitchener, assuming we don't run into problems at the Canadian border." She straightened and turned to address Louise in the backseat. "Louise, where did you book us for tonight?"

Louise sat with her laptop open on her lap. "I've booked three suites at the Homewood in St. Jacobs. It's a fifteen-minute drive north of Kitchener. There are two king-size beds and a kitchen counter in each suite. The hotel boasts a backup generator. That's in case of power blackouts."

"Well planned, Louise," Ashley said. "Pierre gets one suite. You get one, too, so you can work on your laptops without disruptions. Popeye and I get the other suite."

"Am I missing something?" Popeye said.

"Come on, Popeye. Everybody noticed the way you look at me," Ashley said.

"Oh, I didn't realize that. But hey, if that helps you perform at your best, I'll gaze at you as often as I can."

Those in the backseat burst into laughter.

"I understand your hesitation, Popeye. I'll share the suite with Louise. It's probably too early to tell your wife about your crush on me," Ashley said. "But since you insist on sleeping by yourself, I hope you brought something to read."

"I did. Reading in bed helps me to relax and fall asleep."

"Not a bad idea. Did you bring a Swedish noir crime novel? Your favourites. Those with that detective who's tortured by his conscience and depressed all the time? What's his name? Wrangler or something?"

"The name is Wallander. For your information, I've brought two novels. I can lend you one, but there's no romance and no pictures."

The teasing having run its course, everyone returned to their preoccupations.

After an hour on the road, Popeye broke the silence. "I've called Tillman. He's expecting us this evening."

"Why so late? We can be there much earlier," Ashley said.

"He has to supervise a rancher who's picking up some horses this afternoon," Popeye said.

"Has he received any more threatening emails?" Louise asked.

"No, but learning that we can read his emails has shocked him. I explained that the new private policing law allows Reliant to conduct surveillance under strictly regulated circumstances. This was news to him, and he did not like it one bit. I didn't mention we can listen to his phone conversations, as well. That would have really pissed him off."

Popeye continued, "I told Tillman we'd review his security arrangements. He agreed his private security team is no match for military-trained criminals."

Popeye turned to Ashley. "Could you plug in the address for the Kitchener police headquarters? They're called the Waterloo Regional Police Service. Chief Harrington called them yesterday to give them a heads-up about our policing contract. I want to drop by and introduce ourselves. It's part of the protocol our legal boys have prepared for us."

Ashley nodded.

Popeye crossed over the Ambassador Bridge and joined the lineup of cars and transport trucks.

Popeye advanced to the Canadian border inspection booth, and lowered his window the maximum six inches the armoured door would allow. He slipped everyone's passports through the opening.

The border agent asked for everyone's nationality, and he scanned the passports.

"What's the purpose of your trip?"

"We'll be meeting with the former executive of a defunct company called Grenadiers Military Resources. We'll be presenting a security proposal for his family and his property."

"What's the executive's name?"

"Carl Tillman."

"How long will you be in Canada?"

"Four days, a week at the most."

"Will you be selling or leaving any merchandise behind? "

"No."

"Where will you be staying?"

"We're booked at the Homewood Suites in St. Jacobs. Was that a good choice?"

"I'm sure it's a good choice. Can you open the liftgate, please?"

Popeye pushed the release button for the liftgate and handed over a set of keys. "You'll need these to open the armoured door."

The agent took the keys, stepped back, and gave the Suburban the once-over. "This vehicle is armoured? I couldn't tell. Pretty slick." After walking behind the Suburban, he stepped under the liftgate and opened the armoured door. He looked into the cargo area and saw equipment cases and a pile of duffel bags and luggage. After closing the armoured door, he walked back to Popeye's window. "An agent will come over and guide you to secondary inspection." The agent kept the passports.

"You'll want to see the permits for the weapons we're carrying," Popeye said as he turned and took a folder from Ashley, and handed it to the agent. "The weapons are part of our presentation to Mr. Tillman and his security team. We want to show them the assortment of weapons and equipment we'll be proposing."

Another agent walked over from secondary inspection and instructed Popeye where to park. Popeye and the team waited inside the station while more agents combed through the contents of the vehicle.

A half-hour later, a voice on the speaker system called Popeye to the counter.

"Your papers are in order. You're cleared to go," an agent said as he returned the permits, the passports, and the keys, back to Popeye. The agent added, "This may be a coincidence, but you're the second contractor, inside a few days, to be crossing into Canada, with military-grade assault weapons. Do you know something we should be aware of?"

Popeye fixed the agent, with raised eyebrows. "Oh. Which contractor was that? "

The agent read from his computer screen, "Jennings Electric."

CHAPTER 30

RELIANT MEETS INSPECTOR WEBER

Popeye drove the Suburban through the Ontario countryside, along Highway 401, and turned off at the King Street exit. He followed the GPS instructions to the Waterloo Regional Police Service headquarters. After parking the Suburban in the Visitors Parking Area, Popeye turned to address the team. "Louise, you'll come with me to meet the chief of police. The rest of you can wait here or in the lobby."

"I'll wait here," Ashley said, "but leave the fob behind. I want to listen to the radio and keep the ventilation going." She reached over and selected a radio station that broadcast news.

"I'll wait here as well," Pierre said.

Popeye and Louise walked to police headquarters. Automatic doors opened to the entrance of a bright, spacious lobby. Popeye noticed a small police museum in one corner. He approached the reception counter.

"Good day, Officer. We're with The Reliant Detective Agency. We're here to meet with Chief Edwards. He's expecting us."

"Good day to you, too," the officer said. "The Reliant Detective Agency? Yes, I see your name on the log. I'll tell the chief you've arrived."

Moments later, two men in dark blue shirts and pants emerged from the office area. One extended his hand to shake. "You must be Captain Morris?

I'm Chief Edwards." He turned sideways. "And this is Inspector Weber, our Head of Intelligence and Criminal Investigations." Popeye shook the men's hands. He observed with interest the crown and maple leaves on the officers' epaulettes. "Pleased to meet you, gentlemen." Popeye then turned to introduce Louise. "This is agent Louise Jackson, our cyber specialist."

After more shaking of hands, Popeye said, "As my superior, Chief Harrington, must have mentioned to you, we're carrying out a private policing contract for Carl Tillman, former CEO of Grenadiers Military Resources. We're meeting with Mr. Tillman later today. We believe he is a target for a robbery and assassination attempt."

Chief Edwards looked on with a grave face. "Yes, your chief mentioned that."

Popeye continued. "Would you like us to tell you more about our plan of action?"

Edwards nodded and said, "Let's move to a conference room."

Everyone followed the chief.

Once everyone had taken a chair around the conference table, Edwards was the first to speak. "We appreciate your doing this by the book, Captain Morris. This is our first experience with this new legislation. Inspector Weber here will be your contact at the Waterloo Regional Police Service, and he'll keep the Ontario Provincial Police informed. They may need to be involved, as well."

Popeye shared the information his team had gathered about the murder of CEO Jamie Stonely. He then turned the floor over to Louise, who explained how she uncovered information that led Reliant to suspect serial killers were targeting Carl Tillman. She mentioned that a Malcolm Jennings, and his crew from Chicago, were their prime suspects.

Weber's eyes widened at this information. "I've interviewed this Malcolm Jennings and his crew. They're electricians bidding on construction projects in the area. We arrested one of their crew members yesterday for sexual assault, but someone murdered him in his hospital room this morning. He was being treated for injuries inflicted by a pig, at the hobby farm they were staying at." Weber paused, then continued. "The Jennings carry licences to trade in firearms and conduct debt collection. They carry an arsenal in their two cargo vans."

Popeye and Louise exchanged glances. Popeye asked, "We're definitely talking about the same crew. Where are they staying?"

"They were staying at an Airbnb in New Hamburg, but they moved out yesterday. I don't know where to," Weber said.

"We'll talk with that Airbnb owner. Do you have his number?"

Weber handed Popeye a business card from the Homestead. "We're holding the Airbnb owner, Robert Cole, at Central Station, under suspicion of having murdered the rapist, but I can arrange for us to talk to him on the phone?"

"Yes. I'd like that."

"But before we do that, did I hear you say you are meeting with Tillman later today?"

"Yes, this evening. We'll share our information with him, and we'll propose that we carry out a security assessment of his residence in the coming days."

Inspector Weber looked surprised. "There's already a security team in place at the Tillman residence."

"We don't mean to patronize them, but I'm sure they've never encountered the level of sophistication these criminals are capable of."

The two police officers looked at each other with raised eyebrows.

"We'll carry out simulated exercises with his security firm. You may get calls from concerned citizens of some strange goings-on at the Tillman residence," Popeye said. "I'll keep you informed of our plans."

"I appreciate the heads-up," Weber said. "The last thing we need is to dispatch patrol cars on false errands. We've had to do this a few times recently. The military has opened an outdoor firing range, and they sometimes practise late at night. Our dispatcher gets flooded with calls from concerned citizens who've heard gunfire."

Edwards rose. "I'll leave you folks to coordinate together. I must run." He shook hands with his visitors and left.

Weber addressed Popeye, "Let's make that call to Robert Cole, the Airbnb owner. Let's move to a smaller room with a phone."

The three sat in an interview room, and Weber placed the call to Central Station, and had Robert Cole brought to a phone.

"Inspector Weber? You wanted to talk to me?" Robert said.

"Yes. It's about the Jennings. The phone is on speaker, and there are two agents from a detective agency with me now."

Popeye introduced himself. "Mr. Cole. I'm John Morris, team captain with The Reliant Detective Agency in Ann Arbor. Our cyber expert, Louise Jackson, is with me. I'm interested in the whereabouts of Malcolm Jennings' crew. I believe they stayed at your Airbnb recently?"

"Hello, Mr. Morris. Yes, Jennings and his crew stayed at my place for one night. One of the crew, a man called Duke, raped a close friend of mine, and I kicked the Jennings out. Why are you looking for them?"

"We suspect they have murdered a CEO in New York City some three months ago, and we believe they are planning another murder."

"Jesus. My son, Tom, has applied to join that crew."

"Do you know where the Jennings have moved to?"

"No, but my son would know. I can't reach him. His phone is turned off." Robert paused, then said, "Inspector Weber? Can you locate my son and warn him?"

Weber considered, then said, "I'll have the patrol cruisers look for him. We'll start at your place."

"Thanks, Inspector."

Popeye continued, "Mr. Cole, can you remember hearing anything that would show where the Jennings have moved to? What are they planning to do next?"

"Tom mentioned he'll drive a van for them on his first assignment, but I don't know any more than that."

Popeye paused at that news. "How large is the crew, and what are they driving?"

"Jennings, his wife and daughter, and three men. They drive a black Jeep Wrangler and two white Chevy cargo vans. The vans have Jennings Electric logos on them."

"Thank you, Mr. Cole. That's helpful." Popeye looked at Weber and nodded his head.

Weber closed the conversation with, "Thank you for your help, Mr. Cole. I'll send cruisers to look for your son."

"Thank you, Inspector."

Weber ended the call.

Popeye turned to Louise. "Can you locate the Jennings?"

"If they used their credit card to book the lodgings, I can find them, but I need to get my search engines going."

"We'll head to our hotel and let you set up right away."

Weber turned to Popeye. "Before you leave, Captain Morris, could I have the names of your team members, a copy of your licence, and your contract?"

"Certainly." Popeye handed a folder to the inspector. "Would you like to meet the team and look at our equipment? We're parked outside."

"Yes, but give me a second. I'll ask Constable Kidnie to join us."

Weber returned with Constable Kidnie, and all four walked out to Reliant's Suburban.

Popeye introduced his team, then guided the two officers to the back of the SUV. He opened the liftgate and the armoured door, then pulled bags and cases closer. He opened them. They contained assault rifles and associated gear.

"Mother of God! You came prepared for a military operation," Weber said.

"Our prime suspects are Marine veterans with combat experience. They'll be carrying military-grade weapons themselves."

"You're right. I saw those in the Jennings' vans, and I know Tillman's security team doesn't carry that level of weaponry." After a moment of reflection, Weber said, "When are you meeting with Mr. Tillman?"

"At his residence at nine p.m. Mr. Tillman picked the time."

"I'd like to join you for that meeting, if you've no objections."

"I've no objections, but I need to clear it with Mr. Tillman."

Popeye called Tillman, explained the request, then nodded at Inspector Weber. Popeye closed the rear doors of the SUV. "We'll check in at our hotel in St. Jacob, and help Louise set up her computers. Would you like to ride with us to the Tillman residence?"

"Yes, I would. Thank you. Could you pick me up here?"

"Sure thing. We'll be here at eight-thirty." Weber nodded.

Popeye and his team followed a thruway north, through the cities of Kitchener and Waterloo, on their way to St. Jacob.

Ashley, a history buff, shared the fruit of her research with the group. "This region was settled by German-speaking Mennonites and Amish people from Lancaster County, Pennsylvania in the 1800s. The city of Kitchener was called Berlin up until the First World War. If we're lucky, we'll get to see some Amish black horse-drawn buggies."

Everyone raised their eyebrows.

As Popeye turned off the highway and entered St. Jacob, the team saw a huge farmer's market. Bearded Amish men dressed in black were guiding their black buggies into horse sheds.

Popeye parked near the entrance to their hotel. Louise walked ahead to the registration desk and signed them in.

All raced to their suites. Louise set up her two laptops on a worktable and connected to the hotel Wi-Fi. After making a few checks on her main laptop, she called to Popeye, "The internet service is slow here. It'll take me some time to find where the Jennings are staying."

Popeye gave this news some thought, then said, "You keep at it. The rest of us will drive over to the Airbnb where they stayed last and look for clues. Call me when you find where they're staying."

Popeye, Ashley, and Pierre headed for the Suburban. Ashley entered the address of the Homestead on the GPS, and they drove off.

Popeye parked in the driveway of the Homestead. A silver PT Cruiser, an antique, stood near the entrance to the barn. Otherwise, all was quiet.

"Pierre, you check out the barn. Ashley and I, we'll check the house," Popeye said.

Pierre walked by the remains of a make-shift fire pit. From the tire tracks in the grass, he concluded the Jennings had backed up a vehicle close to the fire pit.

He walked by the PT Cruiser and entered the barn. The pungent odour of a pig pen assaulted his nose. He advanced along the main aisle and noticed a large man forking hay into the feeding trough of a white cow.

The man put down his fork and looked at Pierre. "Hello. Are you looking to book a room at the Airbnb?"

"No. Are you an employee?"

"No. I'm a friend helping out. Can I help you with anything?"

"I need to find the previous guests. Jennings Electric. Any idea where they went?"

"No. My name is Bill, by the way."

"Hi. I'm Pierre."

"I know Robert kicked them off the site, but I don't know where they went. One guy from that crew raped a friend of ours, and the bastard was murdered in his hospital room this morning. Wilma had chewed a part of his leg off." Bill pointed at the pig pen where Wilma's head was poking above the enclosure, and grunting. "Serves the bastard right."

"Would you mind coming to meet my supervisor? He'll want to ask you some questions."

Bill considered for a moment, then said, "Yes. I can take a few minutes to answer his questions."

The men walked over to the house where Popeye and Ashley were standing on the porch. Popeye walked down the stairs to meet Pierre and Bill.

Pierre spoke first. "This man is a friend of the owner, and he's looking after the barn and the animals while Robert Cole is detained."

Bill's eyebrows rose. "How did you folks know about that?"

"We're with The Reliant Detective Agency, investigating the guests that were staying here. We've met with Inspector Weber and he told us about Mr. Cole being detained at Central Station. We need to look inside the house and look for any evidence of where the Jennings may have gone. Do have a key to the house?"

Bill was hesitant. "I can't let you in the house without Robert's okay. Don't you need a warrant or something like that?"

"Let's contact Inspector Weber. He may be able to obtain a warrant for us."

Popeye called Weber and explained the situation. Weber asked to talk to Bill. After their conversation, Bill handed the phone back to Popeye, and said, "Inspector Weber said he'll email you a copy of a warrant within the hour, which will authorize you to search the premises. When you receive it, come and get me and I'll open the house for you."

Before an hour had past, Popeye had received a copy of the warrant, and he had Bill open the house for him. He and his team entered and searched the house, room by room, but found nothing that would indicate where the Jennings had moved to.

"Our best hope is for Louise to find them," Popeye said.

Ashley suggested, "Let's go get dinner while we wait."

"Okay. Let's stop somewhere on our way to picking up Inspector Weber," Popeye said. "Can you find a convenient spot?"

"Sure. I'll look on TripAdvisor for a good German restaurant."

Popeye turned to Pierre. He shrugged his shoulders.

"German cuisine, it is," Popeye said.

Pierre almost tripped on something on his way to the Suburban. He looked down and saw a black tomcat. The cat looked up at him and meowed.

"Sorry, pal, but I don't have anything to give you."

When dinner was completed, Popeye paid the bill and the team headed to the Suburban. He steered the SUV toward police headquarters. His cell phone rang. He handed it to Ashley to answer. After looking at the call display, Ashley picked up. "Hi, Louise. It's Ashley. I'll put you on speaker."

Louise said, "Guys. I know where the Jennings are staying at."

CHAPTER 31

THE RAID (PART 1)

Malcolm and his troop climbed in the vehicles and drove off toward the Tillman residence. Darkness had settled over the countryside. The Harvest Moon took pride of place in the sky, against a backdrop of millions of stars. Crickets chirped in the fields, barn owls hooted on the tree branches, and migrating geese honked overhead.

Hydro had scheduled a rotating blackout, and Huron Road was dark. The Jennings caravan drove past the military outdoor firing range. A firearm practice was in progress. Bursts from automatic weapons and the smell of gunpowder filled the air. Thick plumes of smoke rose over the gun range.

The Jennings drove another kilometre. Jim steered the Jeep onto the side road bordering the Tillman property. Tom followed in his cargo van. Malcolm, with Larry and Steve onboard, drove on to the Tillman property entrance.

The guardhouse, the guard booth, and the residence were lit. Malcolm heard the rumble of a gasoline generator located behind the guardhouse.

Malcolm parked in the far corner of the parking lot, beside Moreno's black Camry. The men walked to the guardhouse.

Moreno had taken position in the guard booth. He walked over to greet the men. The men walked inside the guardhouse. Malcolm placed a manila envelope in front of Moreno. "I've brought your new identification papers."

Moreno opened the envelope and examined the documents: a driver's licence, a SIN card, an OHIP card, a credit card, and a passport. "What's the limit on the credit card?"

"Twenty thousand dollars."

Moreno nodded and slipped the envelope inside his jacket. "You guys are ready to do this?"

"Yes, we are. You've instructed your men to take the evening shift off?"

"Yes, I told each one I had overstaffed the shift by mistake, that they could stay home with pay, but to keep their trap shut about it."

"What about the housekeeper?"

"She's babysitting a friend's children in Kitchener." Moreno hesitated before adding, "But there's a problem."

"What problem?" Malcolm asked.

"The family changed their plans. They cancelled their outing and everyone's home."

"Shit!" Malcolm said. "Are there any other evenings this week when they'll be out?"

"No. Not this week."

"Damn."

"It gets worse. There's a reporter in the house right now. She turned up without an appointment. I tried turning her back, but she called Tillman on the spot and he told me to let her through." Moreno pulled a business card from his coat pocket and read it aloud. "Deborah Miner, senior reporter, *Defence Business Magazine*."

Malcolm, Larry, and Steve looked at each other.

"We'll deal with it," Malcolm said.

"Where are the rest of your men?" Moreno asked.

"They're parked on the side road. They'll walk through the fields and meet us at the residence."

"I'll be going inside the house with you," Moreno said.

Malcolm studied Moreno's face. "It will get messy in there. Some things you cannot unsee."

"I want to see for myself what my cut should be."

Seeing that Moreno had his mind made up, Malcolm said, "Okay, let's go."

As the men approached the rear of the van, Malcolm unclipped his walkie-talkie. He pressed the call button, and the device crackled. "Calling Jim. This is Malcolm."

"Jim here. I can hear you loud and clear. We're in position on the side road, awaiting your go-ahead. Over."

"Meet me at the front porch in ten minutes. Over."

"Roger that."

Malcolm turned to his teammates. "Let's suit up!"

Steve opened the two cargo doors, reached in, grabbed an armoured vest, and shrugged it on. He slipped night vision goggles around his neck, stuffed magazines, ammunition clips, two hand grenades, and a walkie-talkie in the pockets of his jacket. He slipped the shoulder strap of the signal scrambler over his shoulder. With an M16 in his left hand and a shotgun in his right hand, he walked hurriedly toward the guard booth.

Malcolm and Larry leaned in and grabbed armoured vests, pistols, spare magazines, and knives. Malcolm turned to Moreno. "You see anything you want?"

Moreno shook his head. "I'll observe."

Malcolm nodded. He noted the lightweight bulletproof vest underneath Moreno's jacket and the pistol inside a holster on his hip.

"Are all closed-circuit cameras turned off?" Malcolm asked.

Moreno nodded.

"The landline. Can you show Larry where to cut it?"

Moreno signalled for Larry to follow him to the guardhouse. The men returned with an extension ladder, a wire cutter, and a navy-blue security team jacket. Moreno pointed at communications cables, which were strung high along the guardhouse wall. Larry set the ladder against the wall, grabbed the wire cutter, and climbed. Moreno walked over to Steve at the guard booth and gave him the jacket. "You should wear this."

After the wires were cut, Malcolm, Larry, and Moreno set off for the residence. Lampposts spilled a subdued and pleasing illumination on the paved laneway. The fruity smell of fresh-cut grass filled the air. Short howls interspersed with yips and yaps pierced the night. A coyote with a scruffy reddish-brown coat appeared ten yards ahead of them. The animal stared at the men with mirror-like eyes. Its pointed ears twitched, it sniffed the air, then trotted out into the darkness.

At the side road, Jim supervised the team as they suited up. Gerta swung the carrying strap of the portable signal jammer over her shoulder. She then handed the satchel with her laptop over to Danielle.

Jim turned to Tom. "You remember where the override switch is for the courtesy lights in the van?"

"Yes." Tom pointed to a switch located low on the dashboard.

"Good. Turn it off now so the van will go dark, and don't turn it back on until we tell you to."

"Understood." Tom reached down and flipped the switch to off.

"Keep your walkie-talkie on at all times. If someone drives by and stops, say you're part of an electrical crew. You're watching over the vehicles while the crew is looking for a break in the power line." Jim paused, expecting some questions. None came. "As soon as you see us returning, open all the doors and sit at the wheel with the engine running. Got that?"

"Got it."

"Can I see your cell phone?"

"I gave it to Gerta," Tom said.

"Good." Jim smiled. He grabbed the tote bag with the assault rifles, and he turned to the women. "Let's go."

Jim, Gerta, and Danielle stepped over a saggy rusted wire fence and trudged through knee-high red clover.

Malcolm, Larry, and Moreno huddled in a shaded area near the porch, out of sight of the windows. Jim and his team appeared, their faces covered in sweat. "Damn clover," Jim said.

Moreno pointed at an Audi sitting by itself in the parking area. "The reporter's car. Tillman's and his son's cars are in the garage."

Gerta turned the signal jammer on. "How many people will be in the residence?" she asked.

"There's been a change," Malcolm said. "Tillman's family is at home, and so is a reporter."

"God. That's four eyewitnesses! Let's abort and pick an evening when Tillman is alone."

Malcolm looked at Gerta. He said with sadness in his voice, "There is no better evening inside our time frame. I'm sorry about that."

The group remained quiet, sombre. Malcolm looked at his team. "We agreed we wouldn't leave any eyewitnesses to an execution behind. This is for everyone's safety." Malcolm paused, then added, "These people partook in the spoils; now they partake in the retribution. We, too, live by that code." He let a moment pass. "But if any of you can no longer live with that decision, now's the time to say so."

All lowered their eyes. No one spoke.

Malcolm turned to Gerta. "There'll be no hanging this time."

Gerta nodded, but looked sorrowful.

Malcolm turned to the rest of his crew. "Load your pistols." He unholstered his Glock, pulled the slide, and released it to chamber a round. He gestured for Moreno to join him as he climbed the steps to the porch. He rang the doorbell.

CHAPTER 32

THE RAID (PART 2)

Dinner was over in the Tillman household. Anita, the housekeeper, had left to attend to some emergency at Moreno's friend's home. Tillman shook his head at Amanda's habit of helping people resolve their self-created problems. At least Anita had cleared the table and loaded the dishwasher before she left.

Amanda's sister had called to cancel her invitation to dinner. She had come down with flu symptoms. When will humanity be free of the variants of this damn influenza virus?

Tillman turned to look at his small-time blackmailer, Deborah Miner, who was sitting in the living room. He wanted her out of the house before the detective agency showed up for their meeting at nine. Deborah had shown up unannounced. Her article about him was set to go to press tomorrow and she wanted her hush money tonight. Tillman didn't want the embarrassing interview with his former executive secretary to be published in a reputable business magazine. The little shyster had brought along a contract for them to sign.

Tillman invited Deborah to sit in the visitor's chair beside his work desk in the den. As he headed toward the den, he noticed his son, Paul, approach Amanda in the living room. Mother and son whispered to each other, while girlfriend Linda watched from the kitchen. Amanda was nodding her head at Paul. She wrote something down on a pad, tore the sheet, and gave it to Paul. His son kissed his mother on the cheek, rose, and headed to the basement. Linda followed him.

Tillman brought up his bank accounts on his laptop. He reached for the contract document Deborah had brought. He found the page he was looking for. "You've left the contract amount blank. How much did you have in mind?"

Before Deborah could answer, the doorbell rang.

Tillman rose and walked over to the entrance door. He peeked through the side panel windows and saw Moreno and a man standing in front of the door. The stranger wore a Kevlar vest and a holster harness. Tillman opened the door.

He stopped short at the sight of a crew of people standing to the side. He raised his eyebrows at Moreno, but before Moreno said a word, the stranger pushed the barrel of his pistol under Tillman's chin. "Let's go inside, Mr. Tillman."

"What the hell is this?"

Malcolm pointed the pistol at Tillman's chest. He pushed Tillman into the foyer and then guided him to the living room.

"Who is at the door, Carl?" Amanda Tillman asked. As everyone stomped into the living room, she stood up. She recognized Moreno. "Luis. Who are these people?"

Moreno stood red-faced and did not answer. Gerta raced up the stairs. Danielle found the basement entrance and vanished down the stairs. Larry walked into the den and locked eyes with reporter Deborah Miner. She sat wide-eyed in the visitor's chair. In a trembling voice, she said, "Who are you people? Is this a robbery?" She looked panicked. "I'm just visiting. I'll stay out of your way while you do what you have to do."

Larry jerked his pistol in the direction of the living room. Deborah rose and joined Tillman and his wife.

"Please sit down," Malcolm said. The three hostages stood, frozen in place.

"What do you want?" Tillman said.

Malcolm didn't answer but pointed to the couch and side chair with a jerk of his head. Deborah picked the side chair, and the Tillmans sat on the couch. Amanda placed her hand on her husband's arm.

Tillman turned to Moreno. "Luis, what's all this about?"

Moreno looked away.

Tillman then looked up at Malcolm. "There's a vault in the basement with cash in it. I'll open it if you promise to leave afterward."

Malcolm said, "Where's your son and his girlfriend?"

"Downstairs." Tillman considered, then said, "They don't know the combination to the vault."

Two gunshots reverberated from the basement stairway.

Danielle reached the bottom of the steps and faced a large, brightly lit recreation room. Couches, side chairs, a bar, and a giant TV screen filled the room. An open doorway led to a side room. She approached and overheard a man and a woman speaking.

"How much money are you taking?" the woman asked.

"Twenty thousand dollars in American bills," the man answered. "Like I told Mom."

"Come on, Paul, take more than that! There's at least two hundred thousand dollars in there. They won't notice the difference."

Danielle entered the room with her pistol drawn. The woman, a tote bag in hand, was leaning over the shoulders of the man called Paul. The man was kneeling in front of an opened floor-mounted vault.

Danielle crept closer and saw two shelves full of bank notes. She noticed a bottom row of metal drawers.

"Hi, guys," she said.

The woman shrieked. She turned around, and froze at the sight of the gun.

"I need you both to follow me upstairs," Danielle said as she waved her pistol in the door's direction.

"Who the fuck are you?" the woman said. Paul remained crouched on his knees, looking on, wide-eyed.

Danielle changed her mind. She pointed her gun at the vault. "Let's see what's inside those drawers."

Paul nodded his head, turned around, and reached for a drawer. His body blocked Danielle's line of sight as he retrieved a pistol. With his right hand firmly wrapped around the gun's grip, he turned, pointed the weapon at Danielle's chest, and pulled the trigger. A deafening noise filled the room.

Danielle fell backward and fired a round into the ceiling as she hit the floor. She lay motionless.

Paul and the woman winced from the pain in their eardrums. Paul sprang up and looked at Danielle, who lay unconscious. He grabbed his companion by the arm. "Come on, Linda. Let's get out of here."

Linda wrenched free, returned to the vault, and stuffed bundles of bills into a tote bag. Paul didn't wait around, but ran out of the room. He sprang up the basement stairs.

He reached the hallway, turned toward the living room, and froze. Two strangers wearing bulletproof vests, pistols in hand, were looking his way. Paul noticed his parents sitting on the living room couch.

A woman, who had run down the stairs from the second floor, stepped into the hallway and stood in front of him. Paul pointed his gun at her chest. The woman backed up a few steps. Both stood staring at each other, standing still like statues.

The two intruders in the living room raised their pistols in Paul's direction, but the woman stood in their line of sight.

Linda burst out of the basement stairs, lugging the tote bag. She saw Paul and a woman facing each other. Paul was pointing a gun at the woman. Linda ran toward the rear entrance, opened the door, and bolted outside.

Paul fired his pistol at the woman's chest and raced out the rear entrance. He bumped into Linda, then steadied himself. Both stood on the rear patio.

"What do we do now?" Linda asked.

Paul looked around. "Let's make for the aircraft hangar."

Lilac bushes lined the path to the hangar. Paul sprinted toward the hangar. Linda followed closely, lugging the tote bag.

Paul reached the hangar's side door, opened it, and held it ajar for Linda. Once inside the hangar, Paul and Linda took shelter behind a large steel column. Paul reached over and opened the door a crack. He peeked in the house's direction. "They'll be on our tail any minute now."

Paul switched on the lights inside the hangar. He turned to Linda. "I'll get the plane ready. You go open the aircraft door. Do you remember how?"

Linda nodded and raced toward the large overhead door.

Linda flipped a switch on the wall, and the large hydraulic door creaked, clanked, and inched open.

Paul grabbed the tote bag and ran toward a small twin-propeller Beechcraft airplane. He pulled down the plane's side door, threw the tote bag inside, and ran up the steps. Paul climbed into the pilot's seat and switched on the cabin lights and the control board. He adjusted his radio headset. "Thank God the fuel tanks are full," he said to himself. He engaged the starter switches. The engines sputtered to life and the two propellers rotated. "Alleluia!"

Linda ran back toward the aircraft and climbed aboard. She pulled the steps back up by the lifting cable, rotated and locked the door handle. She made her way to the co-pilot's seat, sat, and snapped on her safety belt. Paul pointed a finger at his radio headset, signalling to Linda to put her headset on.

"There's no time to go through the checklist," Paul said.

The engines buzzed furiously as the aircraft inched forward. Once the aircraft had cleared the hangar door, Paul pulled the throttle of both engines to the max. The engines roared, and the aircraft sped up.

A woman appeared beside the runway. She raised an assault rifle and sent a hail of bullets slamming against the plane's fuselage. Oil spurted out of the right engine compartment and an oily mist covered the windshield.

"Jesus. I'm hit," Linda said.

Malcolm ran to Gerta, who was lying on her back in the hallway. His hand searched her armoured vest and found the bullet embedded in the fabric. "You okay, honey?"

Gerta grunted. "I don't know. I feel like I've been kicked in the chest by a horse."

Danielle appeared at the top of the basement stairs. "He caught me by surprise. He shot me in the chest. I think I passed out." She crawled on her hands and knees toward Gerta. "Mom! Are you okay?"

Gerta raised her head. "Except for a cracked rib, I think I'm okay. How about you, honey?"

"Okay, I think." Danielle slipped a hand underneath her armoured vest and rubbed at a sore spot. She rose and leaned against the wall. She was still holding her pistol in one hand. "There's a vault down there. The guy and the girl were helping themselves to bundles of bills when I walked in on them."

Malcolm walked over to Danielle and checked on her condition. Once satisfied she was fine, he said, "Danielle. Grab an assault rifle and go after the couple that ran out the back door. They'll head for the aircraft hangar. Don't let them get away."

Danielle took a minute to process what Malcolm had said, then she rose and ran to the tote bag of assault rifles and grabbed an M16. She ran out the rear door.

Gerta tugged at Malcolm's arm. "They can't call nine-one-one from the garage. The range of our jammer will reach that far."

"Good."

Malcolm turned to Moreno. "Can you gather what's in the vault?" Moreno nodded and went looking for a duffel bag.

The roar of small aircraft engines thundered from the backyard. It was followed by bursts from an assault rifle. A voice came over the walkie-talkie. "This is Danielle. I'm calling Dad."

"This is Dad. Go ahead, Danielle."

"The couple is escaping in the aircraft. I've shot at the plane, but it's flying away."

Malcolm considered for a moment. "Clear the hangar in case one of them stayed behind, then return to the house."

Malcolm helped Gerta to a side chair. She let out a deep breath. "I just need a minute and I'll be ready to work."

Malcolm guided Tillman to the den and had him sit at his desk. Gerta rose and reached into the case with the signal jammer. She turned off the separate switch for Wi-Fi jamming, leaving the cell signal jamming in place. She joined Tillman and sat beside him.

Tillman refreshed his laptop. The screen showed his bank's webpage.

"It's as if you knew we were coming," Gerta said. "Let's start with the savings account. You start a transfer of funds and I'll take over from there."

Tillman opened his savings account and started a transfer of funds.

Moreno returned from downstairs. He placed the duffel bag full of bills on the floor. "There was over two hundred thousand dollars in the vault, and some jewellery. I want my cut from the cash and the jewellery." Without waiting for a reply, he pulled a sheet of paper from his pocket and handed it to Gerta. "This is my account."

"You bastard," Tillman said.

Gerta took the sheet of paper, read it, and nodded. After transferring the funds from Tillman's savings, chequing, and TFSA accounts, Gerta said, "Now, let's look at your accounts in the Caymans."

"What are you talking about? I don't have any accounts in the Caymans."

Malcolm looked squarely at Tillman. "Let's not play games. We've read the communications between you and the two Cayman banks. Let's start with the Fidelity Bank."

"Even if I had an account in one of those banks, I wouldn't be able to access it from my laptop. I would need to show up in person and show some ID." Beads of sweat appeared on Tillman's forehead, and his eyes roamed from left to right.

Malcolm looked down at Tillman. "I see you're choosing to do this the hard way."

Malcolm aimed his pistol at Tillman's left knee and pulled the trigger. The shot reverberated in the room. Everyone winced and covered their ears.

Tillman stared in shock. Gunpowder residue surrounded the small, dark hole in his knee. Shattered bone and cartilage raised the skin around the wound. Blood oozed out, and the pain arrived. He howled in agony. Tears filled his eyes. "Jesus Christ!" He rocked back and forth, holding his knee with both hands. The sulfurous smell of gunpowder and the sweet metallic scent of blood filled the air.

Moreno stared in horror. "What the hell! You've shot him in the knee. Jesus!"

Larry brought a cloth and helped Tillman to bandage his knee.

Malcolm looked at Tillman. "Will you bring up those accounts, or shall I continue?"

"No. Fuck." White-faced, Tillman returned shakily to his laptop, navigated to the website of Fidelity Bank (Cayman) Ltd., and opened the page that showed three accounts totalling fifteen million dollars in U.S. funds. "Here they are," he said between clenched teeth.

Tillman started the transfer, and Gerta took over to fill in the destination details. After having completed the transfers, Gerta said, "Now the HSBC Bank."

"I don't have accounts at that bank," Tillman grunted. Sweat dripped from his brow.

Steve's voice blared out on the walkie-talkies. "Steve calling Malcolm."

"Malcolm here."

"A black Suburban has crashed the gate and is heading toward the house. There are four or five people onboard. The vehicle is armoured and the occupants are armed. Over."

CHAPTER 33

THE FIREFIGHT

Louise's voice rose from the speaker on Ashley's phone. "The Jennings are staying at the New Hamburg Country Inn. It's a half hour east of Kitchener."

"Are they at the inn now? Do you know?" Popeye asked.

"I talked with the owner. The Jennings are eating dinner at the inn. They've ordered takeout. They are booked to stay the night."

Popeye considered, then said, "We'll go pick up Inspector Weber at police headquarters and drive over to our meeting at the Tillman's residence. Try to keep track of what the Jennings are doing."

"Will do." Louise ended the call.

Popeye's Suburban, with Inspector Weber onboard, drove up to the guard booth at the Tillman residence at 9 p.m. A guard was standing at the open window. Popeye lowered his window to its maximum. "Hi. We're with The Reliant Detective Agency. Mr. Tillman is expecting us." Popeye handed over his business card.

The guard read the card, nodded, and picked up the receiver of the private phone line. "Mr. Tillman, The Reliant Detective Agency is here."

After a moment, the guard said, "Understood, Mr. Tillman. I will pass on the message." He hung up, then said, "Mr. Tillman regrets to cancel the appointment. A family emergency. He suggests you call tomorrow morning and set up a new appointment."

"I'm sorry to hear that. Could I talk to him?" Popeye said.

"No. I'm sorry. He's attending to an emergency. Please call him tomorrow and set up a new appointment."

Ashley pulled out her cell phone and dialed Tillman's number. She turned to Popeye. "I'm getting an out-of-service message."

The guard, who had overheard, said, "We're having problems with the cell phone system. There's a technical team at the house working on it."

Popeye said, "Okay. We'll call Mr. Tillman tomorrow morning." He backed up the Suburban into the far end of the guardhouse parking lot, out of sight of the guard booth. He turned to Weber sitting in a rear seat. "Something doesn't look right. I saw an assault rifle and some hand grenades in the guard booth. Does that seem normal to you?"

"No, not at all," Weber said. He rubbed his chin and added, "I couldn't see the guard's face from where I sat, but his voice sounded familiar. I can't place it."

"The guard's call to Tillman sounded staged to me," Popeye said.

"Someone could have jammed the cell signal?" Ashley said. "We may have stumbled in the middle of a raid in progress."

"We need to investigate what's going on," Popeye said. "Pierre, you'll stay behind and watch that guard. Grab what you'll need from the cargo area. The rest of us will drive up to the house and check on what's happening up there." He pressed the liftgate release button and handed over the keys to the armoured door to Pierre.

Pierre jumped out and rushed to the back of the Suburban. He unlocked the armoured door, reached in, and retrieved a walkie-talkie, an armoured vest, an assault rifle, a pistol, a knife, cartridges, and magazines.

The roar from small aircraft engines and the rat-tat-tats of an assault rifle arose from the back of the property.

"What the hell is this?" Popeye said.

The guard appeared around the corner of the guardhouse. He stood in the glare of the headlights of the Suburban. He levelled an M16 at the SUV and opened fire. Star-shaped cracks filled the windshield. He aimed the next spray of bullets at the radiator grille and the front tires.

Popeye opened his door halfway, stuck out his left arm and fired his pistol in the assailant's direction.

Pierre had donned a bulletproof vest by now. He closed the armoured door, left the keys in the lock, activated the liftgate to close, and double-tapped the frame of the SUV. Popeye closed his door and floored the accelerator. He aimed the SUV at the guard, who was now racing toward the shelter of the guard booth. The Suburban crashed through the barrier gate and barrelled down the laneway toward the residence.

Steve called Malcolm on his walkie-talkie to warn him about the armoured Suburban heading toward the house.

"Come to the residence to lend a hand?" Malcolm said.

"I can't. They left one guy behind, and he's firing at me. I'm pinned down behind the guard booth, but I can hold my own here. Over."

Malcolm called Jim.

"This is Jim. I'm listening. Over."

"Stop that vehicle and keep the passengers pinned inside. Don't let any of them reach the house. I'm sending Larry to help. We need another fifteen minutes in here, then we'll leave through the back of the house. Over."

Malcolm looked up at Larry. He nodded, took an M16 and four magazines from the tote bag containing the weapons, and raced out the front door.

Danielle had returned from the backyard. Malcolm turned to her. "Close all the blinds."

She ran to the windows that faced the front of the house and closed the blinds.

As Popeye's Suburban reached the house, a man wielding an assault rifle appeared from behind a column on the front porch. Bullets slammed against the SUV's windshield, radiator grille, and front tires. Popeye saw another hostile run out of the house and take position behind a tree. Popeye engaged the reverse gear on the Suburban and backed up behind trees and bushes. He activated the liftgate. Everyone jumped out and ran to the back of the SUV. Ashley and Popeye grabbed armoured vests and weapons.

Popeye turned to Ashley. "I'll make a wide arc and approach from the left, but I can't fire in the house's direction. The Tillman family is in there. You'll have to pick off the hostiles." Ashley nodded.

"I'll approach from the right-hand side," Weber said. He disappeared into the dark.

Ashley walked closer to the front porch, ducking behind trees and bushes. She could see the two hostiles. After resting her Remington 700 sniper rifle on a tree branch, she shouldered the weapon and searched for the targets with the telescopic lens. She sighted the man behind the column on the front porch. The hostile was leaning out from behind the column at regular intervals and releasing a burst from his assault rifle, then ducking back for cover.

Ashley released the safety on her rifle, chambered a cartridge, adjusted her aim for distance and wind. The next time the target leaned out from behind the column, Ashley pressed the trigger. She absorbed the recoil, then looked into the scope. A star-shaped crack radiated from a small hole in the centre of a picture window. "Shit! I missed," she cursed. "I should have double-checked the centring of that scope before we left the shop."

She tweaked the scope settings to compensate for the misalignment, ejected the spent cartridge, and chambered a new one. She shouldered the rifle, aimed, and waited. When the target's head and shoulder next appeared, she pulled the trigger. A red spray burst out the back of the man's head, and he collapsed on the concrete porch.

Tillman kept insisting he had no accounts at HSBC Bank in the Caymans. Gerta looked up at Malcolm and bit her lips. Malcolm leaned forward and looked at Tillman's wounded knee. Tillman was clenching his jaws and grunting from the pain.

Malcolm looked Tillman in the eyes, and said, "Shall I do a balance job?"

"No. For Christ's sake!" Tillman brought up the HSBC Bank's website, navigated to his accounts. They totalled $15 million in U.S. funds. He started a transfer. Gerta took over the keyboard and completed the transfers. She looked up at Malcolm. "We're done here."

Malcolm signalled for Tillman to rise. "I wanted to talk to you about my brother, Eddie, but there's no time."

"What are you talking about?" Tillman said.

At that moment, glass shattered and venetian blinds clattered. Malcolm turned and watched Mrs. Tillman's body roll from the couch onto the floor. Bone fragments, brain matter, and blood had exploded from her head and splattered on the floor.

Tillman gasped in shock, then hobbled to his wife's body.

Malcolm turned toward the picture window. He walked to it in a crouching position. He peeked through the blinds. The glass had shattered. He saw Jim behind a column on the porch. He heard the crack from a rifle, then watched Jim's head snap back and his body crash onto the porch.

"Shit," Malcolm said. His walkie-talkie squawked. "This is Larry calling Malcolm."

"Malcolm here. Go ahead, Larry."

"Jim's down. It looks bad. There's a sniper in that crew. I won't last long here. Over."

"We're done in here. Drag Jim's body inside. Danielle will open the door for you. We're leaving through the back of the house."

"Roger that."

Malcolm called Steve.

"This is Steve. Go ahead, Malcolm." The sound of gunfire filled the background.

"We'll drive around and pick you up in ten minutes. Over."

"I'll be watching out for your van, but take the time you need. I've got enough ammunition to last me a while, and I haven't used my grenades yet. Over."

Malcolm called Tom at the side road. "Tom, do you copy? Over."

"This is Tom. Over."

"We're heading your way. Open all the doors and have the motor running. Over."

"Understood. Over."

Malcolm walked over to Tillman, who was leaning over his wife and whimpering. Malcolm pressed his pistol against Tillman's temple and pulled the trigger. Tillman's body crumpled on the floor.

Danielle opened the front door. Larry dragged Jim's body inside the foyer. Gerta ran over and took Jim's pulse. She turned to Malcolm and shook her head.

Larry had walked over to Deborah Miner. She was in hysterics. "I have nothing to do with this; I'm just here to—" But before she could finish her sentence, Larry pressed the muzzle of his pistol against her forehead and fired. Miner's head snapped back against the chair's back, tilted sideways, and rested on one shoulder.

Moreno, pale and wide-eyed, let out, "Jesus." He bent forward and puked.

Malcolm walked over to Jim's body and, with Danielle's help, lifted Jim in a firefighter carry. He headed down the hallway toward the rear entrance to the house. "Let's go," he said.

Gerta slipped Tillman's laptop into her satchel and gave it to Danielle to carry. She slipped the carrying strap of the signal jammer over her shoulder and followed behind Malcolm. Danielle followed behind her mother.

Moreno spat and cleared his throat, lifted the duffel bag with the cash and jewellery and followed the women.

Larry grabbed the tote bag with the weapons and brought up the rear.

The team stopped on the back patio to orient themselves. Gerta pointed in the side road's direction where their vehicles were parked.

"You lead the way," Malcolm said to Gerta. He turned to Larry. "You cover our back." The team followed Gerta.

It was hard slogging, knee-deep through the clover, especially for Malcolm.

A pistol shot cracked in the darkness, then someone shouted. "Police! Stop. Put down your weapons. Put your hands behind your head."

Malcolm recognized Inspector Weber's voice.

CHAPTER 34

THE ESCAPE

Malcolm and his team froze when they heard Weber's voice. Malcolm looked in the direction the voice had come from. He deposited Jim on the ground, and retrieved the night vision goggles from Jim's neck. He raised them to his face. "It's the police inspector, some hundred yards away," he said.

Malcolm handed the goggles over to Larry. "You hold him off. The rest of us will keep going."

Larry placed the goggles into position, raised his M16, and let off bursts of bullets in Weber's direction. The others trudged onward toward the side road.

At the sound of bullets whizzing past him, Weber dove into the clover and lay prone. After a prolonged quiet, he lifted his head and made out the dark shape of a hostile. *Replacing his magazine,* Weber thought. He raised himself into the two-knee position, brought his pistol up into a two-hand grip, aligned the sight in the centre of the dark shape, and fired three rounds. He then dove forward and lay flat. His gunshots had rattled his eardrums. A deathly silence descended on the clover field.

Larry had finished loading a new magazine when what felt like a sledgehammer struck him in the chest. He fell backward and passed out.

Malcolm, not hearing any covering fire, stopped, turned, and saw Larry lying flat on his back. He lowered Jim's body to the ground and raced back to Larry's side. The night vision goggles were still in position over Larry's face. His hands held his weapon over his chest as if posing for a photograph. Malcolm reached down and confirmed that Larry had a strong pulse. He shouted, "Danielle! Come over quick!" He picked up the assault rifle and sent bursts of bullets in Weber's direction.

Danielle appeared at his side. Malcolm handed the rifle and the goggles over to her. He retrieved a spare magazine from Larry's pocket and gave it to her. "Give me cover. I'll carry Larry back." Danielle nodded. She kneeled down, fitted the goggles into position, and raised the rifle. She searched for Weber's location.

Malcolm lifted Larry over his shoulders in a fireman's carry and made for the side road. Danielle followed while providing covering fire.

When they walked by Jim's body, Malcolm turned to Danielle. "Stay with him. I'll be back to get him."

Weber hadn't returned fire for some time. Danielle slipped the rifle's sling over her shoulder, moved her arms under Jim's armpits, and dragged him toward the side road.

Malcolm laid Larry in the cargo area of the van. Gerta climbed in and examined Larry. She turned toward Malcolm and smiled. "I've located three bullets embedded in his Kevlar vest. "There's no bleeding. He'll be alright."

Larry stirred and groaned. "What the hell happened? My chest hurts." He tried to sit up.

Gerta held him back. "You lie still for a while, Larry. You may have a broken rib. We'll look you over later."

Malcolm ran back to Danielle, and helped her drag Jim's body to the van.

The team piled the weapons and the equipment in the back of the jeep. They climbed aboard the vehicles, and barrelled down the side road, intent on rescuing Steve.

Steve crouched behind the guard booth as the Reliant agent fired at him from the far side of the guardhouse.

BAD KARMA

"Time to bring my grenades into play," he said to himself. He unpinned one and, with a wide swing of his right arm, tossed it toward the far side of the guardhouse where the agent was taking cover. After it exploded, the firing stopped. Steve sat still, resisting the urge to run over and inspect the results of his actions. A few moments passed, and a burst of bullets zipped by him. "The fucker is still standing," Steve said to himself.

The explosion from the grenade sent Pierre's body slamming against the guardhouse wall and knocked him out momentarily. Pierre came to, sitting, his back against the wall. He felt a sting in his neck and a burning sensation in his left leg. He put a hand against his neck. Warm liquid pulsed through his fingers. "Fuck, this is not good," he said to himself.

Pierre dragged himself to the corner of the guardhouse and released a spray of bullets in the guard's direction. He limped to the back of the guardhouse, pulled some tampons from his emergency kit, and pressed them against his neck wound. With his free hand, he retrieved his walkie-talkie. "This is Pierre calling Popeye."

The radio crackled. "This is Popeye. Go ahead, Pierre."

"I'm hurt. Badly. A ruptured artery in the neck. I need to get to a hospital PDQ. Over!"

"Understood. I'm coming over with the van."

"I'm pinned behind the guardhouse, the far back. The hostile is at the guard booth. Hurry!"

Popeye took stock of the situation at the residence. The last man standing had run inside the house. Nobody had returned fire for some time. He raised his walkie-talkie. "Popeye calling Ashley."

"This is Ashley. Go ahead, Popeye."

"You keep your position while I take Pierre to the hospital. If the hostiles are holding the Tillmans hostage, you handle the negotiations, but keep Inspector Weber in the loop. Over."

"Understood. Keep us posted on Pierre's condition. Over."

Popeye ran to the Suburban, fired up the engine, turned it around, and floored the accelerator. The punctured front tires made the steering difficult. *I hope they'll hold together until I reach the hospital,* Popeye thought.

As the Suburban drove past the guard booth, the guard fired at it. Popeye made straight for the far back of the guardhouse. The SUV crunched to a stop. Popeye saw Pierre limping toward him. He jumped out and held the rear passenger door open for Pierre to climb in. Popeye had barely returned behind the wheel when the guard appeared and sprayed the Suburban with bullets.

"The bastard never lets up, does he?" Popeye said. He floored the accelerator and pointed the SUV in the guard's direction. The hostile ducked out of the way. Popeye manoeuvred the Suburban onto the road and steered toward Kitchener. He punched the address of Grand River Hospital on the GPS. The screen posted a trip distance of twenty miles. "I hope the tires will make it that far," he said to himself.

When Malcolm turned into the entrance to Tillman's property, everything was quiet. Steve who was loading his gear into his van, noticed Malcolm's arrival, and he ran to the jeep's open window.

"The armoured Suburban just left with a wounded comrade. They're probably rushing him to the ER. I've put my stuff in the van and ready to go."

"Did you see the logo on their van?"

"It was dark, but I made out Reliant something."

"Hmm . . . I'll ask Gerta to look into this."

Moreno jumped out of Tom's van and walked to Malcolm's window. "I'm getting the hell out of here. You guys are running a fucking execution squad. You can keep my share of what was in the house vault. I hope never to meet any of you again." He walked to his Camry, climbed behind the wheel, and bolted out of the parking lot.

Malcolm smiled at Steve. "You did well. Let's get out of here!"

Steve ran to his van and jumped in. The caravan climbed onto the road and headed for their hideout in Waterloo.

CHAPTER 35

PAUL AND LINDA ESCAPE

Paul watched Linda as she inspected her right leg in the dim lighting of the cockpit.

"My thigh burns as if it's been seared with a hot poker." I can see blood seeping from a gash in the skin."

Paul leaned sideways to look. "I can't see anything. There's a first aid kit behind the seat."

"This stings so badly, I don't think I can get up," Linda said through gritted teeth.

The aircraft picked up speed and lifted off the tarmac. The rat-tat-tat from the assault rifle had ceased. Oil was spewing out of the right engine. Paul shut it off, the plane shuddered, then stabilized. Bullets had pierced the fuselage, but the aircraft seemed airworthy. They had escaped.

Paul piloted the Beechcraft higher in altitude. The left engine purred steadily.

Linda unclipped her belt, climbed out of her seat, wincing from the pain in her right leg, and moved into a passenger seat. She turned on the overhead light and stared at the rip in her pant leg. An angry red wound covered her right thigh. She lowered her pants for a better look. The cut ran deep. She grimaced. After locating the first aid kit, she pulled out antiseptic towelettes, cleaned the wound, and applied sterile gauze pads. The pads turned red, but they staunched the flow of blood. She wrapped gauze over the pads.

"I'm going to need stitches. A bullet has cut a friggin' trench through the skin of my leg."

Paul didn't answer. He was concentrating on the controls and watching the screen.

Linda hobbled back to the co-pilot's seat. "We need to land at the nearest airport and report what happened to the police. And I need medical attention."

Paul spoke on his mic. "Phone nine-one-one on your cell, and say we're hiding in the aircraft hangar. I don't want them to know we're flying away from the crime scene."

Linda looked at him in surprise. "What do you mean, we're hiding in the aircraft hangar? What are you not telling me?"

Paul looked ahead. "We're not going back. We have a tote bag full of money. We're heading to the Caymans, as planned."

Linda stared at him in disbelief. "What are you talking about? What if your parents are hurt? *I'm* hurt."

"The robbers will have roughed up Mom and Dad and scared them shitless. Dad won't let us leave the house unescorted for months. This is an opportunity in disguise."

"I don't believe what I'm hearing. We can't leave your parents after what happened."

Paul did not answer. After a minute, he said, "Are you making that nine-one-one call?"

"Okay, but why not tell them we're escaping in our aircraft?"

"Because I don't want to tip off the police about our flying away. If they see I've filed an international flight plan, they'll block the approval."

"Where are we going?"

"Stewart International Airport in Newburg, New York. They have an aircraft repair centre. I've been there before, with Dad. We need to get the plane repaired before we head for the Caymans."

"How far is that? I'm bleeding here."

"We'll be there in four hours. I'll get you to a clinic as soon as we land."

"And what about your parents? They may need your help?"

"We'll call home from the airport and find out how Mom and Dad are doing, okay?"

Linda considered the plan for a minute. "What if the other engine fails?"

"This aircraft can glide to a landing in an open field if we have to."

"But the plane repairs will cost a fortune. We don't have that much money in the tote bag."

"Let's see how much the repairs will cost and decide then. We can do the minimum repairs that will get us to the Caymans."

Linda mulled this over before adding, "We don't have our passports!"

"I've got them. I slipped them in my pocket when we were preparing our luggage earlier."

Linda stared at Paul. "Aliens abducted Paul Tillman, and a stranger is sitting beside me."

Paul pointed at Linda's cell phone. She tapped the numbers 9-1-1.

As Linda was completing her 911 call, Paul shouted, "Yes. I've received authorization to land the Beechcraft at Stewart International Airport."

The air controller at Stewart International assigned Paul an airstrip dedicated to private jets. Paul affected a smooth landing and taxied toward the terminal. A marshaller waved his wands and guided Paul to a parking stand. The marshaller raised a fist to signal to Paul to apply the parking brakes, and he pushed wheel chocks against the rubber wheels.

Paul unlocked and lowered the stairs, and stepped down onto the tarmac. Linda followed behind him, carrying the tote bag.

The marshaller pointed to the border control office.

It was three o'clock in the morning, and the terminal was empty of travellers. Paul filled out a declaration form and handed it to the border control agent, along with their passports. Paul, who had dual citizenship, presented his American passport.

The agent scanned Paul's and Linda's passports and paused, staring at his screen. He turned to Paul. "There's an alert with both your names on it. Please wait here. Someone will come to take you to an interview room."

CHAPTER 36

WEBER SURVEYS THE CARNAGE

Weber laid low in the grass. The gunfire had stopped. He raised his head above the clover. The criminals were making their way to the side road. He considered giving pursuit, but they outgunned him ten to one. He chose to walk back toward the residence.

When he reached the house, he hugged the wall, turned the corner, and climbed onto the porch. The lights were on in the house, but the residence was as quiet as a funeral parlour. Bullet casings littered the porch. Weber paused in front of a large picture window and noticed the bullet hole in the glass pane. He tiptoed around a patch of blood and brain matter and walked to the entrance door. He peeked through the side panel windows and saw no activity inside. He heard steps behind him, turned, and saw Ashley approaching.

"Are you alright, Inspector?" Ashley asked.

"Yes, I'm fine." He pointed to the fields. "They escaped to the side road." He looked at Ashley. "You okay?"

"Yes, I'm fine. How many were there?"

"I counted at least six. None appeared to be hostages. One of them was carrying a wounded teammate over his shoulders." Weber pointed at the blood splatter on the porch. "Probably this guy." He turned toward the fields. "I shot at and hit one of them. They dragged him or her the rest of the way."

The roar of engines reverberated from the side road. Weber and Ashley saw two sets of headlights dashing toward the main road.

"They had two vehicles posted out there." Weber said. He turned toward the front door. "It's awfully quiet in there. Let's check on the Tillman family."

Holding his pistol in his right hand, Weber grabbed the door handle with his left hand, turned to Ashley, nodded, then entered the house.

There were no signs of the burglars. Ashley headed upstairs, and Weber swept the main floor.

Weber froze at the sight of Mrs. Tillman lying on her side on the living room floor. Blood and brain matter had leaked from her open skull.

Carl Tillman's body was lying beside his wife's. A pool of blood formed a halo around his head. A blood-soaked cloth had been wrapped around his left knee.

Glass shards covered the floor. Their trajectory led back to the picture window. He walked to the window, opened the blinds, and noticed the bullet hole in the glass pane. He returned to the living room.

A middle-aged woman lay sitting on a side chair with her head resting sideways on her right shoulder. A small dark hole marred the middle of her forehead, and her two glassy eyes stared into the distance.

Weber recognized her. A business magazine reporter. "What was she doing here?" he reflected.

Ashley returned from the second floor. "There was nobody upstairs. I'll go check the basement," she said. She located the basement stairs and disappeared from sight.

Returning a few minutes later, she reported, "I've found a vault in the basement. It's been opened and emptied."

As she walked into the living room, she stalled. "Good God."

"They executed these two," Weber said, pointing at Tillman and the reporter. Then pointing at Mrs. Tillman. "I'd say the bullet came in through the window."

Ashley blushed but remained silent.

Weber stood, pensive. "And where the hell was Tillman's security team?"

He pulled out his cell phone and looked at the screen. "We have cell reception. I'm calling the station."

Weber reached the communications centre, reported the details of the crime scene, and requested three patrol cruisers. "And send two Emergency Response vehicles, and a forensics team. Oh, and ask the officer on night duty to locate Tillman's security chief, Luis Moreno. I need Moreno to contact me immediately."

After hanging up, Weber turned to Ashley. "Where's Captain Morris and agent Chamberlain?"

"Pierre's been injured badly, and the captain rushed him to the ER."

"I'm sorry to hear that."

Weber mulled something over in his mind. "Tillman's son and his live-in girlfriend must have left in the aircraft." He considered, then said, "I'll go inspect the hangar and the guardhouse; I'll take your statement later." Ashley nodded. Weber headed toward the door, but Ashley didn't follow him.

Weber stopped and turned. "Don't touch anything. We need forensics to reconstruct what happened in here tonight."

Ashley called Louise and explained what had transpired at the Tillman residence. "Will you be able to trace the computer transactions that took place here tonight?"

"I will, easily enough, if you bring me the laptop or computer they were using. Otherwise, I'll have to search the internet. It could take me days."

"I'll look for them." Ashley headed to the den, all the while thinking, *I hope Pierre will be alright.*

CHAPTER 37

THE NIGHT AT THE HIDEOUT

Malcolm's caravan reached the city of Waterloo and rolled onto Green Acres Crescent. Rows of trees and thick evergreen hedges divided the wide lots. The hydro blackout was still in effect, but exterior lights illuminated the entrance to Robert Cole's house. "Robert must have fitted the property with a Powerwall," Malcolm said.

Malcolm and Danielle climbed out of the jeep and walked to the three-car garage. Danielle walked to the garage's side door and found it unlocked. She entered and turned on the lights. Malcolm followed behind. He smiled at seeing the garage empty.

Danielle opened the two end doors and waved Steve and Tom to drive inside. She closed the doors behind them.

Larry walked unaided by now. He joined the team that had assembled near the front entrance. Gerta pointed at a tricycle and a little red wagon stored neatly on the landing. "There's a young family living here," she said.

"That's a surprise," Malcolm said. He waved Tom over. "Has your dad rented this place in the last few days?"

"No. There shouldn't be anyone living here. I don't know who these people are."

"That's a complication." Malcolm rubbed his jaw. He turned to Gerta. "Can you turn on the jammer?"

Gerta retrieved a signal jammer from a van and turned it on. She slipped the carrying strap over her shoulder.

Malcolm turned to his troop. "Larry, how are you feeling?"

"I'm good. Maybe no weightlifting for a while, but I'll be fine."

"Good. You get the men started on preparing the vans for tomorrow's trip back home."

He turned to Gerta and Danielle. "Let's go meet the new tenants." He placed a hand on Gerta's arm. "Your car broke down and you need to call for a tow."

Gerta nodded.

Malcolm pressed the doorbell and stepped out of sight. They heard sandals tip-tapping on the hallway tiles. Someone engaged the safety chain. The door opened a few inches. "Yes?" came a woman's voice.

Gerta assumed a distraught tone of voice. "Hello, ma'am. Our car broke down and our cell phones show out of service. Do you have a landline we could use to call for a tow truck?"

The woman hesitated, then said, "Please wait here. I'll place the call for you. Do you have a CAA card?"

Malcolm stepped forward and blocked the door with his foot. The woman screamed and ran inside the house. Malcolm shouldered the door and tore the security chain loose. He ran down the hallway and caught up with the woman. She had reached the kitchen and held a phone in her hand. Malcolm grabbed the handset and looked at the screen. It was dialling a number that wasn't 911. He ended the call and unplugged the charger from the wall.

The woman was hyperventilating, but had not shouted for help. Malcolm asked, "Which number have you dialled?"

The woman hesitated, then said, "Mr. Chopra. The landlord."

Malcolm frowned at this. "Why?"

"Mr. Chopra told us to call him first when there is a problem. He programmed a speed dial number on our phone."

Malcolm paused, unsure what to do about that information. He asked, "Is there anyone else in the house?" The woman shook her head. "Just my children. Please don't harm them."

Gerta entered the foyer and looked around. The living room and dining room were open concept. Colourful tablecloths and flowerpots covered side tables. A marble statue of Ganesh sat on a console table and faced the entrance. She sniffed a subtle scent of incense. No sign of a dog. She heaved a sigh of relief.

Danielle followed behind her mother. The two women joined Malcolm in the kitchen.

Malcolm voiced instructions. "Danielle, you check upstairs. Gerta, you check the basement. Collect all the phones and bring them over here."

Danielle headed upstairs. Gerta placed the signal jammer on the dining room table, and headed for the basement.

The young mother's chin quivered as she said, "What do you people want? We have no money in the house."

"What's your name?" Malcolm asked.

"Jaya. Jaya Sharma."

"Where's your husband?"

She hesitated, then said, "He's picking up milk at the corner store, and he'll be back any minute now. When he sees something is wrong, he'll call the police. You'd better leave before he returns."

Malcolm read through the deception. "What does he do? Where does he work?"

"He's an engineer at the car plant in Cambridge." She reddened and bit her lip. She had volunteered more information than she had intended.

Malcolm gave some thought to this answer. "He's working the night shift, from eleven to seven?"

The woman stood, silent, wide-eyed. That was answer enough for Malcolm. "Does he call home during his shift? At what time does he usually call?"

The woman remained silent. She trembled.

"When did you move in?"

Mrs. Sharma found her voice. "One week ago. Mr. Chopra owns the house. He's an important man. If he finds out you broke into his house, he'll be furious. You had better leave immediately."

Danielle appeared at the top of the stairs. "There's two kids sleeping up here." At that moment, a boy and a girl, around seven or eight years of age, appeared at the top of the stairs. They were crying. When they spotted their mother, they raced down and wrapped their arms around her sari. Mrs. Sharma hugged them and calmed them with comforting words.

Danielle descended, cradling three handsets in her hands. She put them on the dining room table beside the signal jammer.

Gerta returned from the basement with one handset. "There's a finished basement down there, a sofa bed, a washroom, and a laundry room."

Malcolm turned to Mrs. Sharma. "You and your children will sleep in the rec room tonight. Danielle will help you bring down what you'll need."

Mrs. Sharma stood frozen, her eyes wide in confusion.

Danielle put her arm around her shoulder. "Everything will be fine." She guided the mother and the children up the stairs.

The doorbell rang.

Malcolm walked over and opened the door. An enormous man with coffee-coloured skin and jet-black hair stood staring at Malcolm. His bulk filled the doorway.

"What is going on here? Who are you people?" the man asked.

"Who's asking?"

"I'm assistant to Mr. Chopra, the landlord. Someone called from here, then the line went dead. Mr. Chopra asked me to come check." He turned his head and pointed at the garage. "And I see people milling around the garage, looking as if they're moving in. Who are you people? Mr. Chopra will be here shortly to sort this out."

The man noticed the broken safety chain. "You've broken in." He pulled out his cell phone, pressed a number, and stared at the screen. "You've fooled with the cell phone service?"

Malcolm pulled out his pistol and pointed it at the man's chest. "Let's go to the garage."

Malcolm led the man through the garage's side door.

Larry and the crew were rearranging things in the vans. They stopped their work and walked over. Malcolm looked at Steve. "Frisk the man."

Steve retrieved a pistol from the man's shoulder harness, and a knife from a sheath strapped to the man's ankle. He tied the man's hands behind his back with tie wraps.

Malcolm guided the captive to the middle of the garage and had him sit on the floor. Steve produced a roll of duct tape and taped the man's legs together, then covered the man's mouth.

Malcolm updated the crew. "There's a couple with two kids living here. The husband is working the night shift at the Toyota plant. This man here works for a Mr. Chopra, who claims to be the landlord." Malcolm looked at Tom. "Did you know anything about this?"

Tom shook his head.

The sound of grinding brakes and the rumble of an engine resonated from the driveway.

"This must be Mr. Chopra," Malcolm said. He signalled for Larry to follow him outside.

An older-model white Cadillac stood in the driveway. A man dressed in a white suit and wearing white patent leather shoes climbed out. He had the same complexion and jet-black hair as their prisoner.

"Hello. I'm Ajeet Chopra, the landlord," the man said in a stern voice. "And who are you gentlemen?"

"Hello, Mr. Chopra. We're friends of the family. We're visiting," Malcolm said.

Malcolm and Larry approached Chopra. They retrieved their pistols, and pointed them at the man.

"Place your hands behind your head and come to the garage with us," Malcolm said.

Chopra froze at first, then he raised his hands, and placed them behind his head. "What's the meaning of this? You need to explain what's going on before I follow you anywhere."

Malcolm stepped behind Chopra and pressed his pistol against the man's back.

Chopra resisted. "What's the meaning of this? What is it you want?"

"Walk into the garage and we'll explain everything," Malcolm said.

Chopra stepped forward as if to obey, but he slipped his right hand inside his suit jacket, pulled out a pistol. He aimed it at Larry's chest, but he fumbled the gun as he tried inserting his middle finger into the trigger guard. Larry kicked Chopra's hand and sent the weapon sliding across the driveway.

"Put your hands behind your head and walk on," Malcolm said. He guided Chopra to the garage's side door. Steve frisked the man and tie-wrapped his hands behind his back.

Malcolm had Chopra sit beside his assistant. Steve taped the man's feet together.

Chopra noticed Jim's body in the cargo van. He looked up at Malcolm. "You guys are carrying a dead comrade. You are criminals running from the law."

Malcolm looked down at Chopra. "How did you come to own this house?"

"What business is that of yours?"

"A man called Robert Cole told me this property was his, and that it sat empty. But there's a family living here, and you claim to be the landlord."

"I bought this property one month ago through Mr. Cole's real estate agent. If Mr. Cole has changed his mind, or whatever story he told you, it's not my concern. I own the title to the property." Chopra puffed out his chest and raised his chin.

Malcolm turned to Steve. "Tape his mouth."

Steve complied.

"What will we do with these guys?" Larry asked.

Malcolm considered, then said, "We'll take out this trash as a courtesy to our host." He mulled something over in his mind, then said, "There won't be time in the morning, so we'll do it tonight."

"How and where?"

"We'll dispose of them and their cars in some quiet parking lot." Malcolm waved Tom over. "Where's a good place to dump cars without being seen?"

Tom mulled this over for a moment. "There's the Conestoga Shopping Centre on King Street. It's deserted at this time of night."

"Is it far enough away? Will it lead the police back to us?"

"It's a ten-minute drive. I think it'll be fine."

"Good." Malcolm turned to Steve and Larry. "You'll dump Chopra's cars there. Tom will drive a van, show you the way, and bring you back. Fill up our jerry cans with gas on your way back. We need to top up all our vehicles."

Larry stepped forward. "What should we do with Jim's body?"

Malcolm mulled this over. "We can't take him with us back to the States, and I don't want to leave him here with this young family. They're traumatized enough as it is. We could leave him in one of Chopra's cars."

Larry and Steve looked at each other and shrugged their shoulders. Tom looked on, wide-eyed.

Steve retrieved the key fobs from the prisoners' pockets. He kept one and handed the other to Larry. Tom rolled up the central garage door as Steve and Larry backed up the two cars. Malcolm and Steve placed Jim's body in the rear seat of the Caddy. Afterward, they swung Chopra and his assistant into the trunk of the Buick, like sacks of feed. Steve slammed the lid shut.

Malcolm gave some last-minute instructions to his men. Larry then walked to a van and retrieved a silencer, while Steve and Tom rounded up two jerry cans.

Tom climbed in his van and took the lead, Larry followed in the Cadillac, and Steve brought up the rear in the Buick. The Buick sat low, betraying its heavy payload.

Malcolm went into the house to check on Gerta and Danielle.

Tom led the caravan into the Conestoga Mall parking lot, to a far corner sheltered with trees on two sides. Larry and Steve climbed out and walked around to the back of the Buick. Steve popped the trunk open. Chopra and his assistant were wriggling, attempting to break free from the tie wraps and the duct tape.

Larry turned to Tom. "You go and stand watch." Tom took position outside the treed area, where he had a clear view of the entrances of the parking lot.

Larry leaned back against the trunk. He paused, breathed deeply, unholstered his pistol, screwed on the silencer and chambered a cartridge.

Larry turned, leaned into the trunk, and grabbed Chopra by the collar. He pressed the tip of the silencer behind the man's right ear, and pulled the trigger. The detonation sounded like the strike of a hammer on a wooden beam. Dark liquid and bone grit jetted from the top of Chopra's head and splattered on the back of the car's seat.

Chopra's sidekick groaned and wriggled furiously. Larry moved in closer and repeated the procedure.

His gruesome task completed, Larry straightened, leaned back against the car, and let the tension leave his body. Silence settled over the parking lot.

Steve raced to the van and returned with a jerry can.

"We don't need to burn the Buick," Larry said.

"I'm improvising." Steve poured fuel over the men, closed the trunk lid, then doused the car's interior. He walked over to the Caddy, and poured fuel over Jim's body, as well as the inside of the car.

"I want to say a few words," Larry said. "I'll be quick."

Steve nodded.

Larry lauded the courage, comradeship, and loyalty of his departed pal. Larry then lowered his head as if in prayer. Steve stepped forward. "So long, pal. Safe journey!"

Larry called to Tom, and pointed to the van. Tom ran to the vehicle and climbed behind the wheel.

Steve produced a butane lighter and set the Caddy and the Buick ablaze. The two men raced to the van.

Larry rode shotgun, and Steve sat on the bench seat. Tom sped out of the parking lot. They were two blocks away when the gas tank of one car exploded, followed moments later by a second explosion. Flames lit the dark night.

Steve leaned forward and placed a hand on Larry's shoulder. "That was unpleasant work you took care of back there. Thank you for that."

Larry stared ahead. "I don't know how many more of these jobs I can do."

Everybody went quiet.

Tom held the steering wheel in a death grip. His face was pale. The van straddled the white line and an incoming car blared its horn.

"Careful!" Larry said.

"Sorry." Tom steered the van back into his lane.

Larry let a moment pass, then said, "It's normal for you to be upset by what you saw, Tom. You'll harden to it in time."

Tom stopped at a gas station. Steve climbed out, ball cap lowered to cover his face, inserted a gas card in the pump, and filled the two jerry cans.

Once back in the garage, Larry said, "Let's finish prepping the vans."

Steve pulled out a roll of plasticized blank white labels and rubber rollers. He unrolled a label for Tom to see. "We'll peel off the plastic film backing and we'll roll the labels on the sides of the vans. When we're finished, I'll rub some dirt on them so they don't look brand new." Steve and Tom began labelling.

Larry installed Ontario licence plates on all three vehicles. He retrieved three sets of registration papers, insurance certificates, and VIN labels from a manila envelope. He placed each item in its corresponding vehicle.

With their task completed, the three men stood back and admired their work. They returned to the house.

"How did it go?" Malcolm asked.

"It went well," Larry said. "We said a few words in remembrance of Jim."

Malcolm nodded his approval. "How about the labels on the vans?"

"All done. Looks good."

Gerta walked over and joined the men. "Danielle has set up the young family in the basement rec room. Poor Mrs. Sharma. She has the children calmed down, but nobody's sleeping."

Gerta took Malcolm aside, and in a soft voice, she said, "This woman and her children have witnessed nothing that will make our situation any worse."

"I agree. All they've witnessed was a break-in. We don't need to silence them. We've done far more killing than I had planned for." Malcolm rubbed his chin. "But they will identify us from photographs."

"The police need time to organize this and get our photos to the border. We'll have cleared the border by then. And besides, the agents at the check booths don't have time to check photos against those on the FBI's Most

Wanted site. They only do that at secondary inspection. If we avoid secondary inspection, we'll be fine."

"You're probably right."

"I'll check the FBI's Most Wanted site as we approach the border. If our photos are up on the site, I'll call you. We can decide what to do then." Malcolm nodded.

Gerta put a hand on Malcolm's arm. "There's one more thing. I feel bad about retiring on dirty money. I want to give my share to help the families that were hurt by the CEO's financial schemes. Let's just keep enough for us to buy a small business somewhere." She looked into Malcolm's eyes.

"It's okay by me, but let's hang onto our share for a few years. If the police catch one or more of us, we'll need money for lawyers, or worst case, to plan a prison break." Gerta nodded, then leaned over and kissed him.

Larry approached Malcolm. "When's the husband returning from his shift?"

"After seven this morning, but we'll be gone by six-thirty."

"What if he returns earlier?"

"We'll put him in the basement with his family. But it's critical he not go into the garage. Whoever's on watch will need to watch out for him." Larry nodded.

Malcolm turned to Gerta. "Let's distribute the new passports and the documents now."

"Right." Gerta left for the garage and returned with a satchel. She distributed the new identities: Canadian passports, U.S. Work Permit EAD cards, Ontario driver's licences, OHIP cards, and short bios.

Malcolm commanded everyone's attention. "We're crossing into the States as Canadians. Learn your new identities carefully. You must sound convincing at the Detroit border or at a highway roadblock."

Gerta added, "A word of warning. These passports will pass the scanners at the border inspection booth, but they won't stand up to scrutiny if you're sent over to secondary inspection. If you enter that building, you won't be coming out."

Everyone stared at Gerta with raised eyebrows.

"I'd prefer going back to the States as an American," Larry said.

"So would I," Malcolm said, "but the police and border control will be on the lookout for Americans in vans with Illinois plates."

"Why take three vehicles?" Larry said. "We can all fit in two."

"It spreads the risk. Those that make it through can help those that don't," Malcolm said.

Larry nodded.

Malcolm turned to Tom. "Are you sticking with us, Tom?"

Tom turned to Danielle. The two looked into each other's eyes, then Tom said, "Yes. I'm in."

"Good. Do you need to inform your father about your absence tonight? Is he likely to come looking for you here?"

"No. I've already told him I'll be staying with the crew for a while. He'll be thinking of a motel." Tom looked worried. "But I don't have my passport with me. Can we stop home on our way out?"

"Too risky, and you can't use your passport, anyway. Your criminal record will raise a flag at the border." Malcolm turned to Gerta. "Can you put together new identity papers for Tom?"

Gerta considered the request, then said, "I'll doctor the ones intended for Jim." She looked up at Tom. "I'll need to scan your photograph from your driver's licence." She turned to the group. "I need help to transport some equipment and supplies from the van."

Malcolm turned to Tom and Steve. "Go with Gerta."

Malcolm turned to Larry. "Can you put together a roster for the lookouts tonight? One in the basement and one by the front door. And bring some M16s and ammunition in the house in case the police show up."

Larry nodded.

Gerta, Tom, and Steve returned, arms loaded with equipment and supplies. They placed everything on the dining room table.

Gerta scanned Tom's photograph from his driver's licence and touched it up using Photoshop. Steve loaded holographic polycarbonate film in the laser printer, and Tom went looking for an extension cord with which to plug in the portable laminator.

CHAPTER 38

RELIANT AT THE HOSPITAL

Popeye felt relieved as he drove the damaged Suburban into the emergency entrance of Grand River Hospital. The front tires of the vehicle had held. Pierre, his face white, laid unconscious on the backseat.

Popeye had called ahead. Two attendants ran over and transferred Pierre to a collapsible stretcher. They rushed him to the pre-op room.

Popeye parked the vehicle and rushed to Admission to fill out the paperwork. He then made his way to the surgery waiting room.

Popeye's cell phone rang. It was Inspector Weber. He walked over to the hallway to answer the call. Weber and a forensics staff sergeant were on speaker phone. They questioned Popeye about the events at the guardhouse. Popeye passed on the little he knew.

After that conversation was over, Popeye called Ashley.

"Popeye. Finally. How's Pierre?"

"He's in the operating room. Shrapnel from a grenade nicked an artery in his neck. He lost a lot of blood. I'm waiting to hear from the surgeon."

"That sounds serious. I hope he'll be okay." She was silent for a moment, then said, "The Tillmans are both dead, and so is a visiting reporter."

"Yes. I just talked to Inspector Weber, and he mentioned it. I told him the Jennings were staying at the New Hamburg Inn. He's sending a patrol cruiser over to check the place out."

"Good thinking." Ashley hesitated, then added, "I'm sure one of my bullets struck Mrs. Tillman. The scope on my rifle was off, and my first shot went through a window. The CSI team is onsite now and they'll figure it out."

"Don't beat yourself up over this. We'll deal with that when their report is out." Popeye paused, then said, "Where was Tillman's security team during all this?"

"There's no sign of them anywhere. Inspector Weber is trying to locate their security chief."

"What about the airplane noise we heard?"

"Inspector Weber believes it was Tillman's son, Paul, and his live-in girlfriend, who must have escaped in the family's light aircraft. But it's not confirmed yet."

"Those are the only eyewitnesses to the murders. It's critical we find them."

Both were silent for a moment.

"Have you called Chief Harrington yet?" Ashley asked.

"Right. I'll do that right away. Thanks for reminding me." Popeye paused, then added, "Keep your spirits up. I'll call you with the results of the surgery." He ended the call.

Popeye called Chief Harrington's cell phone. He had awakened him. Popeye apologized and updated him on the events of the evening.

Harrington was silent for a moment, then said, "Call me when you have the results of Pierre's operation, no matter how late." He paused, then said, "I'll review with legal, what our responsibilities are, now that our client is dead. Get Louise to set up a video conference for ten a.m. tomorrow. I should have an answer from legal and new instructions for you by then." He ended the call.

Soon after Popeye had returned to the surgery waiting room, the surgeon appeared. Blood splatters speckled his white gown. He stopped short at the sight of Popeye in his bulletproof vest. "Are you with the patient with the neck injury?"

"Yes. How did it go?"

The surgeon seemed to weigh his words. "I'm sorry, but Mr. Chamberlain died during the operation." The medical man stood quietly, then added, "We reconstructed the artery, but we lost him before we could replenish all the blood he had lost. We attempted resuscitation, without success. I'm sorry."

Popeye's face turned pale, his eyes moist.

The surgeon continued. "That was a serious injury. How did it happen? An accident at the firing range?"

Popeye described the raid on the Tillman residence, and what he knew of the firefight at the guardhouse, of Pierre being struck by shrapnel from a hand grenade thrown by one robber.

The surgeon pondered this for a moment. "We're required to notify the police department about injuries of this type."

"I understand," Popeye said. "The police will know of the incident when the hospital calls. Their Inspector Weber was at the crime scene. What will happen next?"

"We'll notify the coroner's office, and we'll keep your friend's body in the hospital's morgue for the time being."

The surgeon waited for more questions, but none came. He nodded in sympathy and left.

Popeye walked to the hallway and called Ashley with the news. "Pierre didn't make it."

"Oh, God, no."

"The surgeon said they did what they could, but he had lost too much blood."

The two exchanged comforting words. They reminisced about Pierre's friendly personality, his steadfastness through all their past assignments with Reliant and in the military.

"I'll see you at the Tillman residence shortly," Popeye said.

After composing himself, Popeye called Chief Harrington. Both men expressed their grief over the loss of a team member and a friend. "I'll have instructions for you tomorrow morning," Harrington said. "Can you get a certified copy of Pierre's death certificate and find out when we can return his remains to his family?"

"Will do."

After a moment of silence, Harrington said, "I'll inform Pierre's immediate family, and I'll commit to giving them a full explanation after we've held our debriefing tomorrow."

Harrington paused, then added, "Pierre was a Marine veteran. I'll coordinate with Veterans' Affairs about his funeral. They'll want a flag-draped casket, and for 'Taps' to be played at the burial ceremony." He ended the call.

Popeye walked through the hospital lobby to the parked Suburban. He stopped short at the sight of the vehicle. The tires were in shreds, the windshield and the side windows cracked, and the body panels riddled with bullet holes.

Shit, I forgot about that, Popeye thought. He called Louise.

"Popeye. God, I just heard from Ashley. I can't believe it. Pierre is dead?"

"Yes. The surgeon could not save him."

"This is awful." She went silent, then added, "Ashley said the criminals killed the Tillmans during the raid."

"Yes. Ashley told me, as well. Chief Harrington wants us on a video conference call at ten a.m. tomorrow."

"I'll set it up."

"I want to head back to the Tillman residence to pick up Ashley but the Suburban is out of action. The tires are punctured, the windshield's cracked, and the body panels are riddled with bullet holes. Can you get us a rental?"

"I'm on it."

"Great. Thanks. I'll wait for your call."

Ten minutes later, Louise called back. "I've located a Suburban at a twenty-four-hour car rental company at the local airport. It's not armoured, of course. A rental agent is on their way to the hospital." Louise paused, then added, "Do want our vehicle towed somewhere? I've located a repair shop for armoured vehicles in Kitchener."

"We need to get it back to our office. The technical team and Chief Harrington will want to inspect it before the repairs are done." Popeye considered, then said, "The local police might want to impound it as part of their own investigation. I'll talk this over with Inspector Weber." He let a moment pass, then said, "Thanks, Louise. We'll see you later tonight." He ended the call.

Popeye waited by the hospital entrance for the rental vehicle to arrive.

"Now to untangle the mess at the Tillman's residence," he reflected.

CHAPTER 39

BACK AT THE CRIME SCENE

Popeye drove past the forensics officers, who were working behind the yellow tape that encircled the guardhouse. An officer stopped him, took down his identity, cleared it with Inspector Weber by radio, and waved him through.

As he approached the residence, Popeye noticed a news broadcast vehicle parked behind the police cruisers. A crew member was pointing a shoulder-held video camera at a news anchor who stood, mic in hand, with the Tillman house in the background.

Popeye spotted Inspector Weber and Ashley standing beside a police cruiser. He parked and walked over. Ashley saw Popeye, ran over, and hugged him.

"I can't believe Pierre is dead," Ashley said.

"It hasn't sunk in yet."

They stayed close to each other, sharing in the ache of loss. Ashley rested a hand on Popeye's arm.

Weber stood aside for a few minutes. He now approached Popeye. "Please accept my condolences for your loss. I'm sure agent Chamberlain was a fine man."

"Thank you, Inspector. Yes, Pierre was a good man. We'll miss him."

The three turned toward the residence, where forensic officers were processing the crime scene.

Weber spoke first. "Mr. and Mrs. Tillman did not fare well, and neither did a third person. A visiting reporter. The ambulances have just left with the bodies."

"Ashley mentioned she killed one perpetrator?" Popeye said.

"Yes. Your colleague shot one criminal. You can see the spot where he fell on the porch. We're sure he didn't survive. The criminals carried his body to the side road. I hit one of them in the clover field, a lucky shot. They dragged the body to their getaway vehicles." Weber paused. "We've alerted all the local emergency rooms and clinics, but no sightings so far."

"Any sign of the robbers' vehicles?" Popeye asked.

"We know they had two vehicles parked on the side road. I remember seeing a white cargo van in the guardhouse parking lot, but it's gone. All our road patrols, and those of the Ontario Provincial Police, are on the lookout for any vehicle behaving suspiciously. They'll stop all vehicles with Illinois plates."

"Any sign of the Jennings at the New Hamburg Inn?"

"They cleared out of the Inn at eight o'clock, and the Innkeeper has no idea where they went. They're my prime suspects at this time."

"What of the black Camry that was parked by the guardhouse?"

Weber rubbed his chin. "That was Security Chief Moreno's car. He's gone missing. We've contacted the security crew that was on duty tonight, and they all reported that Moreno had given them the evening shift off with pay. We've sent a patrol car to Moreno's residence, and they've found his car parked outside his apartment building. No sign of Moreno. He must have switched cars."

"And you believe Tillman's son escaped in the aircraft?" Popeye asked.

"Yes. Paul Tillman and his live-in girlfriend, Linda Atchison, have flown away. She called nine-one-one around nine-thirty p.m. and reported the assault on the house. The emergency operator could tell the call came from inside the cockpit of a small aircraft in flight. The local airport received a flight plan from Paul Tillman, giving Newburg, New York as his destination. We've alerted border control at Newburg airport and requested they hold the couple for questioning when they land." Weber shook his head. "I can't figure out what they're up to."

Popeye let a few moments pass, then asked, "Do you know when we can bring home agent Chamberlain's remains?"

"The coroner will decide if an autopsy is required. I'll let you know."

"Will you need to keep our Suburban as part of your investigation?"

"Yes, we will, and I'm not sure when we can release the vehicle back to you. This new private policing law may address this situation. I'll have our legal department look into it and I'll get back to you." Weber looked past Popeye. "I see you're driving a rented SUV. Where did you leave your vehicle?"

"It's in the hospital's emergency parking lot."

"Could you hand me the keys? I'll have it picked up. I'll give you a receipt for the vehicle."

Popeye handed over the key fob. "The registration and insurance papers are in the glove compartment."

Weber looked up at Popeye. "I need to take down your statement. Can you follow me to a patrol car?"

After he had given his statement, Popeye told Weber, "We'll be at our hotel in St. Jacob. Call me anytime, if I can help with anything."

"I will." Weber shook hands with Popeye.

Popeye lay in bed, reading a crime novel to help him fall asleep, when Inspector Weber called. "Hello, Captain Morris. This is Weber. Something came up and I could use your team's help."

CHAPTER 40

PAUL AND LINDA IN THE U.S.

Border officer O'Grady appeared out of the back offices of the Stewart International Airport and greeted Paul and Linda. O'Grady was tall and healthy looking, red-haired, mid-twenties. He took Paul's and Linda's passports and said, "Please follow me."

O'Grady guided the couple to an interview room. Everyone took a seat.

"Do you know what this Canadian police services alert is about?" O'Grady said.

Paul feigned ignorance.

"The police in Waterloo, Canada, need to talk to you both." He noticed Linda's bandaged leg and leaned in for a closer look. "Do you need this injury looked at? We have a first aid station in the terminal."

"Thank you, Officer, but no, we'll visit a clinic later," Linda said.

O'Grady nodded. He swivelled in his chair, reached for a phone on the nearby desk, and dialled a number. When the other party answered, O'Grady introduced himself and asked to speak with Inspector Walter Weber. After a few moments, Weber was on the line, and the officers held a brief discussion. O'Grady then passed the handset to Paul. "This is Inspector Weber of the Waterloo Regional Police on the line. I'll leave the room and give you some privacy. I'll return in fifteen minutes. Okay?"

219

"Okay," Paul said nervously. He lifted the receiver to his ear.

"Hello. This is Paul Tillman."

"Hello, Mr. Tillman. This is Inspector Walter Weber of the Waterloo Regional Police. I need to talk to you and your companion, Linda Atchison. But before we start, are you both alright?"

"Yes, we're alright."

"Good. Could you please put the phone on speaker so all three of us can talk?"

Paul found the designated button and pressed it. The phone crackled. Weber introduced himself to Linda, then said, "Were you both in the house when the robbers broke in?"

"Yes, we were," Paul answered.

"Can you describe what happened?"

Paul spoke first. "We were in the basement rec room when this young woman surprised us. She was brandishing a gun. I retrieved a pistol my father keeps hidden in the basement, and I fired at her. She fell, and we ran upstairs. That's when I saw a group of robbers in the living room. They were holding Mom and Dad at gunpoint. A woman appeared in the hallway in front of me. She was armed. I fired at her and I ran out the back door. Linda ran out with me. Are Mom and Dad alright?"

Weber ignored the question. "So your father and your mother were standing in the living room when you and Ms. Atchison escaped through the back door?"

"Yes!" Paul tensed, sensing bad news.

"I'm sorry to inform you that your mother and your father have been killed."

Paul froze with shock. Linda moaned, "Oh, no!" They hugged each other. Linda sobbed loudly, and tears rolled down Paul's cheeks. They remained embraced for some time.

Inspector Weber waited for a minute, then said, "I'll leave you two to absorb this news in private. When Officer O'Grady returns, he will assign a separate room for each of you, and I'll take down your statements." Weber paused, then added, "You must both return to the Waterloo Police Station at the earliest to assist with our inquiry. This is required by law. Do you understand?"

"Yes, Inspector," Paul said.

"Good. I'll be talking with you both shortly."

Paul replaced the handset back in its cradle. He and Linda conferred and agreed they would not mention the money from the house vault and their plan to fly to the Cayman Islands. Paul tucked the tote bag underneath Linda's chair.

O'Grady returned, and he assigned separate interview rooms to Paul and Linda.

Weber's first question to Paul was, "Explain to me why you flew to Stewart Airport in New York State instead of one of the local airports?"

Paul hesitated before answering. "I was confused, in shock. The robbers were shooting at us and at the aircraft. I've accompanied Dad to the Stewart Airport before, to have the Beechcraft serviced and repaired." Paul paused, then added, "I had planned on calling Mom and Dad as soon as we landed and cleared customs. I never imagined the robbers would murder my parents."

Paul answered all of Weber's questions, and promised he would return to Kitchener at the earliest. He sat and waited for officer O'Grady to return. After fifteen minutes, O'Grady appeared. He brought Paul back to the previous room. Linda was already sitting there. Paul looked at her with raised eyebrows. She said, "Inspector Weber interviewed me. I told the inspector what I saw, that I experienced confusion and shock, called nine-one-one, and deferred to you for all decisions."

Paul nodded and took her hand in his.

O'Grady turned to Paul. "Inspector Weber asked me to deny you both entry into the U.S. because you are a prime witness in a murder investigation back in Canada. I informed him you had American citizenship and I would not refuse you entry, that he would need a court order to have you extradited back to Canada." O'Grady turned to Linda. "I could refuse you entry, but Inspector Weber said he trusts you both to do the right thing and return home promptly."

Paul and Linda looked at each other, then back at O'Grady and nodded.

O'Grady accompanied Paul and Linda to the border control counter, and gave them back their passports. The counter agent handed Paul the keys to the aircraft. "Customs has cleared your aircraft. Welcome to the United States."

Paul and Linda walked to the Alamo counter and rented a car. They asked for directions to the nearest twenty-four-hour medical centre.

The medical centre's waiting room was empty, and they admitted Linda immediately.

An elderly doctor examined Linda's cut on her thigh. "Young lady, this is a bullet wound. You're lucky an artery wasn't cut. How did that happen?"

"I was handling a friend's handgun when I accidentally disengaged the safety and shot myself in the leg. It didn't look so bad at first."

The doctor looked at Linda. "I'll pretend I believe your story, and I won't report the injury to the police." He cleaned the wound, stitched it closed, applied antibiotic ointment, and wrapped it with gauze. He took her temperature. "You have a low-grade fever, young lady." He gave her some antibiotics to ingest immediately, and he filled out a prescription. "Keep those bandages clean, get lots of rest, and follow a proper diet for the next two weeks."

Paul paid the bill and purchased the prescribed medicines at the clinic. He then booked a room at the local Comfort Inn. They drove over, registered, and settled in. Linda undressed, climbed into bed and was dead to the world. Paul undressed, took a shower, and turned in.

Paul rose at eight the next morning. He had no razor, and left unshaven. *Dad called this the* Miami Vice *look,* Paul thought. *Where did Dad get that expression from?* he wondered. He left without waking Linda.

Paul drove to the small-aircraft terminal at Stewart International Airport and asked about having his aircraft towed to the service centre.

The service centre supervisor looked at the aircraft and shook his head. "I won't ask. What would you like done?"

"Can I get a full inspection of the airplane, a detailed cost estimate for the repairs, and a schedule for completing the work?"

The supervisor considered. "We'll have an estimate to you by five p.m. today."

Paul hitched a ride back to the terminal. He ordered breakfast at a concession. While sitting at his table, his thoughts settled on the death of his parents and its implications. *I must be in shock,* he thought. *I feel nothing. I must be a cold, ungrateful bastard.*

His thoughts moved to the fortune he stood to inherit. I'm the sole heir to the Tillman estate. I'll need to hire a lawyer and an accountant to help me manage the inheritance and to fight off Dad's business associates and relatives. It will take months to sort out Dad's affairs. Can I get an advance on my inheritance—not just a living allowance but a substantial sum?

A dark thought surfaced: Did the robbers clean out Dad's offshore accounts? That's where most of the money is. Paul rubbed his eyes. Jesus, this is giving me a headache.

Paul finished his meal and drove back to the hotel. He entered the room quietly. Linda was sleeping. He sat and rested his head on the high-back chair, and he returned to his ruminations. He dozed off.

An hour later, Linda stirred. She raised herself on an elbow and looked around the room. She focused on Paul, yawned, and said, "You're up already."

"Yes. I've been to the airport, and the service centre is looking at the plane. They'll have a cost estimate and a repair schedule for us by five o'clock. How are you feeling?"

"Much better. I think my fever is gone. My stitches are itching and sore, but that's a good sign, right?"

"I think so. You want to go down for breakfast? They serve a buffet downstairs. I've already eaten, but I'll have a coffee."

"Good idea. I'm hungry, but I need to get cleaned up first." Linda looked up at Paul. "It's nice of you to think of me like that. What happened to the body snatcher who was flying the aircraft yesterday?"

"My life has become so damn complicated that the body snatcher got spooked and ran off. It's just plain old me again."

Linda rose and planted a kiss on his lips. "Ouch. You haven't shaved." She hobbled to the bathroom and closed the door behind her. Paul heard the water running in the sink. The bathroom door opened an inch. "Could you go to the front desk and ask for some toiletries?"

Paul returned minutes later with a courtesy bag filled with toothbrushes, toothpaste samples, a disposable shaver, shaving cream, and more.

At the breakfast buffet, Linda loaded her plate with scrambled eggs, sausages, and a croissant with strawberry jam.

"Someone's feeling a lot better." Paul said as he nursed his cup of coffee. Paul and Linda exchanged a look that said 'What the hell happened?'

"What should we do now?" Linda asked.

Paul sipped some coffee, stared into the distance, then said, "I think we should return home. We'll be walking back into a circus, but that's what we should do. What do you think?"

"I agree. Going back is the right thing to do. Let's catch the next plane back, as we told Inspector Weber we'd do."

"There are no direct flights to Kitchener from here. It'll take at least a day to get back home. Let's fly out early tomorrow morning. Mom and Dad are dead, so we're not holding back anything critical."

"Well, we can help identify the women you've shot at. We may remember some faces we saw in the living room, although that's all a blur to me now. And there's the funeral arrangements, people to call, aunts and uncles. I can help with those."

"You're right about helping the police identify people. The two women I shot, they had a family resemblance, probably mother and daughter. And I think I saw Security Chief Moreno in the living room. He was standing on the side. What the hell was he doing there?" Paul paused. "Thanks for offering to help to call relatives." Paul reached over and squeezed Linda's hand.

Paul lowered his head as if burdened by the tasks that lay ahead. "I'll go to the hotel's business centre and book the flights home."

"When you're done, let's find a Target. I need to buy some clothing and supplies."

"Wow. You *are* feeling better." Paul smiled at Linda.

They headed to the hotel's business centre.

CHAPTER 41

RELIANT DISCOVERS THE HIDEOUT

Popeye read Inspector Weber's name on the call display. He sat on the side of his hotel bed and picked up the receiver. "Yes, Inspector, how can I help?"

"It's about an incident that happened around midnight, in the parking lot of a shopping mall, in Waterloo. Someone set two cars ablaze. The firefighters discovered two bodies inside the trunk of one vehicle. Both had been hogtied and shot in the back of the head, execution style. In the other vehicle, they discovered a man lying in the rear seat. He was wearing a Kevlar vest. He had been shot in the face. This last victim could be connected to last night's firefight."

"Any identification on the victims?"

"No documents survived the flames, but both cars belong to Chopra Properties Inc. of Kitchener." Weber paused before adding, "Did that name come up during your research on Carl Tillman and the Jennings?"

"Not that I know of, but I'll ask Louise to look into it. I'll get back to you as soon as she finds something."

"Much appreciated." Weber ended the call.

Popeye called Louise's room and updated her on Weber's call.

After a moment's reflection, Louise said, "No. I've never heard of Chopra Properties, but I agree the man wearing a bulletproof vest could be the one Ashley killed during the raid on the Tillman residence."

"There has to be a connection between the Jennings, Tillman, and Chopra Properties," Popeye said.

"Leave this with me. I'll find the connection, but it will take time. The internet service is slow here."

"Much appreciated, Louise." Popeye hung up and returned to reading his crime novel. But he couldn't concentrate on his reading. His mind was analyzing all that had happened during the previous day.

At 5:30 a.m., Popeye's phone rang.

"I found the connection," Louise said.

Popeye rubbed his eyes. "Go ahead. I'm all ears."

"The connection runs between Chopra Properties Inc. and Robert Cole, the owner of the Airbnb the Jennings were staying at. Cole owned a suburban house in Waterloo, which Chopra Properties purchased a month ago. That house had been sitting empty for two years. The Jennings could have learned about the house from Cole himself and crashed there for the night. That would explain why there's been no sightings of them on the roads, and I found no trace of them booking lodging anywhere."

Popeye mulled this over, then said, "And if two employees of Chopra Properties confronted the Jennings squatting on their newly acquired property, it's no surprise if they end up dead in the trunk of their cars. The location and the timing jibe." Popeye considered, then said, "Give me the address of that house and I'll pass it on to Inspector Weber. Could you wake the whole team up and tell them to meet in the lobby in twenty minutes, ready to roll?"

As Popeye steered the Suburban onto Green Acres Crescent, he spotted a black Jeep Wrangler pulling out of number 210. Two white cargo vans followed close behind. Popeye floored the accelerator and caught up with the last van. He attempted to pass and crowd it to a stop, but the driver of the fugitives' van swerved and blocked his path.

One rear door of the criminals' van swung open and flashes burst out from the dark cargo area. Bullets thudded against the radiator grille and the front wheels of Popeye's SUV.

"Everybody duck!" Popeye said as he lowered his head.

The punctured front wheels of his vehicle pulled the Suburban to the left. Popeye could not straighten the steering wheel, and the vehicle careened over the sidewalk, across a front lawn, and crashed against a concrete porch. The chase was over.

"Did anybody get hurt?" Popeye asked. Everyone answered in the negative.

"I couldn't see any logos on the van," Ashley said, "but I got the licence plate. They've switched to Ontario plates."

"I'm calling it in to Inspector Weber," Popeye said.

Weber answered the call, took down the information, then said, "Stay where you are. I've two patrol cruisers heading your way. They'll arrive any minute now."

Everyone climbed out of the Suburban and checked on each other's condition. Everyone was fine, but the vehicle was out of action. Steam whistled out of the radiator and coolant leaked on the ground. Bullets had shredded the two front tires.

Two patrol cruisers arrived and four officers walked over. Popeye described what had happened. One officer inspected the Suburban, another took photographs, while two others positioned orange traffic cones on the street and set about marking the spots where bullets had struck the ground.

The lead officer called Weber on his radio and described the situation. He then turned to Popeye. "We're impounding your vehicle."

Popeye turned to Louise. "Can you get us another one?"

Louise dialled the car rental agency, described the damage to their existing rental, that it was being impounded by the police.

"Jesus. You guys are hard on cars," the rental agent said. "I can't allow a replacement before checking with the manager."

The rental manager came on the line. "I'm sorry, but I can't lease you a replacement."

"Put the district manager on the line, please," Louise said.

After a few minutes, the district manager came on the line. Once Louise agreed to purchase the full collision damage waiver and leave a $20,000 deposit, the manager agreed to have a replacement vehicle sent over shortly.

Twenty minutes later, a rental Ford Expedition arrived. Popeye and his teammates transferred their belongings into the new vehicle.

A tow truck appeared. The driver had the lead police officer sign some papers, then he hooked up to the damaged Suburban and towed it away.

Popeye phoned Chief Harrington and explained the situation.

After listening to Popeye's description of the events, Harrington said, "I reached our lead lawyer last night. He advises we wait for instructions from Tillman's estate lawyers. Drop the chase and head back to Ann Arbor immediately. We'll hold a debriefing upon your arrival."

After hanging up, Popeye turned to his team. "We're heading home." He turned to Ashley. "You'll drive. I need to work on the phone and on my laptop."

Ashley climbed behind the wheel of the Expedition, dropped off the rental agent at the airport counter, and steered the vehicle toward Ann Arbor.

Popeye called Inspector Weber and told him Reliant was off the case for now and were heading to Ann Arbor.

Weber replied with, "The OPP are running roadblocks on all major highways leaving the area. They assigned patrol cruisers to drive the side roads, but they don't have the personnel to set roadblocks on all secondary roads. I've alerted the U.S. border control points—land, air, and water. We'll catch them."

CHAPTER 42

THE RUN FOR THE BORDER

When six o'clock arrived in the hideout, the moonless night still covered the skies, but a hint of pinkish twilight peeked over the horizon.

Malcolm awoke from a nightmare five minutes before the alarm beeped. His body was dripping with sweat. In his dream, Michael Stonely was hanging from a rope under the bridge in Fallujah, He looked down at Malcolm below. "What have you accomplished by killing me, you naïve fool? Did your father not warn you to leave justice to God? Now, you and your family are running for your lives. And for what?"

The bastard is right, Malcolm thought. Killing him and Tillman did not bring him the satisfaction and the closure he was yearning for.

Malcolm appraised his new life as a criminal. His team had overcome every setback so far, thanks to their military training and Gerta's cyber expertise, but the amount of research, planning, and costs had surprised him. Three months of his and Gerta's time had gone into planning Stonely's execution. The same for Tillman's. And the execution of the bastard that had harmed Larry's mother remained to be done. Malcolm felt weary.

He nudged Gerta awake gently. She lay in a deep sleep. She had stayed up late preparing identity documents for Tom. Malcolm toured the house, summoning everyone to get ready to leave.

Larry and Tom had slept in a separate bedroom. Steve was keeping watch by the front door, and Danielle slept in the rec room, keeping watch over Mrs. Sharma and the two children.

After hasty visits to the washrooms, the team gathered in the dining room. They had brought down their belongings and piled them on the table.

"Let's load everything in the vehicles," Malcolm said.

Each person grabbed some weapons, equipment, tote bags, satchels, and they carried their load to the vehicles.

Larry and Gerta took position in the garage and instructed everyone as to what went in which vehicle.

Malcolm did a last walk around. He peeked into the downstairs rec room and saw Mrs. Sharma propped up on pillows with both children huddled against her. Three pairs of eyes stared back at him. Malcolm nodded his head, and Mrs. Sharma stared back, wide-eyed. He closed the door and left to join the others.

Larry had opened the garage doors and was waiting. At Malcolm's signal, Tom and Steve climbed behind the wheel of their respective vans and drove out of the garage. Larry closed the garage doors and climbed into the jeep. Gerta climbed in with Tom, and Danielle climbed in with Steve.

Malcolm's instructions were for them to drive south as far as Highway 2, following side roads. They were to drive at normal speed, a kilometre apart, and make their way to the Windsor–Detroit border crossing. Malcolm took the lead, Tom followed, and Steve brought up the rear.

As Steve steered his van onto Green Acres Crescent, he caught sight of a black Suburban speeding in his direction. The SUV attempted to overtake him, but Steve steered sharply to the left side of the street and blocked it. The SUV kept trying to pass him.

"Shit! Not those fuckers again," Steve said. "They must have switched vehicles. This one doesn't have a scratch on it."

"Are you sure it's them?" Danielle asked.

"Ninety-nine percent sure."

"I can take care of this," Danielle said. She undid her seatbelt, climbed over the bench seat, and slipped into the cargo area. She retrieved an M16 from a rifle bag, inserted a thirty-round magazine, and chambered a round. "Hold the van as steady as you can. I'm going to open a rear door and blow out their tires."

Steve slowed down and hogged the middle of the street. Danielle swung a rear door open, aimed the rifle at the front wheels of the Suburban, and pulled the trigger. Bullets sprayed across the front tires and the radiator grille. Strips of rubber peeled off the front wheels and green liquid spurted out through the front grille. The SUV swerved toward the sidewalk, climbed over the curb, and crashed against a porch.

"That takes care of them," Danielle said. "They didn't have bulletproof tires, that's for sure." She reached over, closed the rear door, and climbed back into the front passenger seat.

"That was well done," Steve said, "but the bastards must have seen our plates. We need to replace them ASAP. Call Gerta. I hope she's got spare plates."

Danielle called her mother.

"Yes, I've got spare plates in our van. Let me find a parking area where you can switch the plates." She was silent for a moment, then said, "Drive to Stanley Park Mall on Ottawa Street in Kitchener. We'll be there first, and we'll wait for you by the entrance to the parking lot."

"Understood," Danielle said. She located the mall on the van's GPS.

As Steve drove south on Highway 8, he spotted two police cruisers hurtling northbound with sirens wailing and roof lights flashing.

Steve reached the mall within ten minutes and spotted Tom's van. Tom waved for Steve to follow him, and he drove to the far end of the lot.

Once parked, Steve and Danielle raced to Gerta's open window. She handed over new plates, new ownership papers, and a stick-on VIN label. "Hurry," she said. She raised her window and Tom drove off.

Steve retrieved a large Phillips head screwdriver from the van and switched the plates. Danielle replaced the documents in the glove compartment, and pasted the new VIN label on the dashboard. Steve stuffed the old plates into a toolbox. They climbed aboard and rolled out of the parking lot.

Malcolm's jeep was now far ahead of the others, and within sight of the city of London. He called Gerta. "Change of plans. Larry and I will drive through the Sarnia–Port Huron border crossing."

"Why the change?"

"To reduce the risks. The U.S. border agents will be on the lookout for a black Jeep Wrangler and two white Chevy cargo vans. You guys continue to the Detroit crossing."

"Okay," Gerta said. "Do we rendezvous at the Pilot Travel Center in Monroe, as planned?"

"Affirmative. You'll get there first. Our route is longer. Let's keep each other posted on our progress."

"Understood. I'll call you when we've reached the border." Gerta hung up.

Malcolm steered in the northwest direction along the side roads. They had not encountered any roadblocks, but they were still an hour and a half to the Sarnia–Port Huron border crossing.

As Tom's van approached the city of Windsor, Gerta asked him to park in the St. Clair College campus parking lot. She retrieved her iPad and logged onto the FBI website. After a minute, she let out a deep breath. "They haven't posted our photos yet." She turned to Tom. "Onward to the border, driver. I'll phone Malcolm with the good news."

CHAPTER 43

THE BORDER CROSSING

As Tom approached the Ambassador Bridge, he followed behind a lineup of eighteen-wheelers that stretched as far as the eye could see. It was stop-and-go traffic, but soon the line split between passenger vehicles and transport trucks. The passenger vehicle line moved faster.

Tom reached his turn at the inspection booth. He lowered his window and handed over his and Gerta's passports.

The border agent looked at Tom. "The purpose of your trip?"

"We're reporting for work at a construction site in Detroit." Tom handed over the forged copies of a contractor licence and work permits.

"I need to inspect the cargo area," the border agent said.

Tom climbed out and opened the rear doors for him.

Gerta turned in her seat and watched Tom and the border agent. She saw Tom's face turn white, and beads of sweat formed on his brow. She realized her mistake. The equipment and the tools in the van were for electrical work, and the contractor licence read plumbing work.

She locked eyes with Tom and nodded, signalling for him to stay calm.

Lady Luck smiled at their enterprise. The border agent handed the documents back to Tom and nodded.

Tom climbed behind the wheel. His hands and his legs were shaking. Tom pressed softly on the gas pedal and steered the van out of the U.S. Customs area.

Gerta put a hand on Tom's arm. "I'm sorry, Tom. My heart stopped when I realized my mistake. We got lucky. I'd better alert Steve."

Steve was standing in the long lineup to the border control stations when Gerta called to tell him that the work permits did not match the equipment onboard their vans. After hanging up, Steve tuned to Danielle. "We need a backup plan. Our paperwork doesn't match the equipment onboard. We may get sent to secondary inspection."

Danielle looked at him with raised eyebrows.

"Climb out back and bring over two hand grenades and four spare magazines for our pistols." Steve and Danielle carried their Glocks in their shoulder harnesses.

"Holy cow! Are we going to shoot our way through the border?"

"No, no. This is just a Plan B, and I hope to hell we don't have to use it."

Danielle climbed into the cargo area and returned with the grenades and the ammunition.

They slipped the magazines inside their jackets. Steve slipped the grenades into a large pocket.

As the van inched forward in the lineup, Steve worked on the GPS. He studied a street map and a satellite view of the neighbourhood. He turned to Danielle. "Call Malcolm and put your phone on speaker."

"This is Malcolm. Is there a problem?"

"There could be," Steve said. "Our paperwork and our tools don't match. We may get sent to secondary inspection."

"Shit. What are you proposing?"

"To run the border if we have to. Can you pick us up if we do?"

"I'm on Interstate 75, about twenty minutes north of Detroit; I can pick you up if need be."

"Roger that," Steve said. Danielle ended the call.

Steve's turn finally came, and he advanced to the inspection booth. He handed over their passports.

The agent compared Steve's and Danielle's faces with those in the passports. "Nationality?"

"Canadian," Steve and Danielle said in unison.

"Where do you live?"

"Chicago—no, Kitchener," Steve said. His face blushed.

The border agent stared at Steve. "Which one is it?"

"Kitchener."

"Why did you say Chicago?"

"I spent part of my childhood in Chicago. My father worked as an electrical technician at the Ford plant for some years. That's why I said Chicago."

"Do you have American citizenship, then?"

"No, no. We stayed in Chicago under a work permit and returned to Canada when I was a teenager."

"What's the purpose of your trip?"

"We'll be working on a local construction project." Steve handed over the work permits and the contractor licence.

"I need to look at the cargo area. Could you release the lock on the doors?"

The agent walked to the back, opened one door, looked inside, and returned to the booth. He studied the work permits and the contractor licence, then looked up at Steve. "Are you electricians?"

"Yes. No. We're plumbers."

"Which one is it?"

"Plumbers." Steve blushed. "I had my electrician's license at one time; that's why I answered electrician."

The agent stared at Steve. "I need you to go to the inspection building. An agent will show you where to park." He picked up the intercom and called for an agent to come over.

Steve put the van in drive and rolled at normal speed toward the exit to the customs area.

The agent ran out of his booth and shouted for Steve to stop.

Danielle stared at Steve with raised eyebrows. "Plan B?"

Steve nodded. "Call Malcolm."

Malcolm came on the speaker. "Yes?"

Steve spoke. "We're making a run for it."

"Okay. Where should I pick you up?"

"On West Jefferson Avenue, next to West Riverfront Park. We'll be watching out for you."

"Okay. Give us fifteen minutes tops."

Danielle hung up.

Steve continued at a normal speed until he reached the first intersection. He turned right on 21st Street and floored the accelerator.

Danielle placed one hand on the dash to steady herself. "We won't get far before they catch up to us. They'll set up roadblocks."

"That's why we need to ditch the van."

Steve turned on Bagley Street. He saw a point in the street with delivery trucks parked on both sides. He yanked the steering wheel hard to the right and slammed on the brakes. The van swung crosswise and screeched to a stop, blocking the street.

Steve turned to Danielle. "We're going on foot from here."

Two border patrol cruisers had rounded the corner onto Bagley Street with sirens wailing, roof lights flashing.

Danielle jumped out and ran.

Steve climbed out, pulled open the fuel filler door, and removed the gas cap. He retrieved the two grenades from his jacket, removed the safety clips, and pulled the pins. He placed one grenade on the fuel-filling pipe and threw the other grenade into the cargo area of the van. He ran.

After counting three seconds, Steve shouted "Frag Out!" and ducked behind a parked delivery truck. The first detonation sent flames, glass, and steel pieces flying, striking nearby vehicles. A second explosion followed, blasting more hot air and debris. The heat ignited cartridges in the cargo area of the van, sending bullets in all directions. Steve rose and ran to catch up to Danielle who had hunkered behind a car when he had shouted "Frag Out." She stood up and waved at him.

Steve pointed at an alley between buildings. "This way. We need to find shelter under the trees before they get a chopper in the air."

They followed back alleys, crisscrossed through empty lots, and headed in a northeast direction.

When they reached West Jefferson Avenue, Steve looked around for the shelter of trees. The faint *wop-wop-wop* of a helicopter filled the air.

Steve led the way underneath tree cover along Rosa Parks Boulevard and stopped at the edge of West Riverfront Park.

He spotted Malcolm's Jeep Wrangler rolling in their direction along West Jefferson Avenue. He turned to Danielle. "You stay here." He walked in the open toward Malcolm's jeep.

As Malcolm's car rolled closer, Steve gestured for Malcolm to drive onto Rosa Parks Boulevard and to park underneath a massive silver maple. Danielle and Steve climbed aboard. They sat sweating and panting.

Malcolm looked in the rear-view mirror and smiled at them. Larry turned, shook his head, and chuckled. It was contagious. They all broke out laughing.

Malcolm drove at the speed limit along West Jefferson Avenue, then steered onto side streets, always heading south. A helicopter hovered above the neighbourhood arteries, and police sirens filled the air. He left the Detroit city limits, encountering no roadblocks.

Malcolm asked Steve to call Gerta with an update. "You can embellish the story. We'll back you up." They all laughed.

Arriving at the Pilot Travel Center in Monroe, Malcolm spotted Tom's van and parked beside it. Tom and Gerta were standing beside their vehicle. They waved.

The teammates greeted each other and embraced.

Malcolm looked at Gerta. "I see you've switched your plates already?"

"Yes. We stopped along the way and we switched to Missouri plates. The cameras at border control will have captured our plates. You need to switch yours, as well."

Gerta retrieved a set of Missouri plates and matching documents from her van and handed them to Malcolm.

Malcolm turned to Steve and handed over the package and the key fob. "Can you find a sheltered spot and switch the jeep's plates? Join us at Denny's when you're done." He pointed in the restaurant's direction. Steve nodded, took the plates and documents, climbed in the jeep, and drove off.

Malcolm turned to the team. "We need a new plan. Let's go eat and talk." He led his team toward the restaurant.

CHAPTER 44

WEBER RELEASES ROBERT

The clocks were soon to strike noon, and Weber was waiting impatiently for the reports from Forensics and from the OPP.

His own patrol cruisers had driven the roads all night and morning and seen no signs of the Jennings' vehicles. The Reliant team was last to have seen the criminals at 6:30 a.m.

The Ontario Provincial Police's report arrived first on his computer. Weber scrolled eagerly through the document. The OPP had set up roadblocks on Highways 400 and 401, but none on the secondary highways because of a lack of manpower. They had, however, heightened the surveillance on the secondary highways leading out of the Kitchener-Waterloo area. They reported no sightings of the suspect vehicles.

The fugitives must have slipped through our net, Weber thought.

An attachment to the email contained a report by Customs and Border Protection in Detroit. It stated that a white cargo van with Ontario plates and two individuals onboard, bearing Canadian passports, had run the border at 10:30 a.m. The occupants had abandoned their vehicle, set it on fire using hand grenades, and escaped on foot. The vehicle had exploded and prevented the police cruisers from pursuing the two fugitives. Border Control had dispatched a helicopter, but it failed to locate the escapees.

The suspects' passports and work permits were highly sophisticated counterfeits. The van bore no logos, and the plates were fakes. Cameras captured the vehicle and the faces of the occupants. The FBI was working at identifying the suspects. At the OPP's request, Border Control was sifting through the morning's computer records, searching for more fake passports. They were scanning their cameras for another white van and a black Jeep Wrangler. They put all neighbouring police departments on high alert.

Now we know the Jennings have returned to the States, Weber thought. It's up to the FBI to find them.

Weber sent Captain John Morris at the Reliant Agency a copy of the OPP's and Border Control's reports. He and Morris had agreed to a quid pro quo concerning the sharing of relevant information regarding the robbery and murders at the Tillman residence.

The preliminary report from forensics arrived five minutes before noon, as promised. Weber read it carefully. There was no evidence implicating Robert Cole in the murder of Douglas Ferguson.

The inspector drove to Central Station. Seconded by a station officer, he walked to Robert Cole's jail cell.

"Good morning, Mr. Cole. Good news! You're free to go." Weber signalled for the officer to open the cell.

"Thank God this nightmare is over." Robert breathed a sigh of relief. "Have you reached my son? Is he alright?"

"We could not locate him. We tried to, but he turned off his cell phone yesterday afternoon. That was at the New Hamburg Inn, where the Jennings were staying. We sent an officer to the inn and to your residence, but there was no sign of him."

Worry wrinkled Robert's face.

"I'll walk you back to the front desk," Weber said. "Once you've recovered all of your belongings, we'll sit in an interview room for a debriefing."

Robert picked up his belongings at the front desk and followed Weber to the interview room.

"Forensics found nothing to connect you with Mr. Ferguson's murder," Weber said. "Moreover, our technicians' calculations indicate you would have had to drive at two hundred kilometres an hour from Ms. Doyle's farm to the hospital and back in order to commit the crime. Your alibi holds."

"No surprises there. I wasn't at the hospital yesterday morning," Robert said.

Weber looked directly at Robert. "But your son, Tom, was."

Robert's face went pale.

"The hospital cameras caught him entering and leaving. Any reason your son would have visited the hospital yesterday morning?"

Robert shook his head. "You'll have to ask him."

"Why would he have turned off his cell phone for all that time?" Weber asked.

"I don't know. Like I told you yesterday, Tom was to work as an apprentice electrician with the Jennings crew starting yesterday. He said he'd be staying with the crew for the next while."

Weber raised his eyebrows. "What do you know about last night's assignment?"

"Not much, except that Tom would drive a van. Why are you asking? Did something happen last night?"

Weber didn't answer, but asked instead, "Did Tom mention where the Jennings were going next?"

"No, but I expect him to call me today to let me know how he is making out in his new job. Why all these questions? What happened last night?"

Weber paused for a moment, then said, "We believe the Jennings robbed and murdered Carl Tillman last night. I and the Reliant Detective Agency stumbled upon the raid in progress, and a shoot-out ensued. Mrs Tillman and a visitor died during the altercation. The Jennings killed one agent from the detective agency. They are now on the run."

Robert froze, in shock.

Weber fixed him. "The Jennings used your house in Waterloo as their hideout last night. Had you rented the place to them?"

Robert turned pale. "I had offered to rent the house to them, but nothing came out of it. And that was before I knew Chopra had purchased it."

"We believe the Jennings murdered two of Chopra's employees. Firefighters discovered the two bodies in the trunk of their company car in the parking lot of the Conestoga Shopping Mall. That is some coincidence."

Robert stared at Weber, speechless.

Weber rose. "When your son calls, tell him he needs to call me. He's in way over his head with the Jennings. He will need my help if he wants to come out of this alive. Give him my cell number." Weber gave Robert his business card. "And try to find out where he's calling from and where the Jennings are going next. For your son's sake."

Robert sat quietly, looking despondent.

"Constable Kidnie will drive you back. Your vehicle is at Ms. Doyle's farm, isn't it?"

Robert stared back, looking confused for a moment, then he nodded.

As Constable Kidnie drove him to Sharon Doyle's farm, Robert turned over in his mind what Weber had told him. Had Tom been angry enough to kill Duke? But the murder showed premeditation, not a spur-of-the-moment thing. And now that the Jennings crew has raided the Tillman residence, is Tom an accessory to murder? With a charge for aggravated assault already on the books, the courts will sentence Tom to the maximum penalty. He needed to discuss this with Tom, but the police would be monitoring his calls. *Fuck.*

Constable Kidnie turned into Sharon Doyle's farm and parked behind a red Honda Civic.

"Sharon must have a visitor?" Robert said. He thanked the constable, climbed out of the cruiser, and watched the officer leave. He walked toward the house.

Sharon's son, Patrick, walked out the front door. Patrick was a mirror image of his mother with his brown hair, hazel eyes, freckled cheeks, and amiable smile.

"Patrick! What a pleasant surprise! I'll bet Sharon is pleased to have you visit."

Patrick shook hands with Robert. He looked worried. "When I called Mom last night, I sensed such despair in her voice." His voice faltered. "I was worried as to what she might do to herself. I drove over immediately and spent the night with her."

"Good God. Let's go see her." Robert rushed to the front door and entered the house.

CHAPTER 45

PAUL AND LINDA RETURN

The airport limousine drove Paul and Linda from Toronto Pearson Airport to their residence on Huron Road. As the car steered onto the property, Paul gawked at the pockmarked walls and broken windows of the guardhouse. Yellow police tape surrounded the building. The limo proceeded to the guard booth.

Paul lowered his window as a guard from his father's security team walked over.

"Good day, Mr. Tillman." The guard nodded and looked embarrassed. "My condolences," he said.

"Thank you, John. How is everything here?"

"It's weird. Chief Moreno has disappeared. The police are looking for him. The place looks like the abandoned set of a disaster movie, except it's real." He looked at Paul. "They roped off your house and haven't released it yet. I'm sorry."

"Inspector Weber told me I could pick up my car, but not to go inside the house," Paul said. The guard nodded, reached through the open window of the booth and pressed a button. The recently replaced security gate lifted.

The limousine drove up to the house and stopped. Paul and Linda climbed out. The driver retrieved two tote bags from the trunk. One bag contained the bills from the house vault. Paul asked the driver to wait. He peeked through a window in the garage and saw his car. He turned and paid the driver. The limousine left.

Paul and Linda stared at the yellow police tape and the sign that read "No unauthorized entry." All was quiet except for the chirping of birds.

Paul noticed the bloodstains on the concrete porch and the bullet hole in the picture window. The venetian blinds blocked their view of the interior of the house.

"Let's go check out back," Paul said.

They each grabbed one bag and walked to the rear of the house. They approached the aircraft hangar. Bullet holes marred the hangar walls. The overhead door stood open. Brown autumn leaves had blown inside.

"I can't believe we survived this," Linda said as she instinctively rubbed the bandage on her leg.

They walked to the rear entrance of the house. Paul pulled the tape away and said, "Fuck this. I'm going in." He punched in the code that unlocked the door. He dropped his tote bag and entered. He reached over to a wall panel and disarmed the security system.

Linda dropped her tote bag and followed Paul inside.

Paul walked down the hallway to the living room. He froze. Dark brown and yellow stains covered the carpet. He turned to a side chair where dark stains marred the seat cushion and the backrest. He noticed the bullet hole. A whiff of ammonia, puke, and feces permeated the room.

Linda caught up to Paul and took in her surroundings. She put a hand to her mouth, turned, and raced to the rear entrance. She crossed the stone patio and puked in the flowerbed.

Paul joined her. His face was ashen. He put a hand on her shoulder. "Is there anything you need from the house? I'll get it for you."

"No, there's nothing I want in this house. Thank God we're staying at a hotel tonight."

"I'll go get the keys to the car and we can leave."

Paul returned with the keys and locked the rear entrance door behind him. He entered the code on the garage's rear door and walked in. Linda followed, carrying the tote bags.

The garage looked undisturbed. Carl Tillman's black Audi 8 occupied one spot. Paul's white Porsche Cabriolet sat beside it. He opened the passenger door and threw the tote bags on the rear seat.

Linda climbed in and Paul sat behind the wheel. He pressed the remote and the garage door inched open. He pushed the Porsche's start button, and the engine rumbled. The gas gauge showed half full. He exited the garage, clicked the remote to close the overhead door behind him, and sped down the laneway.

Paul and Linda reported to Inspector Weber on the next day. The inspector displayed photographs of the members of the Jennings crew for Paul and Linda to look at. "Do you recognize any of these people?"

Paul pointed at the photos of Danielle and Gerta. "I fired at these two women. In self-defence." He then pointed at Malcolm's and Larry's photos. "I think I remember those two. They were in the living room."

"You hesitated?" Weber said.

"They were pointing pistols in my direction, and I focused on their weapons more than their faces. The older woman stood between me and them. That's what saved my life."

Weber nodded, then turned to Linda. "How about you, Ms. Atchison? Do you recognize anyone in these photos?"

Linda immediately pointed at the photo of Danielle. "That's the young woman who surprised us in the rec room downstairs. But for the others, I don't know. I walked upstairs, saw a bunch of people in the living room. Paul was pointing his gun at that woman. I ran out the rear entrance door. My memory of who was in the living room is blurry."

Weber considered where to go next. "The investigators found a vault in the basement. It was open and empty. Nobody had forced the combination lock." He paused and looked into Paul's and Linda's faces. "Did the young woman force you to open the vault?"

Paul looked at Weber and shook his head. "No. The robbers must have extracted the combination from Dad?"

They've rehearsed this, Weber thought.

"Do you know what was in the vault?" Weber asked.

Paul hesitated before answering. "I know Dad kept some cash, some legal documents. Mom's more expensive jewellery, maybe."

Weber nodded, then said, "Have you been to the house yet?" Weber knew the answer already. The guards kept a log of the visitors to the property and Weber had checked.

"Yes, yesterday afternoon, to pick up the car," Paul said.

Weber nodded. "Where are you staying now?"

"Homewood Suites in Cambridge."

"Are you eager to move back home?" Weber watched Linda reach over and squeeze Paul's arm. He noticed the distress on her face.

"We're in no hurry to move back in. In fact, we may not return to live there. At least that's how we feel right now."

Weber nodded. "I'll let you know when the coroner will release your parents' remains." He looked at Paul. "Again, I offer my condolences. I can't imagine what it is like to lose both parents in such a violent way." Weber let a moment pass before adding, "The region of Waterloo offers a victim's counselling service. Can I introduce you to them? They can be very helpful in times like these."

"Yes, that's a good idea." Paul turned to Linda. "We're both confused and in shock. What happened hasn't completely sunk in yet."

"That's understandable," Weber said. "They can help with funeral arrangements, as well. And they'll give you names of crime scene cleaning contractors you can hire."

"Yes, we'll need help with all that," Paul said.

"Okay. Let me introduce you to these folks." Weber then left some closing comments on the recording machine and turned it off. He rose and guided Paul and Linda to the victims' counselling service.

Paul visited his father's law firm that afternoon. Cameron Brodie was the solicitor and executor for Carl and Amanda Tillman and their living wills. Brodie addressed Paul from behind his mahogany desk. "You, Paul, are the sole inheritor of the estate of your father and your mother. The estate comprises the property on Huron Road, which is estimated at ten million dollars, and shares of different companies, which are estimated at five million dollars. There is approximately five hundred thousand dollars in your mother's bank accounts. Unfortunately, the criminals have emptied your father's bank accounts. Oh. And there are no life insurance policies."

"What about Dad's overseas account?" Paul asked.

Brodie hesitated, looked embarrassed, then said, "I am not supposed to know about those accounts, but I can tell you the criminals emptied those during the robbery. I'm sorry."

Paul stared at Brodie. "How much was in those accounts?"

Brodie fidgeted in his seat. "Please keep this information confidential. Your father had thirty million dollars in the Caymans."

"Damn." Paul mulled something over in his mind, then said, "What about this criminal lawsuit against my father?"

"My colleague, Everett Myer, leads the criminal defence for your late father, and you'll meet him shortly."

Brodie changed the subject. "What are your immediate plans?"

"I'll sell the house. Linda and I will move into a condo in the city. How soon can I put the house up for sale?"

Brodie blushed, then said, "Let's have you meet with Everett. He'll apprise you of your father's legal situation, and we'll talk again afterward?"

Paul suspected Brodie had left something unsaid. "Is there some problem you're not telling me about?"

Brodie paused before saying, "Everett knows the details of the lawsuits. I only handle estate planning matters."

Paul, apprehensive, followed Brodie to Everett Meyer's office. Brodie knocked with what sounded like a code on Meyer's office door, and they heard a muffled invitation to enter. Paul followed Brodie. His shoes sank into a plush carpet. Dark mahogany furniture was the unifying theme in the office, and all the wooden surfaces sparkled. Floor-to-ceiling windows filled the wall behind Meyer's desk. Paul gazed at the Kitchener skyline. The office faced north. There were no blinds to impede the view.

Meyer, dressed in a dark grey suit, white shirt, and sky-blue tie, rose to greet Paul. A full head of distinguished grey hair topped the senior barrister's six-foot frame. His smile was broad and his handshake was firm. Paul sat, but Brodie remained standing.

"Everett, this is Mr. Paul Tillman, the son of the late Mr. Carl Tillman." Brodie gave Meyer time to extend his condolences, then continued. "I've gone over the will with Paul, but he needs to be brought up-to-date on the criminal and civil lawsuits facing his father."

"Civil lawsuit?" Paul turned to Brodie with raised eyebrows.

"Mr. Meyer will go over that with you. I'll leave you gentlemen to it." Brodie shook Paul's hand and left.

Paul gave Meyer an inquiring look. Meyer returned the eye contact, coughed softly into his raised fist, and said, "The criminal suit ended with the death of your father, but there is a civil lawsuit on the books." Meyer cleared his throat and continued. "The civil lawsuit doesn't end with the death of your father. It gets transferred to his estate."

"What civil lawsuit?"

"Your father never mentioned this to you?" Meyer asked. Seeing Paul's confused look, he continued, "A group of investors, in the company your father founded, have filed a civil lawsuit for mismanagement and fraud."

Paul looked stunned.

Meyer continued. "Your uncle, Alvin, is heading the lawsuit. The mismanagement part we can fight off easily. After all, the board of directors approved the closure of the company and the sale of its assets and patents. But fighting the fraud part will be trickier." Meyer let Paul catch up.

"What fraud?"

"The plaintiffs claim your father accepted a kickback of thirty million dollars from the buyers in return for selling below market value."

"What proof do they have?" Paul asked.

"Your father's executive secretary gave the plaintiffs some documents and records that are very damaging. She was present during the negotiations. The documents show your father having negotiated a kickback."

"Doesn't that incriminate her, as well? Make her an accomplice?" Paul said.

"Yes. She admitted having accepted hush money from your father."

"Why did she come forward now?" Paul said.

"She claims your father had promised to leave your mother and marry her but had changed his mind. She produced the records in exchange for a reduced sentence. Her intentions are clearly to sully your father's memory and ruin his legacy."

"What are my uncle and his group suing for?"

"Thirty million dollars. They've tabled expert market evaluations that support that claim." Meyer bit his lips.

"Didn't the board of directors approve the sale?" Paul said.

"Yes, they did," Meyer said. "But they voted themselves generous bonuses and parting compensation packages prior to the sale. That will weaken our defence." Meyer paused, then looked Paul in the eye. "And there's the injunction."

"What injunction?"

"Your uncle and the plaintiffs have got a court injunction that prevents the sale of any assets in the Carl Tillman estate until the court has ruled on the lawsuit."

"What the hell?"

Meyer said. "Is your car in your name?"

"Yes."

"Good. They can't touch that, at least." Meyer paused, then added, "Mr. Brodie will help you empty your mother's bank accounts immediately. You will need those funds to cover legal costs."

"Jesus! What are our chances of beating this?"

Meyer lowered his gaze to his hands, which lay flat on the surface of the desk. He looked up into Paul's eyes. "Do you want the Norman Vincent Peale answer or my honest opinion?"

"Your honest opinion, for God's sake."

Meyer stared at Paul. "You're fucked."

Paul and Linda dined at King Street Trio in downtown Kitchener. They ordered sea scallops for appetizers.

Linda said, "You looked so down when you returned from the lawyer's office, I held back from peppering you with questions until you'd rested. Can you talk about it now? You're not the only inheritor; is that it?"

"No. I'm the sole inheritor."

"That's good, right? You will inherit a fortune, no?"

"It's complicated. My Uncle Alvin and a group of shareholders are suing the estate. They claim Dad sold the company below market value in exchange for a kickback. Uncle Alvin got a court injunction and I can't touch any assets or funds until the courts settle." Paul swallowed hard. "I get to keep my car, and whatever is left of Mom's savings. But I'll need those funds to pay the legal fees. The lawyer said the plaintiffs are sure to win. I'm broke."

Linda looked on, open-mouthed. "I don't understand what you're saying. You will get nothing? How is that possible? Your father was loaded."

"The criminals who murdered Dad have emptied all his bank accounts, here and offshore. My uncle and his pals will seize Dad's assets: the house, his car, any shares he owns. There'll be nothing left."

"How can the lawyer claim you will lose? The board of directors, dozens of company accountants, and lawyers would have signed off on this deal. Get another lawyer," Linda said.

"Dad's executive secretary spilled the beans. Dad accepted a kickback and hid the money in the Caymans. No lawyer can fight that."

Linda sat staring at her plate of appetizers. The server walked over and asked, "Is the food alright?"

Paul looked up at him. "Everything is fine. Could you please take our plates away and bring the main course?"

The server cleared the half-empty plates from the table. He returned with a plate of seafood paella for Linda and veal osso bucco for Paul. He brought white wine in an ice bucket and served it.

"I'm not hungry," Linda said with downcast eyes.

"I'm not that hungry, either," Paul said. "Let's eat what we can."

They picked at their food and emptied the bottle of wine.

"What are you thinking?" Linda asked.

"That I'm going to have to work for a living, and that sucks."

Linda looked at him with sympathy. "What would you like to work at?"

Paul thought about it for a moment. "I have a chemical engineering degree with a specialty in environmental science." He reflected, then added, "The government has approved a lot of environmental projects lately. I'll apply to the engineering firms doing the design."

"That sounds positive," Linda said. "I've a bachelor's in education. I'll look around and see where I can fit in."

Paul and Linda looked at each other and smiled.

"Excuse me, I need to visit the washroom." Paul rose and left the table.

Linda's cell phone rang. The call display announced her former flame, Derek Meyer.

"Hi, Derek."

"Hi, Linda. I called to find out how you're doing. Were you hurt during the raid on the Tillman residence?"

"No, nothing serious. We were lucky to escape in Mr. Tillman's aircraft. Paul flew us to safety, but the violent death of his parents was quite a shock."

"Yes, that's all my friends and I are talking about. You were one lucky couple." Derek paused, then added, "I guess Paul isn't that lucky, after all."

"What do you mean?"

"Well, Dad's legal firm is handling the Tillman estate. He told me a civil lawsuit will clean up the estate. Paul is broke."

Linda remained silent.

"Hey, what about you and I getting together to talk about your future?"

Linda hesitated before answering, "I'll be busy for a while, helping Paul with the arrangements for his parents' funeral, getting settled in a new home, and such. I'll call you when things have settled down. Okay?"

"Yeah. Sure. Call me anytime."

"Bye, Derek. Thanks for your concern." Linda ended the call.

Paul returned to the table. "I feel better. I'm in the mood for a wicked dessert and strong coffee."

"Me, too," Linda said. She rose, walked around the table, and kissed Paul on the lips. "If I can't sleep, you'll have to entertain me."

"How's your leg?" Paul asked.

"Still sore, but we'll manage." Linda gave Paul a teasing smile.

CHAPTER 46

SHARON'S RECOVERY

Robert entered the house and looked around for Sharon. Not seeing her downstairs, he rushed upstairs. Patrick followed close behind. They padded through the open bedroom door. Sharon laid curled up in the bed, facing away from them. Robert approached softly.

"Hi, Sharon."

She turned. "Hi, Robert." Her eyes were red. "I don't know what's wrong with me. All I want to do is sleep. I want to crawl into a deep hole and hide."

Robert brought a chair and sat by the bedside. He put a hand on Sharon's arm. "That sounds reasonable after what you've been through." He noticed a sadness in Sharon's eyes he hadn't seen before. "You have medication you can take?"

She nodded.

Robert added, "Has the hospital assigned a doctor to follow-up on you?"

"Yes. Dr. Whitfield recommended I start behaviour modification exercises at her office. I'm in such a funk right now, I can't concentrate on anything."

Robert rested a hand on her arm. "I'll call Dr. Whitfield right now."

Sharon rolled over to face the wall. She pulled the duvet over her shoulders and ducked her head underneath it.

Robert reached Dr. Whitfield. "Can you bring her to the clinic at two p.m. today?" she said.

"Yes, we'll be there for two."

Robert walked down to the kitchen, made coffee, buttered a toast, spread peanut butter on it, put everything on a tray, and brought it upstairs. Patrick was still sitting near the foot of the bed. Robert whispered to Sharon, "Do you think you can eat something?"

Sharon turned and pulled herself up on the pillows. She looked at the tray. "My favourite treat, but I'm not hungry." She looked on with pouted lips. "But I'll have a nibble and a sip of coffee because you are such a nice person." She smiled at Robert, who leaned over and kissed her on the forehead.

"Dr. Whitfield will see you at two. Patrick and I will help you get down the stairs." Robert turned to Patrick. "Are you coming to the appointment with us?"

"Absolutely!"

"You're a wonderful son," Sharon said.

After nibbling on the toast and sipping some coffee, Sharon walked to the bathroom, looked at herself in the mirror, and groaned. *My hair is all matted, my eyes lifeless, my cheeks so pale.* Sharon brushed her hair and applied rouge, eyeliner, and lipstick. She walked to the closet and slipped into fresh clothes. She looked at herself in the full-length mirror and sighed. *It'll have to do.*

"You look very presentable," Robert said, and he guided her down the stairs and out the front door. The three climbed into the Leaf, and they headed toward the Grand River Medical Clinic.

Patrick asked, "Where is Tom?" Robert and Sharon looked at each other. Robert answered, "I don't know."

"Mom told me he joined an electrical contractor as an apprentice electrician? The contractor that stayed at your Airbnb."

"Yes. They're called Jennings Electric. I believe Tom is with them," Robert said.

"Holy cow! I heard on the news they're accused of robbing and murdering Tillman and his wife. That they're on the lam, somewhere in the States. Is Tom with these guys?"

Robert looked up at Patrick's reflection in the rear-view mirror. "I believe so." Robert paused, then added, "And it gets worse. The police suspect Tom of murdering Duke, the man who raped your mom."

"Jesus!" Patrick said. After a moment, he added, "If it's true, I don't blame Tom. I wish I had done it."

Sharon turned in her seat. "Patrick! Don't say that. Murder is a serious matter. You don't want to spend most of your life in jail."

After a moment of silence, Robert said, "There's a warrant out for Tom's arrest. When he calls, I'll encourage him to return and face the music." Robert released a deep breath. "But he has to make that call."

"I'm worried for his safety," Sharon said. "What if he gets hurt when the police catch up with the Jennings?" She placed a hand on Robert's arm.

Patrick mulled this over in his mind. "But why is he staying with that crew? They can't be doing electrical work anymore. They're just running from the law."

Robert looked out the window, stared in the distance, bit his lips, then said, "I think he's in love with Jennings' daughter, Danielle. The two got along well and grew close. I don't expect him to return home willingly."

They drove the rest of the way to the medical clinic in silence.

When Robert, Sharon, and Patrick walked into reception, an attendant directed Sharon to Dr. Whitfield's office. Robert and Patrick sat in a waiting area.

Twenty minutes later, Dr. Whitfield came out. She invited Robert and Patrick into her office. Sharon looked up at them with tearful eyes.

Dr. Whitfield addressed the group. "Sharon is experiencing depression, anxiety, nightmares, self-guilt, and fear of being alone." She paused, then added, "That is to be expected after the trauma she experienced. But, with medication and regular sessions of behaviour modification therapy, those symptoms will lessen with time." She gave Sharon a tender look. Sharon bit her lips.

"From my discussions with Sharon, I've learned that you, Patrick, your brother, and you, Mr. Cole, are Sharon's support system. You can help her recover by being present, cheerful, and supportive."

Dr. Whitfield rose and gave Sharon a parting hug.

Robert led his friends back to the Leaf and drove back to Sharon's home. He stopped at a Tim Hortons and picked up a dozen muffins.

The three sat around the kitchen table. Patrick served coffee, and each selected a muffin. Robert made a mental note to go grocery shopping and replenish the fridge and the cupboards.

Robert turned to Patrick. "If you need to return to work, don't worry about your mom. I'll visit every day and I can prepare meals until she's well enough to take over the cooking."

"Hold on, you guys! I'm not an invalid yet," Sharon said. "Patrick, you return to your work and your life. Depressed or not, I can work." She turned to Robert. "I'll help with the barn chores tonight. I feel a lot stronger already."

Patrick hesitated, but seeing Robert and Sharon sitting close together, forming a team, he said, "Alright. My supervisor will be happy to see me back. He's short-staffed."

Patrick walked up to his room and returned a few minutes later, lugging a large sports bag. "I leave you in expert hands, Mom." Mother and child hugged and kissed.

Sharon walked her son to the porch. Robert followed close behind. They waved Patrick goodbye as he drove off.

Sharon turned toward Robert. She hesitated, then said, "Could you stay overnight? You could sleep in a spare bedroom. I would feel safer and sleep better. I'm not imposing too much, am I?"

"No. You are not imposing. And I will feel better knowing you are not alone in the house."

Sharon put a hand on Robert's arm and looked up at him. "This is not a romantic invitation. You understand that?"

Robert placed his hand over Sharon's hand. "I understand."

Robert's phone rang. The call display read "unknown caller." Robert picked up. "Hello?"

"Dad. It's me."

CHAPTER 47

MORENO IN COSTA RICA

Moreno let out a sigh of relief as he drove out of the Thousand Islands border crossing. That fake passport the Jennings had given him had worked like a charm. The stolen car with fake papers and plates had been worth the $10,000 he had paid for it, even if he planned to dump the vehicle shortly.

He steered his car toward Syracuse where his cousin, Fernandez, was waiting with a replacement vehicle, a four-door black Chevrolet Malibu, also with fake plates and fake papers. Fernandez had purchased a fake passport and fake papers for him. The $100,000 cash advance from the Jennings had made all these preparations possible. If it weren't for the cold-blooded assassinations he had witnessed, he would admire the Jennings.

Moreno's destination was Playas del Coco on the Pacific coast of Costa Rica. He faced eighty hours of driving, but he was in no hurry. He allowed himself ten days to get there.

After crossing the border into Costa Rica, Moreno was appalled at the condition of the roads. Upon reaching Playas del Coco, Moreno checked into the Coco Beach hotel and Casino.

He spent his days swimming and sunbathing, and his evenings gambling in the casino.

He purchased a beachfront house for $550,0000, a fraction of the $6 million now sitting in his bank account. The quaint renovated bungalow featured a vaulted ceiling, an open concept living, dining, and kitchen area. A veranda faced the pristine sandy beach.

Moreno had set himself a daily stop loss limit at the casino. He began each evening at the stud poker table, and when he reached his set limit, he moved to the blackjack table where the odds were better. Moreno often came away even or slightly ahead.

Life was good, but one thing was missing: a woman companion. Prostitutes were plentiful and cheap, but he yearned for a serious relationship.

In time, Moreno befriended Sofia, a server at the Coco Beach hotel dining room. He asked her out for dinner, and they went dancing afterward. They ended up at his beach house, and Sofia agreed to stay overnight. They repeated the experience regularly and Moreno fell in love.

He confided to Sofia that he had no attachments, no ex-wife, no children. The couple began making plans for a future together.

Sofia would join Moreno at the casino when she wasn't working. She rejoiced in his winnings and commiserated over his losses.

One evening, a lucky star shone on Moreno. He won big at poker: $100,000. "You brought me luck," he said to Sofia, and he kissed her. He brought his chips to the cashier window and instructed the cashier to deposit the funds in his bank account. The cashier, whose nametag read Emiliano, took down Moreno's bank details, made the transaction, and handed over a deposit slip.

Moreno and Sofia left the casino and walked along the beach on their way to the beach house. The moon shone brightly and reflected off the ripples in the ocean. Sofia sat in the sand in a secluded area of the beach. She signalled for Moreno to sit by her side. The lovers commented on how beautiful the moon was and how good life was.

Moreno noticed a lone shape appear some distance away. The person quickened the pace as he drew near as if he had been looking for them.

Moreno recognized Emiliano from the casino. He stood and said, "Hi. Did we forget something at the casino?"

Emiliano approached, pulled a knife from underneath his shirt and plunged the blade repeatedly below Moreno's ribcage. Moreno fell forward on the sand. He turned on his side, curled up, moaned, and pressed his hands over his wounds. He felt weak, but he could hear the conversation between Emiliano and Sofia.

"What took you so long?" Sofia said.

"My replacement was late."

"Do you have the bank account details?"

"Yes. This guy has over six million dollars in that account. Can you believe it? You've got his password?"

"Yes. I've got all his passwords, even those for his credit cards. The idiot keeps them all in a Word file on his laptop. I searched and found them when he left his computer running and unattended."

Sofia kneeled and searched Moreno's pockets. She retrieved his wallet.

Moreno heard a small outboard motor approaching, followed by the sound of a boat slipping on the sandy beach. He heard feet splash in the water.

"Mateo. Come help me. Quick," Emiliano said. "Let's get him in the boat. The sharks are waiting." Both men laughed.

Moreno groaned from the pain when the men dragged him by the underarms. He didn't have the strength to defend himself or to shout for help. His body tumbled into the boat. Everything went dark.

CHAPTER 48

TO ST. LOUIS AND A NEW LIFE

Malcolm led his team into Denny's and picked a large table away from the other diners and with a clear view of the parking lot. Larry had brought a tote bag containing assault rifles and 30 round magazines. Steve had thrown in some frag and smoke grenades.

All were ravenous. They ordered overflowing plates of eggs, bacon, sausages, home fries and toast. Steve arrived shortly and ordered the same.

Malcolm looked in Tom's and Danielle's direction. They sat next to each other, and Danielle had rested a hand on Tom's arm. Malcolm was pleased to see Tom's affection for Danielle. Malcolm had watched Tom grow more comfortable with his new companions. He felt gratified that Tom respected his leadership—a leadership he shared with Gerta and Larry.

Malcolm surmised that what Tom had witnessed last night would have shaken him to his core. He watched Danielle turn, look into Tom's eyes, and give his arm a squeeze. Tom leaned over and kissed her.

A calm settled over the table. Gerta broke the silence and spoke in a melancholic tone. "It feels strange not having Jim at the table. Even Duke. He's dishonoured himself, but he was family for a while."

All lowered their eyes, and sadness passed over the assembly. Malcolm noticed Tom blushing. He caught Gerta's eye. She had noticed, as well.

Everyone returned to their food, and spirits lifted.

Larry asked Malcolm, "Is it safe to return to Chicago? You mentioned a new plan?"

Malcolm turned to the group. "We can't return home. This last job has burned our names and that of Jennings Electric. We've left a ton of evidence in our wake, and the FBI—and, I presume, that detective agency—will find out where we live, and they'll come hunting for us. We need new identities." Malcolm let the group digest what he had said before adding, "I suggest we split up while we're ahead."

"But what about getting the bastard that hurt my mother?" Larry said. "That was my condition for joining this revenge project."

Everyone looked at one another with raised eyebrows.

"Who's that guy again?" Steve said.

"Michael Tyler. The CEO of Retail Conglomerate in New York City."

Everyone remained silent. Malcolm spoke first. "You're right, Larry. Count me in. We'll get that bastard."

Gerta nodded to Larry. "I'm onboard, as well."

Larry looked at the rest of the team. Steve, Danielle, and Tom looked worried and uncertain.

Larry scrutinized every face, paused, then said, "That's okay, guys. I have enough funds for Mom to enjoy a comfortable retirement and for me to start fresh. We can split up. I'm good with it."

Steve, Danielle, and Tom let out a sigh of relief. Malcolm put a hand on Larry's shoulder. "You're a good man, Larry. If you change your mind, call me. Gerta will show you and the team how you can always reach us."

Malcolm commanded everyone's attention. "Gerta and I have devised an emergency plan in case we couldn't return to Chicago. She's rented a five-bedroom house and an empty warehouse in St. Louis. We will lodge there until Gerta creates new identities for all of us."

"How long will that take?" Steve asked.

Malcolm turned to Gerta. She pursed her lips, then said, "One week. Ten days at the most. I'll need the printing equipment and supplies brought over from Chicago."

"What about police surveillance?" Steve said.

"I've kept the equipment in a rented office under a false name. The FBI won't know about it."

Steve looked impressed. "And what's our take so far?"

"After putting aside twenty percent for the victims' fund, we are left with thirty-eight million to split equally amongst ourselves," Gerta said.

Everyone did mental calculations as they chewed their food. Malcolm noticed Tom looking perplexed.

Malcolm announced, "I suggest we give Tom an equal share. He performed well since he joined us, and now he shares equally in the risks of getting caught. Everyone okay with this?"

Larry and Steve looked at each other. They nodded their heads.

"That leaves me with over five million. That's enough for me to retire in Casablanca," Steve said as he leaned back and looked into the distance. "I can picture myself at Rick's Café, sipping orange glamour cocktails, listening to blues music."

All smiled and shook their heads.

"We'll need to plan this carefully," Gerta said. "There'll be cameras with face recognition software in the airports. I'll need to hack into the camera system and jumble the software while you get through the terminal."

Steve pursed his lips and bobbed his head.

"Morocco's a good choice," Malcolm said. "They have no extradition treaty with the U.S., but don't forget the warning by the famous actor, Jim Carrey. It goes something like this: 'I think everybody should get rich and famous and do everything they ever dreamed of so they can see it's not the answer.'"

"I don't think his advice applies to me—not the part about becoming famous, anyway."

"I doubt sitting in a café and listening to music all day will satisfy you for very long," Malcolm said.

"I'll try it, and report back," Steve said. "What about you? What do you want to do with the rest of your life?"

Malcolm sipped from his cup, stared into the distance before answering. "I've accomplished my mission, to avenge my father and my brother. As for the rest of my life, I want to retire with Gerta by my side, manage a small business, and help Danielle build a good life for herself."

Malcolm raised his eyebrows as if surprised by his own words. He turned to Gerta. "You okay with this?"

Gerta smiled, reached for Malcolm's hand, and pressed it. "Buy me a quaint house with a large garden where I can grow flowers, for as long as my strength will allow me to."

Malcolm refocused his attention on the group. "We know what Steve, Gerta, and I want to do, but what about the rest of you guys?"

"I'm going with Tom," Danielle said. She turned to look at Tom.

Gerta stared at Malcolm with raised eyebrows. He smiled back.

Tom straightened his shoulders before answering, "We're thinking of settling on a farm outside Vancouver and growing marijuana and other crops. Nobody knows us down there, but just in case, I'll grow a beard." He rubbed his chin and turned to Danielle with a questioning look. Danielle returned the look and rested a hand on his arm.

"I know someone who can help you get across the border from Seattle to Canada," Gerta said. "He runs boat tours to Vancouver Island and knows how to avoid the border control. I'll call him."

"Thanks, Mom," Danielle said.

Malcolm turned to Larry. "How about you, Larry?"

"I'm thinking San Francisco, where old hippies go to die. I'll grow a beard, wear shades, and keep my hair long. I'll blend right in. Yeah." Larry bobbed his head.

Everyone smiled as they savoured their coffee.

"Wherever everyone ends up," Malcolm said, "let's stay in touch. Gerta will show us how to do it without leaving a trace. If anyone needs help, call us."

Everyone nodded at this.

As the new reality sank in, Malcolm read a rising anxiety on everyone's faces.

"I realize you're leaving a lot behind," Malcolm said. "We'll settle in our rented house in St. Louis tonight, and we'll hold a meeting tomorrow morning and plan everyone's disappearance in more detail."

"What about my bank account? Is it safe?" Steve asked.

Malcolm turned to Gerta. She gave the matter some thought, then looked up at the group. "The FBI will seize all of our bank accounts as soon as they figure out where they are. Once we're settled in tonight, I'll transfer all your funds to a hidden account for now. I'll set everyone up with your own account when your new identities are in place."

"You're not planning on leaving the country without telling us, are you?" Steve asked, faking an anxious look. Everyone chuckled.

Gerta continued, "The first item of business for tomorrow's meeting will be to transport our security printing equipment and supplies to St. Louis. I know the firm who can do it for us. It belongs to my Uncle Karl. He delivered the equipment to our rented office in Chicago in the first place. I'll contact him."

Malcolm took the floor and issued instructions. "Everyone, turn your burners over to Gerta. The FBI will eventually figure out our burner numbers and the location of the calls. Gerta will issue new burners once we've settled in St. Louis."

Tom raised his hand. "Can I call my dad?"

Malcolm looked at Gerta. She looked up at Tom. "You can make one last call, but do not mention where we are and where we're going!"

Tom nodded. He stepped outside to make the call.

The server came around to replenish everyone's coffee, and he left the bill. Malcolm, rose, picked up the bill, and headed for the cashier. He then joined the group outside. They had formed a circle out of earshot of the restaurant entrance. Some lit cigarettes.

Gerta took Malcolm aside. "About Duke's murder. I hacked into the Grand River hospital's cameras. Tom was there that morning."

Malcolm looked in the distance. "I'm not surprised."

"What do you think we should do?"

"Does Danielle know?"

"Yes. She's okay with it."

"Good. I'm okay with it, too," Malcolm said.

Gerta stared wide-eyed at him for an instant, then put a hand on his arm. "Good."

Tom dialled his father's number. "Hi, Dad. It's me."

"Tom! Are you alright? Where are you? I was crazy with worry."

"I can't say much over the phone, Dad, but I'm well and I'm safe. I will not be returning home. I'll contact you as often as I can and let you know how I'm doing."

"Return home, Tom. It's the safe thing to do. The police are after the Jennings." He hesitated, then said, "Inspector Weber is looking at you for the murder of Duke. They caught you on the hospital's cameras. Come home and we'll face this together. We'll get legal help. Let me give you Inspector Weber's number. Talk to him. He can bring you in safely."

"Dad, I've got to go. Love you." Tom hung up.

Malcolm watched Tom walk over to his side. Tom said in a heavy voice, "I've reached Dad. He's very worried. I can't wait until Gerta shows me how to communicate with him safely." He paused, then added, "The police are looking at me for the murder of Duke."

Malcolm looked Tom in the eyes. "I wouldn't blame you if you did it. Neither would Gerta." Tom stared back wide-eyed. He blushed but remained silent. Malcolm said, "Have you told Danielle?"

Tom looked at his feet, then raised his eyes. "Yes. And she's okay with it."

"Good." Malcolm put a hand on Tom's shoulder and guided him toward the crew. He added, "Gerta and I will help you and Danielle get established and put this behind you."

Malcolm addressed his crew. "We've reached the last chapter of our lives as a team. We'll regroup at our safe house and prepare our disappearing act." He turned to Gerta. "Could you give Tom the address and the keys to the warehouse?" He turned to Tom and Steve. "You two will drive the van to the warehouse. Follow secondary roads all the way. I'll drop off the others at the house first, then I'll drive over and pick you up." Tom and Steve nodded.

Tom climbed behind the wheel of the van, and Steve sat in the passenger seat. They drove off.

Malcolm and the others walked to the jeep. With everyone aboard, Malcolm headed back to the highway. He steered the jeep along Highway 24, toward St. Louis, and a new life.